ROMANTIC TIMES PRAISES *USA TODAY* BESTSELLING AUTHOR CONSTANCE O'BANYON!

HALF MOON RANCH: MOON RACER

"Kudos to Constance O'Banyon!"

RIDE THE WIND

"Ms. O'Banyon's story is well written with well-developed characters."

TYKOTA'S WOMAN

"Constance O'Banyon delivers a gripping and emotionally charged tale of love, honor and betrayal."

TEXAS PROUD

"*Texas Proud* is another good read from Ms. O'Banyon. With its excellent characters and strong plot, readers will find enough action and surprises to fill an evening."

LA FLAMME

"Constance O'Banyon tells a tale replete with action-adventure and glorious romance."

SONG OF THE NIGHTINGALE

"Mesmerizing, engrossing, passionate yet tender and richly romantic."

DESERT SONG

"Constance O'Banyon is dynamic. Wonderful characters. [She is] one of the best writers of romantic adventure."

TASTE OF PASSION

"This has never happened to me before," she admitted, more confused than ever.

His lips feathered softly across her cheek. He was trembling when he realized her mouth was just a breath away from his. Sweet torment tore at him, and he felt like a man dying of thirst.

He had to have her, all of her, or he would drift forever with nothing to live for. He could feel her body soften against his, and he knew she wanted him too. His mouth touched the edge of her full lips, and they trembled against his.

Casey felt his breath on her mouth and an incredible sweetness touched her heart. He hadn't kissed her yet, but merely brushed his lips across hers.

What would she do if he actually kissed her?

Other *Leisure* books by Constance O'Banyon:

MOON RACER
THE AGREEMENT (SECRET FIRES)
RIDE THE WIND
SOMETHING BORROWED, SOMETHING BLUE (anthology)
TYKOTA'S WOMAN
FIVE GOLD RINGS (anthology)
SAN ANTONIO ROSE
TEXAS PROUD
CELEBRATIONS (anthology)

HEART OF TEXAS

CONSTANCE O'BANYON

LEISURE BOOKS NEW YORK CITY

A LEISURE BOOK®

June 2004

Published by

Dorchester Publishing Co., Inc.
200 Madison Avenue
New York, NY 10016

ISBN 0-8439-5365-9

Printed in the United States of America.

Visit us on the web at www.dorchesterpub.com.

This one is for you, Jennifer Dawn Gee, my little redheaded daughter-in-law. I am so glad my son chose you.

And my son, Jason, why do I always have to smile when I see you? You are the light of my life.

Kimberly Melton, my dearest daughter, I treasure every day I have with you. We so often walk the same path.

My son, Rick, the rock that so often holds this family together. Words are inadequate to thank you for your strength and devotion to those you love. We all benefit from your caring nature.

Pamela, my first born and sometimes writing partner. We think so much alike it's scary. Especially when the words you write are also in my mind.

ACKNOWLEDGMENT

To my uncle, Henry Hoyle. Once again you came to my rescue when I needed advice on ranching. What would I do without my favorite uncle?

Dr. R. N. Gray. I tapped into knowledge of Texas once more. Thanks for letting me know how to do away with a large number of cattle in the 1800s.

HEART OF TEXAS

Chapter One

Colorado Wilderness
June 1867

The day was bleak and dreary, and it had been raining off and on all morning. But the weather didn't seem to dampen the spirit of the young woman who stood ramrod straight, her pale blue eyes intense and unflinching as she stared at the wagon master.

"I'm not going back!"

Her unrelenting demeanor somehow made her seem formidable for such a small slip of a girl. She came only shoulder high on Marty Grimshaw. The stubborn tilt of her head warned Grimshaw that she was going to give him trouble. He felt pity for Casey Hamilton because her life had taken a devastating turn—only yesterday they had buried her pa after several of the men had recovered his mangled body from the floodwaters that had crushed him between two wagons.

Grimshaw respectfully removed his hat, then shifted from one booted foot to the other, knowing he was only adding to her pain, but he had no choice. It was his duty to do right by everyone under his protection, and if that meant sending her back to Virginia, then that was what he would do.

He stared at her, assessing her features. She was a pretty little gal with a mass of red-gold hair that curled around her face in ringlets. There was a light sprinkle of freckles across her nose, and she had the most unusual and beautiful turquoise-blue eyes he had ever seen. She was delicately built, her mannerisms those of a fine lady.

Grimshaw knew some of her history from what her father had told him. Her mother had died some years back, and the family had, at one time, owned a bank in Charlottesville. From what he could tell, the Hamiltons had lost everything in the war. He couldn't conceive what fool notion had driven John Hamilton to embark on such a dangerous venture with his motherless family. There was no way in hell Miss Hamilton could make it to Texas on her own. Her brother, Sam, was barely thirteen, and little Jenny was somewhere around four or five years old. That alone was a lot of responsibility for one little gal to contend with, without adding the hazards of the two-month journey still ahead of them.

"I'm sending you back to Virginia, Miss Hamilton, but you needn't worry. Joe Franks will be going with you. He's a good man—he'll see you safely home."

Casey was fighting back tears along with feelings of anger and frustration. "Virginia isn't our home anymore, Mr. Grimshaw. Our house is gone, and our land was taken for back taxes. But we do have a home and land waiting for us in Texas—and that's where we are going to go, no matter what!"

She paused, and he realized that she was choosing her words carefully.

"You have every right to refuse to let us stay with the wagon train, but you can't prevent us from going to Texas on our own."

Grimshaw thought he'd seen everything in the fifteen years he'd been wagon master, but the accident that had left the three Hamilton offspring without a father had gotten under his skin. Maybe he felt partly responsible because he should have prevented John Hamilton from swimming to help the Larsons' two stranded wagons. The pain in this little gal's eyes, her helplessness, and her desire to keep her family together made him feel guilty. It was hard for families to rip up their roots and leave everything that was familiar to them. But it was near impossible to make the crossing without a man to do the heavy, backbreaking work that kept the wagons rolling.

"This land can be a mighty cruel place for those who don't know what they're doing, and you don't have any idea what hardships still lie ahead of you. How do you expect to take care of yourself, let alone your brother and sister?"

In some ways Mr. Grimshaw reminded Casey of her father—he was about the same age and build and had the same color brown eyes. She blinked back the tears that threatened to fill her own eyes at the thought of her father. Right now she had to concentrate on the problem at hand.

She had to admit that Mr. Grimshaw was making a good argument, and it scared her some. In truth, she didn't know how she was going to make it without her father, but she wasn't going to give up.

Life in Virginia had not been easy for her family since the Yankees had laid siege to Charlottesville. They had survived for three years in a small two-room cottage, living on little more than hardtack and beans. Still, they had been fortunate, because they at least had a cow, so Jenny and Sam could have fresh milk, and the family could have butter.

No matter what faced them on the journey ahead, it couldn't be harder than living through war and its devastating aftermath. They had come through hard times before; somehow, they would have to get through their father's death, too. No matter how much it hurt to think about going on without him.

Texas was where her father had wanted to take them, and Texas was where they were going to go, although she had no idea what would await them when they got there.

"My uncle, my mother's brother, left us some land. I don't know much about it, but I do know that it's more than what we left behind in Virginia."

Her story was becoming a familiar one to Grimshaw. Since the war had ended, the migration west had become the only hope for many Southern families. But he couldn't allow himself to be swayed by sentimentality.

"The plain truth is, you've got to go back to Charlottesville. We'll be pulling out in the morning . . . without you."

"I'm eighteen years old, and I'm strong for a woman," Casey stated emphatically. "I *will* make it, because if I don't, my father died for nothing. It was his dream for our family to start a new life in Texas and put the old life behind us."

.Grimshaw slapped his battered hat against his thigh in frustration. "Miss Hamilton, I've seen many families that had to turn back, and there's no shame in it. Everyone has a dream of a better life, but sometimes those dreams are buried along the way like the broken carcasses of the deserted wagons you've seen littering the trail. And sometimes those who reach their destination find it more of a nightmare than a dream."

Grimshaw watched Casey flinch at his hard words. He didn't feel good about wrenching her heart out, but he had to drive the truth home to her. He already had her father's death on his conscience; he didn't want to be responsible for this courageous young woman's death as well.

"I got to know your pa pretty well, and I liked him. It didn't take me long to understand that he took real good care of his family despite hard times. I think he would want you to go back to Virginia."

Casey was distracted for a moment as she watched her brother try to unharness the horses—a task he usually performed with their father. Sam was struggling to complete the task alone. He was too young to be doing a man's job, but he was determined to do it. It was only the three of them now, and they had to take care of each other, because no one else would.

"You didn't know Papa at all if you think he would expect his children to turn tail and run."

Grimshaw had little doubt that she had the courage to push on, but that alone could get her killed, along with her brother and sister. He had twenty families to look after, and he couldn't let her have her way. She had a power of persuasion about her, though, and he felt himself wavering in his resolve.

If he did allow her to stay with the wagon train, he would be breaking a rule he'd never broken before: letting a woman make the trek without a man to help her. He watched her chin angle upward, and he could see that her fingernails were digging into the palms of her clenched hands.

"Why don't you sleep on it, and we'll talk more about it in the morning," he advised her, hoping that when she'd had a chance to think it over, she'd realize he was right.

"There's nothing to talk about. We are going on to the Spanish Spur, and neither you nor anyone else is going to stop us. You only have to decide if you'll let us go part of the way with this wagon train."

Grimshaw's mouth thinned to a narrow line. "Did you say the name of the ranch was the Spanish Spur? I've heard of it—and from what I remember, it's quite a spread."

"I don't know much about it." Casey studied his face. She reasoned that the longer she kept him talking, the less likely he was to tell her they had to leave the wagon train. "What have you heard about it?"

"Was your uncle's name Bob Reynolds?"

"Yes. Did you know him?"

"Never met him. But he was well respected, and his name is known to me."

"He was my mother's brother. Papa said Uncle Bob never married and had no family of his own. I guess that's why he left everything to us. The will said the property is located on a river. Do you know anything about that?"

Grimshaw grinned. "I'll say it's located on a river—the Brazos!" He scratched his head and then shook it. "I don't know what you're going to do with all that land."

Casey flinched at his hard tone, but never took her gaze from his. "We'll do just fine. It belongs to us, and we are going to settle there."

"Lord help you." Grimshaw felt grudging respect for the young woman's temerity—she just wouldn't let go. "I don't guess it would do any good to ask you to think about what's best for your brother and sister?"

"What's best for them is to have a home," Casey said stubbornly.

"As I said, we'll talk more on this in the morning." Grimshaw put his hat back on his head and nodded as he courteously touched the brim. "Good evening to you, Miss Hamilton."

Only when Casey watched him walk away did she allow her shoulders to droop and uncertainty to settle over her. She might have sounded confident when she had been talking to Mr. Grimshaw, but she wasn't confident at all. She was more frightened than she had ever been in her life. But she had to hold the family together—she just had to. Casey summoned her courage, refusing to give in to the tears that burned behind her eyes. She had to be strong for Sam and Jenny.

Sam was hobbling the team horses when she reached their campsite. Instinctively, she moved forward to help him. She lifted a bucket of water for the horses to drink. "You do that just like Papa did," she said encouragingly.

"No, I don't," he answered, knowing his sister was trying to bolster his courage. "Not yet, anyway." His shoulders straightened, and he met her gaze. "But I'll learn, because I helped Papa plenty of times."

Sam was so much like their father, with the same soft brown eyes, and the same smile that made a person want to smile back. His dark hair fell in an unruly manner across his forehead, and he needed a haircut. At thirteen, Sam came only to her chin, but her father had claimed that Sam would do most of his growing in his sixteenth year, just as he had.

Sam watched Casey closely as he asked, "Did Mr. Grimshaw agree to let us stay with the wagon train?"

"Not yet. But I think . . . I hope he'll change his mind. He's a reasonable man."

Casey moved on to the next horse with the water bucket while her brother tightened the tether rope.

"What if he refuses?"

She wanted to cry, she wanted to scream, she wanted to sit down and quit, but she couldn't. She turned and faced Sam squarely. "Then we'll go on to Texas on our own. I want you to start practicing with the rifle tomorrow. I know Papa taught you to fire it, but you need to be good enough to hit what you're shooting at."

"Are you scared, Casey?"

"Yes, I am," she admitted, because she thought Sam deserved complete honesty from her. She set the bucket on the ground and ruffled his hair.

"But I'm a Hamilton, and we Hamiltons don't give in to fear, and we don't give up—ever!"

He nodded and looked at her hopefully. "Then we go on regardless."

"Regardless," she answered solemnly, wrapping her arms around him.

When Sam moved away, Casey dropped her head in her hands, feeling as if the world were crushing down on her.

It was quiet throughout the camp, except for an occasional whinny from restless horses. The storm that had hung over them all day had moved on, allowing soft moonlight to filter in through the canvas flap and fall on her little sister's face as she lay curled up next to Casey. Casey felt her heart swell with love for the tiny girl who had never known the mother who died the night of her birth. Now her father was dead as well.

The child was too young to understand the tragedies that had touched her life. Jenny had asked several times today why their father wasn't with them, but so far, Casey had managed to guide her questions in a different direction, because she just didn't know what to tell the child.

Casey had been only fourteen at the time of her mother's death; since then, she had tried to teach her brother and sister some of the things her mother would have wanted them to know. In truth, she could not imagine loving her own children any more than she loved Sam and Jenny.

And she was the only mother Jenny had ever known. She had to be strong for all of them.

Just the night before Sam had started sleeping under the wagon, with their father's rifle by his side. Casey had tried to comfort him since their father died, but Sam would have none of it. She realized that he was trying, in his own way, to assume responsibility as the man of the family.

With troubles weighing heavily on her mind, Casey was still awake when the first light of dawn filtered through the wagon flap. As quietly as possible, she dressed and crept out of the wagon in search of Mr. Grimshaw. As she approached his campsite, she found him shaving. He smiled at her reflection in the mirror he'd hung from a tree branch.

"I'd have bet money that yours would be the first face I saw this morning, Miss Hamilton. You have the look of someone who is ready to dig her heels in and do battle."

She stared back at him. "Do I have to do battle with you?" she asked crisply.

He snapped his razor shut and slowly turned toward her. "If I let you stay with the wagon train, you'll have to keep up. If you lag behind, I *will* leave you. The rest of these people are going on to California, and they don't want anyone holding them up."

Casey saw the fixed expression on his face, and she knew he meant what he said. "You won't have to worry about us."

"Miss Hamilton, I have to get these people safely through, and to do that, I've got to beat the winter storms in the Sierra Nevadas—if that means leaving you behind, I'll do it."

Casey could hardly contain her excitement, but she managed to speak past the lump that had formed in her throat. "You needn't worry about us, Mr. Grimshaw—we'll keep up with the rest of you. You'll see."

"You know, I just bet you will." His grudging smile turned into a boisterous laugh. "In fact, I'd be willing to bet my last two bits on it."

Chapter Two

It had been a week since they had split off from the wagon train at Cimarron Crossing. There had been many tearful good-byes with people they would never see again, people who had become almost like family to them.

Casey knew she would miss Mr. Grimshaw. He was a man she had grown to like and respect. It was frightening to go out on their own, but so far, they had met with no mishaps. The only person they had come across had been a grizzly old buffalo hunter who lingered with them long enough to have five cups of coffee before he rode off into the night. Jenny looked upon their situation as a new adventure, while Sam, who was ever vigilant, kept his rifle beside him at all times.

It was late afternoon when they came to the edge of a canyon that looked down upon the snaking, mud-colored Brazos River. If the map Mr. Grimshaw had drawn for them was accurate, and if they hadn't somehow miscalculated, the Spanish Spur was just on the other side.

Sam was ensconced in the driver's seat as they approached what appeared to be a shallow place to cross the river. Casey saw that he was tense when his hands tightened nervously on the reins. She realized he was probably remembering that their father had been killed in a river crossing very much like this one. She patted his hand.

"It's all right—you can do it."

Deciding he would be less distracted if she left him alone, she climbed inside the wagon and settled Jenny on her lap so she could brush the tangles out of the child's hair. Pulling the red-gold curls away from her sister's face, she tied it with a blue ribbon. Little Jenny was weary from their long months of traveling. Casey would be glad when they were settled in their new home so she could attempt to make a normal life for the family.

"My hair is like yours, Casey," the child said, looking up at her with pride in that fact.

"Indeed it is. And our mother's hair was the same color. Sam has Papa's dark hair."

The child's forehead furrowed. "Will Papa be waiting for us at our new home?"

"No, he won't." A lump tightened in her throat, and it took her a few moments to be able to speak. "Remember when I explained to you that Papa is with Mama now?"

Jenny's frown deepened. "Why can't they live with us? Didn't they like us?"

Casey was saved from answering when a sudden jolt tilted the wagon, propelling her and Jenny forward. In a frantic attempt to keep Jenny from being slammed against the back of the wagon seat, Casey clutched the child to her chest, then somehow managed to land Jenny on top of a stack of folded quilts, but Casey herself was slammed against the seat's iron support.

Everything shifted from the impact, pinning her between the seat and a heavy trunk. Pain shot through her shoulder, and she was unable to move.

Sam scrambled inside and quickly assessed the situation. He shoved the trunk aside so that Casey could free herself. She ignored her bleeding arm and the bump that was already rising on her head and gathered her frightened sister to her. With Sam's help, she managed to climb down into the river, carrying Jenny in her arms.

"What happened, Sam?"

"I'm not quite sure. The river is so muddy, I can't see whatever it is that bogged us down."

Casey held Jenny close and waded through knee-deep water, ignoring the fact that her gown was sopping wet and her shoes were probably ruined. When she reached the back of the wagon, she handed Jenny to Sam and bent down to examine the damage.

"It's listing pretty badly, Sam." She felt along

the bottom of the wheel. "It appears to be wedged between two rocks."

Sam bent down beside her and nodded. "It's all my fault. I should've seen the drop-off, but I didn't."

"It's not your fault," Casey assured him. "You probably kept the wagon from tipping over." She felt around the wagon spokes and was relieved to find that none of them were broken. "We are fortunate the wheel didn't come off."

"That's something, anyway," Sam said in a pained voice. "I feel real bad about this, Casey."

"Don't." She tried to sound cheerful. "Let's see if the horses can pull us free of the rocks."

Sam looked crestfallen. "They can't do it tonight—they're too tired." He sounded defeated. "Maybe in the morning we can lighten the wagon and pull it free."

Casey judged the position of the sun and nodded. "We'll have to spend the night here."

Sam looked so dejected that she placed her arm around his shoulders. "I told you not to worry. You have nothing to feel bad about. I'm so proud of you. Just look at what you have done—you brought us safely home, Sam."

He gave her a weak smile. "Almost home."

She took Jenny from him and climbed up the bank, where she sat Jenny on the grass while their brother unhitched the team. Her shoulder was throbbing with a pain that was becoming difficult to ignore.

She bent down and spoke to her sister. "Jenny, you must stay right here while I help Sam. Don't go near the river."

The child, unaware of the gravity of their situation and looking at it only as a new adventure, curled up on the grass and yawned. Her eyes drifted shut almost immediately.

For two hours they unloaded the wagon and carried everything onto the riverbank.

As Casey and Sam carefully lowered the wooden crate that held their mother's china, their gazes met, communicating the unspoken worry that the dishes might have been broken in the mishap. Their mother had valued her Spode china above all her other possessions; therefore, the delicate dishes were important to her family. The trunk that Casey's mother had brought with her when she married her father had fallen into the river when she and Sam tried to carry it to shore. The fine linens inside were soaked and had to be hung across branches to dry.

Daylight was fading fast, and it was after dark when they finally rescued everything from the wagon. Casey carefully unpacked and examined every piece of her mother's china. Fortunately, none of it was broken, so with the same care she packed the dishes back in the crate.

It was a bedraggled brother and sister who stood amid their few possessions as afternoon turned into evening.

They had been so busy they hadn't even had time to observe their surroundings.

Casey stretched her cramped muscles and winced in pain. Her shoulder ached, but she tried to sound cheerful. "We are on our land now, Sam."

"Yeah, I guess so," he answered wearily. "But so far it isn't going all that well, is it? We're just lucky the river isn't swift, or it would have carried everything we own downstream with the current."

Thunder rumbled in the distance and lightning flashed across the sky. "Pray it doesn't rain tonight."

It was late when Casey spread quilts on the grass while Sam tended to the stock. "I hope today isn't a sign of troubles to come," she mumbled to herself.

Jenny woke up the minute Casey lifted her onto the quilt. Childlike, she smiled as if the day's tragedy had not touched her world.

"I'm not going to have a cookfire tonight, Jenny," Casey told her. "You'll have to eat one of the biscuits and bacon from this morning."

The child nodded and settled next to her. "Casey, will you tell me about Mama and Papa and when you all lived together in the big house?"

Sam joined them and sat with his back braced against a tree, staring broodingly in the direction of their wagon as if he could will it up the embankment. "Jenny, Casey's tired, and besides, you have heard that story a hundred times. Let her rest tonight."

"It's all right." She smiled down at her sister, who never tired of hearing about a brighter time in their lives. The child snuggled closer to her, melting Casey's heart with her sweetness. "Well, let me see," Casey began. "Papa's family had owned a bank in Albemarle County, Virginia, for generations."

"Charlottesville," Jenny supplied. "That's where we lived, wasn't it?"

"That's right. Our house was on a wide boulevard with many trees. It was a big house with an upstairs and a downstairs. There was a fireplace in every room, and a wide veranda surrounded the house on all sides."

"Tell what happened to our house," Jenny urged. "Tell how it got all burned up."

Sam smiled faintly and shook his head. He knew Jenny could have recited the story word for word if she chose to. But Casey patiently continued, hugging the child to her. "You were born in that house, and so was Sam, and so was I. Papa bought the house when he married Mama."

"And Mama was born in Texas and traveled all the way to Virginia to meet Papa. Then she stayed with him in Virginia." Jenny's eyes clouded. "Then she left us."

"Yes. But she didn't want to," Casey said softly. "Mama had to go away."

"Tell about the soldiers that came to town and what they did to our house."

Casey drew in a deep breath. The memory of that awful day still haunted her, and it probably always would. For Jenny's sake, she had managed to sugarcoat the tragedy. "There was a war raging and soldiers in blue uniforms came to Charlottesville and burned Papa's bank."

Jenny nodded. "They were Yankees. And they burned the house, too. Tell about that, Casey."

"There had been a long siege. Papa had heard that the Union soldiers had broken through our lines and would soon be in Charlottesville. He was packing us up to take us to the country, where we would be safe."

"But the soldiers got there before we could leave, didn't they, Casey?"

"That's right. They burned most of the businesses in town. I don't think they really intended for the fire to spread to family homes, but the flames were out of control and went from rooftop to rooftop. The soldiers quickly started a bucket brigade and tried to help us save our house—but it was too late."

"I want to hear how Papa saved our mama's Spode dishes. Tell about that next."

"Well, Papa was very brave and went into the house many times to rescue our belongings, and the soldiers even helped him. They saved three quilts that Grandmother Ruth had given Mama as a wedding present. And Papa saved Mama's

Spode china, the very dishes her great-grandmother brought over from England when she came to this country as a young bride. And one day those dishes will belong to you, Jenny."

"When I'm a bride, like Mama was when her mother gave them to her?"

"Uh-huh." Casey winced when she tried to move her shoulder. It had been hurt worse than she'd thought, and the pain was getting more severe. But there was no reason to worry Sam about it. He had enough on his mind. "That's right. Mama's dishes will be yours when you become a bride."

"When can I be a bride?"

Sam looked serious for a moment; then he managed to smile. "When you grow up and find a man who can love you as much as we do."

"Casey's grown-up, and she isn't a bride," Jenny said, yawning and laying her head in her sister's lap.

Sam chuckled. "That's because she hasn't found a man who will love her as much as you and I do."

Casey pulled a quilt over her sister, glad that Jenny was too young to realize the gravity of their situation. "You are far too inquisitive. Now close your mouth and go to sleep."

The child was silent for a moment, then finally asked, "You mean close my eyes, don't you?"

Casey kissed her forehead. "Yes. Close your eyes and dream beautiful dreams."

"About the big house?"

"No, Jenny—that's gone. Dream about growing up strong and happy in our new home. That's what Papa and Mama would have wanted for you."

"That's what you are going to do," Sam said in a determined tone.

"Let's all go to sleep and see what great adventure awaits us tomorrow," Casey said.

"We'll just be trying to get the wagon out of the river," Sam reminded her.

Chapter Three

The four team horses pulled and strained so hard that Sam had to stop to rest them. The wagon groaned under the stress, then rolled back into the deep rock bed. It didn't seem possible that they would ever be free of the river.

Wet, muddy, and discouraged, Casey and Sam sank down on the grass to rest before they tried again.

Jenny was picking wildflowers, and she had several varieties clamped in her chubby little fist. She giggled when a butterfly landed on her hand, and then went chasing after it when it fluttered away. She did not hear the rider approaching, and he didn't see her, since she was mostly hidden by the tall grass.

The man reined in his horse just in time, guiding the animal sideways to avoid the small child.

With a heavy hand, he managed to bring his skittish mount under control.

"Look," Jenny said to the stranger, holding up her flowers for his inspection. "These flowers are growing just everywhere. Do you want to smell them?"

The man uttered a curse under his breath and dismounted. "Where are your folks?" he asked, kneeling beside her, anger coiling inside him because someone had allowed this child to wander off by herself.

Jenny pointed toward the river. "Right back there. Do you want to see them?"

His lips tightened. He supposed she belonged to one of the steady stream of sod busters who had migrated to Texas since the end of the war.

"Come on. I'll take you to them," he said, lifting her in his arms. He had never held a child before, and it felt awkward to him. He was certainly going to let the parents know how close their daughter had come to being trampled to death.

He remounted his horse, and she laughed up at him when he settled her across his leg. "Papa used to let me ride on his horse with him."

The stranger was taken by surprise when she turned to him and shoved a bright yellow flower behind his ear. "Now you're pretty," she told him.

He ground his teeth and jerked the bloom from behind his ear, crushing it in his fist. He felt a prickle of regret when he saw the disappointment on her beautiful little face and the trembling of her chin as if she were about to cry.

"Let's find your folks," he said gruffly, nudging his horse forward.

Casey gripped the wooden spokes and pushed forward as hard as she could while Sam maneuvered the horses. She could feel the wheel give a bit, but it rocked back again, and the impact of it threw her face-first into the river. She went underwater and came up sputtering, while rivulets of mud trailed down her forehead and stung her eyes.

"Someone's coming," Sam said, reaching behind the seat for his rifle.

Casey was coughing up river water, and at the moment she couldn't see anything. By the time she could catch her breath, she saw the rider dismounting with Jenny in his arms.

Like a mother hen protecting her chick, Casey quickly waded out of the water, flew up the embankment, and grabbed her sister out of the man's arms.

"What do you think you're doing?" she asked, clutching her sister tightly to her.

When she saw the man's murderous expression, Casey quickly stepped away from him.

"I'll tell you what I've been doing, ma'am—I've been rescuing your child. Something I wouldn't have had to do if you'd been watching her. There's no telling what could happen to her out here."

Fear climbed up her spine, and she took another tentative step away from him, not sure what his intentions were.

The stranger was tall, powerful, and lean. His dark hair was coal black, and, like Sam, he also needed a haircut. His black hat was pulled low over his forehead, so she could see only the bottom part of his face, which was covered by several days' growth of stubble. He looked exactly like she imagined a gunfighter would look—right down to the holster that was laced about his leg as it cradled a dangerous-looking black-handled gun. Suddenly he shoved his hat back on his head, and she stared into cold, silver-gray eyes that were riveted on her in an intimidating manner.

A quick glance at Sam relieved her mind. His rifle was aimed directly at the stranger.

"Where did you find her?" Casey demanded. She frowned at her sister, who was certainly going to be reprimanded as soon as the man left.

"She was about a half a mile from here. I'd say with her short legs it took her quite a while to get that far. You should have missed her by now—why didn't you?"

Casey stood there dripping wet, attempting to wipe the mud from her face, but merely smearing it more. "We were trying to get the wagon out of the river, and I thought she was asleep."

Gabe scowled at the woman. Her gown was wet and clung to her soft curves. She certainly was not a beauty. But she did have the most unusual blue eyes he'd ever seen—they were turquoise. He couldn't tell what color her hair was, and there wasn't a clean spot on her face.

Gabe's attention suddenly focused on the boy, who rested a rifle in the curve of his arm and was watching him closely. With a quick assessment of the situation, he realized that they had real trouble.

"Where's your husband, ma'am?"

Casey was suspicious of the stranger, or, more accurately, downright frightened of him. "My husband is nearby," she said quickly, not wanting the man to think they were without protection. "He should be back any moment."

She saw the expanse of his chest when he took a deep breath of irritation.

"You'll need to put something underneath the wheel to get leverage, or you'll never get that wagon out of the river. We need branches. I suppose you have a saw or an ax in there, boy?"

Sam nodded, looking from Casey to the man. "Yes, sir, I have an ax."

"Ma'am, you need to stay out of our way and keep the child safe," he ordered.

She was so irritated with him that she considered telling him they didn't need his help.

He took the ax Sam handed him. "You people come out here with no notion what you're in for. Why didn't you just stay where you were?"

Casey was soaking wet, in pain, and accustomed

to being treated with more respect. Her temper flared. "We aren't asking for your help or your advice. Why don't you just go away and leave us alone?"

The man brushed past Casey, ignoring her outburst. She held her breath when his hand went to his gun belt, until she realized he was only unbuckling it. She was relieved when he tossed it across his saddle.

"Keep the kid away from my horse," he ordered, turning away. Without hesitation, he waded into the river to discover what was holding the wagon wheel.

At the point of admitting defeat, and feeling so bone-weary she could cry, Casey carried Jenny up the riverbank and sat down to watch the stranger examine the wheel.

Casey kept a watchful eye on Sam as he accompanied the man a short distance from the river to help him chop branches off a mesquite tree. Without realizing she was doing it, she had become fascinated by the way the stranger's muscles rippled across his broad shoulders while he worked. There was power behind the ax he wielded, and some anger as well. Her gaze followed him as he waded back into the river and drove several stakes between the rocks and the wheel.

"Pull forward slowly," he instructed Sam. "Keep one hand on the reins, and the other on the brake. When I tell you to, push the horses hard."

Casey held her breath as the wagon inched forward. She wanted to shout for joy when it pulled out of the river and onto solid ground, but she didn't. She watched the stranger wade out of the water to stand dripping on the bank. She should thank him for helping them, but she was still seething from the unkind remarks he had made.

"I'd like to pay you," she said instead.

"You can pay me by keeping a closer watch on your daughter. Anyone could have come along and carried her off. It's dangerous out here, ma'am."

He was the most dangerous person Casey had seen so far. She turned her back to him, allowing him to believe that she was Jenny's mother.

"You have our gratitude," she said in a voice that implied the opposite. She felt some satisfaction in the fact that he was as soaked to the skin as she was. She hoped his boots were full of water.

"Your gratitude and a nickel will get you nothing out here. This country is no place for folks who don't even know how to cross a river."

She turned and glared at him.

"Ma'am, if your husband were from around here, he'd have known there were rocks in this part of the river. If you had gone fifty yards downstream, you could have crossed with no trouble at all."

He had driven the point home. She watched him adjust his hat as he gave her a dark look. "If you are figuring on camping around here, I think

I should warn you that you are on private property."

She returned his frown with one of her own. "Are you saying you own this land?"

"Nope. I'm just riding through. And, if I were you, when your husband returns, I'd advise him to do the same."

"This is the Spanish Spur ranch, isn't it?" Sam asked.

"That's what they call it. If you are wise, you'll load up and keep going until you are clear of this place."

It was on the tip of her tongue to tell him that this was their land, and he was the trespasser. Instead, she watched him mount his horse and ride away.

"Sam, if that was what they call 'Texas hospitality,' I want none of it."

"He did do us a good turn," her brother reminded her. "But he didn't give his name, and he didn't ask for ours."

"I hope we have seen the last of him," she answered. "He is an overbearing, arrogant man." She frowned in contemplation. "What do you suppose he meant by warning us off our own land? It's strange, don't you think?"

"Maybe we should have asked him."

Jenny drew back as she studied her sister. "You look so funny with mud all over your face. I wish I could have some on mine."

"Little girl," Casey said in annoyance, "don't

you ever run away again. You could have been lost. What if that man had taken you away from us?"

Jenny lowered her head—she wasn't accustomed to Casey scolding her in such a hard tone. "He wouldn't wear my flower," she said forlornly.

Casey set her sister on her feet. "You stay right here while Sam and I load everything back in the wagon—and don't move from this spot."

Glaring, the child sat down hard and folded her arms across her chest in defiance. "I'm not going with you to our new home. I'm staying here all by myself. Then when I get hungry, I'll probably die, and you'll be sorry you talked so mean to me."

Casey was already sorry. To make amends she bent down and placed a kiss on the child's cheek, which did nothing to soften Jenny's expression.

"Let's get busy," Sam interjected, laying his rifle on the wagon seat so he could get to it in a hurry. "It'll probably be dark before we reach the house."

Casey knelt at the river and washed the mud from her face, then spoke encouragingly to her brother. "We made it, Sam. Just like Papa would have expected us to."

A smile tugged at Sam's lips. "Papa would have been proud of us, wouldn't he?"

"That he would."

By the time they were finally ready to leave, the sun shone on the high cliffs on the other side of the river, washing them in a red glow. As they got farther away from the Brazos, the land leveled off to scrub brush, mesquite trees, and cactus.

Sam balanced Jenny on his knee, watching as Casey drove the team. "This country is not a bit like Virginia," he said, reflecting her own thoughts.

"No, it isn't. And we are all feeling somewhat lost at the moment. We know next to nothing about ranching and raising cattle."

"We can learn," Sam said hopefully.

"We didn't know how to survive on the trail, but we did it. We came this far against almost impossible odds. We'll learn what we need to know, and figure out the rest as we go along." She tightened her hands on the reins. "We'll do whatever it takes to make this our—"

"I see a house!" Jenny cried, waving her arms. "Casey, Sam, it must be like our big house back home—the one the soldiers burned up."

Casey reined in the team, and they all quietly stared at the scene before them as their excitement turned to disappointment. The house was a Spanish-style structure that had long been neglected and stood in desperate need of repair. In the distance there was a large barn, as well as several outbuildings she couldn't identify.

As far as Casey could tell, there were no animals and no people about. The place looked as if it had been deserted for a long time.

As Casey urged the horses forward, she noticed there was a brick well with a wooden bucket hanging from a tattered rope. That was something, anyway—at least they wouldn't have to depend on the river for their water—if the well water was still good.

She met Sam's gaze and felt his discouragement.

"The house we lived in after ours burned was much smaller than this one," she said brightly. "And this is our home—that one wasn't. Think of it this way: we have all the time in the world to make repairs."

Sam knew she was trying to be cheerful for his sake, but he was old enough to be told the truth. "How much money do we have to make those repairs?"

She nodded at Jenny, who was scrambling over the side of the wagon. When she dropped to the ground and ran toward the house as fast as her little legs would take her, Casey answered her brother. "I have in my possession forty-seven dollars. In the letter Papa got from that attorney, Mr. Murdock, he wrote that we were to come to his office as soon as we arrived. The letter was mailed from a town called Mariposa Springs. I think it's possible that Uncle Bob may have left us in debt, and there may even be back taxes to pay on the ranch."

Sam looked around. "It certainly doesn't appear to have been a prosperous ranch."

"No, it doesn't."

Jenny came running back, laughing with

delight. "This is the best house I have ever seen! And you will never guess what! We get to live with chickens!" She was so excited, she was jumping up and down. "I saw them right there in the house!"

Casey and Sam exchanged glances as Sam lifted Jenny up in his arms.

"Our welcoming committee," Sam observed with irony.

"Chickens," Casey said in a stunned voice.

Chapter Four

Casey stepped over broken glass and scattered debris to reach the rickety porch step. A slight breeze caught the door, and it creaked back and forth with only one good hinge to hold it in place. Her heart plummeted as she stepped into the dark interior. There was no furniture at all, and she could not identify the awful odor that permeated the air, making her want to gag.

She moved cautiously through the first room, holding her hand over her nose. She didn't take a deep breath until she moved into the kitchen. She rushed for the window, which was stuck. She pushed and tugged until she was finally able to shove it open, letting in fresh air.

She hung herself out the window for a moment. Then she glanced about the kitchen. Mercifully, there was a large cookstove and an open hearth. It must have once been a nice kitchen. There even appeared to have been water at one time, because there was a broken pump handle on the floor.

She backtracked through the front room and found what must have been her uncle's bedroom. It was now dreary, dismal, and empty. With a heavy heart, she returned to the main room and almost stumbled over a ladder that led up to a loft, which must have served as a second bedroom. At the moment it seemed to be serving as a chicken roost.

Jenny had been right. Huddled in the rafters, clucking their annoyance at being disturbed, was a flock of chickens! She closed her eyes and tried not to think about what she had just stepped in that squished beneath her shoe. She tried to imagine the house as it might once have been, but she could think only about the work it would take to make it livable once more.

Sam stood in the doorway, holding Jenny's hand. "The barn is in bad shape and will need a lot of repairing. The corrals are not too bad, though—they just need a few boards replaced. And, Casey, there is a small two-room cabin on the other side of the bunkhouse, and someone is living in it. There was a pot of coffee on the back of the stove, and it was still hot. But no one seemed to be around at the moment."

"I wanted to wait for them. Sam wouldn't let me," Jenny said, jerking her hand from her brother's.

"It's probably someone who worked for Uncle

Bob." Casey tried to gather her wits about her. "It's too late to do anything tonight, so it looks like we'll be spending another night under the stars."

Jenny had broken away from Sam and was headed for the ladder. "I'm going to sleep with the chickens."

Sam caught up with her and swung her into his arms, but not before she had stepped in chicken droppings.

Casey groaned as she untied her sister's shoes and held them away from her nose. "The first thing I want you to do tomorrow is to fix that door. I'll be evicting the chickens."

Jenny seemed to be the only one who was happy about their situation. This was certainly not the welcome they had hoped for.

"Did you see any sign of stock, Sam?"

"None whatsoever—not cattle or horses. And it doesn't look like there has been any here in a long time."

Casey let out her breath. "It's just as well. We wouldn't know what to do with—"

"Don't no one move!" A female voice cut through the silence and echoed around the empty house. "I got a gun aimed at your back, and I know how to use it."

Casey turned slowly to face the newcomer, who certainly did have a rifle trained on her. "Who are you?" she asked, hoping the woman wasn't deranged.

"Now, seeing as how you three are the intruders, I'll be the one asking the questions. There ain't going to be no squatters on this land. I drove a family off last month, and I'm telling you to leave right now."

The woman was the most unusual person Casey had ever seen. She could not be over four feet tall; she was angular and thin, her chin sharp and prominent. She wore a gray skirt with the hem tucked into her belt, showing a pair of cowboy boots and a pair of men's red long johns. Her gray hair was braided and then twisted into a knot on the top of her head. Her eyes were dark, maybe brown—it was hard to tell in the dim light.

Sam moved closer to Casey, and she handed Jenny to him, then stepped in front of them.

"We aren't intruders; this is our land," Casey stated clearly.

A doubtful expression moved over the woman's face, but she loosened her grip on the rifle, aiming it at the floor. "Now, I know who this ranch belongs to, and the last time I looked, it surely wasn't you three. You have the look of squatters to me."

"You are mistaken," Sam said, setting Jenny down and pushing her behind him. "The Spanish Spur belonged to our uncle, and he left it to us in his will. What we want to know is, who are you and what you are doing here?"

"Never you mind about me. How do I know you aren't from the Casa Mesa ranch, sent here to stir things up? Cyrus Slaughter is just mean enough to send someone 'round to cause more trouble for me."

Casey took a step toward the woman. If she was crazed, she wanted to be standing in front of Sam and Jenny. "You are on our land," she said cautiously. "You are the one who is the intruder."

"Now that ain't the way of it. I've been living here way before you were even born. Do you have some kind of proof to back up your claim?"

"I have a letter from my uncle's attorney in the wagon. His office is in Mariposa Springs, and his name is Mr. Bartholomew J. Murdock. My uncle was Bob Reynolds."

The woman's hard expression eased a bit, and she nodded. "Why didn't you say so straight off? You'd be the ones I've been expecting. Where's your pa?"

Casey stepped even closer and lowered her voice so Jenny wouldn't overhear her answer. "My father . . . died on the way here. Jenny doesn't understand, so I would appreciate it if you wouldn't mention it in front of her."

The woman blinked her eyes and nodded. "Honey, you don't mean to tell me that the three of you think you can run this place alone?"

"We went through a lot to get here. I will do whatever I must to make this a home for my brother and sister."

The woman's eyes softened, and so did her voice. "Why, you are hardly more'n a young'un yourself." She walked around each one of them. "I should of knowed you right away from all your uncle told me 'bout you."

"This," Casey said, nodding at her brother, "is Sam. My name is Casey, and the child is our little sister, Jenny. Our last name is Hamilton."

"Your uncle called you by different names. He called you Cassandra, you'd be Samuel, and the little one there would be Jennifer."

Jenny peeked her head around Sam's leg and said in a disgruntled voice, "I'm mad at my sister. I want to sleep with the chickens, and she won't let me."

The woman chuckled and then laughed so hard she had to wipe her tears on the sleeve of her shirt. "Lord have mercy on us all. I have three children on my hands."

"I didn't quite get your name," Sam said, stepping closer, and asserting his authority.

Casey knew by the set of his shoulders that he was tired of people pushing them around. First it had been the wagon master who tried to send them home, then the man at the river, and now this woman.

"Well, young man, my name is Kathryn Eldridge. Folks hereabout just call me Kate."

Casey had a million questions to ask the woman. "Mrs. Eldridge—"

"Not Mrs. I ain't never been married. Never found a man I could stand to be 'round for more than a week at a time. Just call me Kate."

"Kate, what happened here? My mother had wonderful memories of growing up on the Spanish Spur. This looks nothing like the place she described to us."

"Honey, this house has been sitting vacant for more'n two years. Thieves took most of the furniture, 'cept the few things I managed to lock in the storage shed. All your uncle's papers are there, and a few family things you might be interested in."

Casey glanced about her in distress. "I don't even know where to start cleaning."

"Now that ain't your biggest worry. Your worry is going to be Cyrus Slaughter, the meanest, orneriest, most cantankerous old man you'll ever meet up with. He owns half of Texas and won't be satisfied until he gets the rest. Now, this here ranch stands between his Casa Mesa ranch and the Brazos. He's had his eye on this spread for quite a spell. Your uncle always let him water his herd at the river, but that wasn't good enough for Cyrus—he won't stop until he drives you off or buries you."

"No one can be that mean," Sam said in disbelief.

"Well, you may think different when you get to know him. I have a notion he's been driving off some of your cattle, and I suspect, although I can't prove it, he's been sticking his own brand on some of 'em."

It was too much for Casey to absorb all at once.

"If he's that bad, he should be arrested."

"Hell, gal, ain't no lawman going to go up against him. He'll do whatever it takes to drive you away." She cradled her rifle in her arms. "Your uncle wanted you to know about Cyrus, so I told you right off. And, honey, he's going to run right over you three youngsters like you weren't even there."

Sam slid his arm around Casey's waist to comfort her and to find comfort for himself. "This is our home now, and we'll do whatever we have to do to protect it."

Kate looked as if she would like to say more, but she turned away and called over her shoulder, "After you've tended the horses, come on up to the house, and I'll feed you. I got a big garden behind my house, and my guess is you three ain't had any fresh vegetables in a spell. You look like you could use a good meal."

Sam and Jenny had been asleep for over an hour, but Casey had too much on her mind to sleep. And with her shoulder hurting, it was hard to find a comfortable position.

She tried to find a bright side to their situation, but there didn't seem to be one. If it had been Kate's intention to frighten her with talk about Cyrus Slaughter, she had certainly succeeded. Should she take the initiative—visit the rancher and introduce herself—or should she wait for him to make the first move? She wondered how much repair work would be necessary before they could move into the house.

Casey recalled her mother mentioning the fierce weather in this part of Texas. They had to make the house livable before winter set in. According to Kate, they had about two months before the weather turned bad.

And how were they going to live in the meantime? They hadn't much money. Maybe the best thing to do would be to sell the Spanish Spur to Mr. Slaughter, if he wanted it so badly. But that would leave them without a home, and she wasn't ready to admit defeat—not yet. And perhaps Mr. Slaughter wasn't as bad as Kate had said.

Casey pushed the covers aside and felt around in the dark until she found a shawl to throw over her nightgown. There was no need to get dressed, because there wouldn't be anyone about. She slid her feet into her slippers, then climbed down from the wagon as quietly as she could so she wouldn't disturb Sam and Jenny.

She noticed a light was still burning in the cabin. It seemed that Kate couldn't sleep either. Casey stared up at the stars and wished she knew what her father would expect them to do. There was no one she could turn to for help.

She made her way to the house and seated herself on the top step, unwilling to go inside the dark interior. She felt the cool breeze on her cheeks and pushed her hair away from her face. She had made so many choices since her father's death; suppose she had been wrong in insisting they come to Texas? If only they could somehow manage to hold on to this ranch, it would one day belong to Sam—and she wanted that for him.

"I see you didn't take my advice."

Casey jumped to her feet at the sound of the man's voice. "What . . . who . . ." Although she saw only his shadowy form, she knew who it was. She would never forget that voice. He was the man who had helped them with the wagon. "What are you doing here?"

"I might ask you the same thing."

Even if she couldn't see his face, she imagined the look of disapproval etched there. She suddenly remembered that she was wearing her nightgown and gathered the shawl tighter about her. He took a step toward her, and all she could focus on was the gun in his holster. She thought about calling for help, but Sam would be no match for this man.

"The Spanish Spur belongs to my family, and you are trespassing." Her legs were trembling with fear, and she didn't think she had ever been so frightened. If only she had thought to bring the rifle—if only she had taken the time to dress—she wouldn't feel quite so vulnerable and at such a disadvantage.

Casey felt his gaze on her, as if he were weighing her words. "How can you say the ranch belongs to you when I know Bob Reynolds would never sell the Spanish Spur?"

Although she was afraid of him and she wanted to run away, she stood her ground. "Bob Reynolds was my uncle. I would have told you before if you hadn't been so rude."

He stepped into the moonlight, and she tried to pull away when he clamped her chin and raised her face to his. Refusing to allow him to intimidate her, she met his gaze defiantly. In that moment, she saw a look of puzzlement in his eyes, and his touch was gentle as he brushed his hand through her hair.

"It seems the females in your family have a tendency to wander into danger," he remarked.

He dropped his hand to his side, and in that moment Casey knew instinctively that he would not harm her.

The young beauty stood before Gabe, the moonlight washing her pale skin with an ethereal light. She touched something deep inside him, and he wanted nothing more than to stand between her and any trouble that might come her way. How could he have mistakenly thought she was homely when she had the kind of beauty that pulled at a man's insides, made him want to touch her skin to see if it was as soft as it appeared?

Suddenly he stiffened; he had forgotten she had a husband. "I see you washed the mud from your face," he said, trying to distance himself from her.

"I . . . had fallen in the river."

His gaze strayed across her soft mouth, and he

mentally shook himself. "You have a lot to think about, ma'am." He didn't trust himself to be near her, so he moved farther away. "I'll be seeing you."

She took a guarded breath as he moved past her and disappeared into the night. With hurried steps, she ran toward the wagon and climbed inside. Her heart was pounding so fast she could hardly breathe.

She lay back beside Jenny and took the child's hand in hers, hoping she could find comfort in her sister's nearness.

Something deep and meaningful had happened to her when the stranger had touched her.

But what?

He had stirred feelings inside her that she had never felt before. It was as if he had opened a door and all her emotions had come rushing out. She didn't even know his name or anything about him. She was confused and troubled, and hoped never to see him again, and yet, if she didn't, something very precious would be lost.

Chapter Five

Kate laid her book on the wobbly table beside her chair and rubbed her tired eyes. Her sight was getting worse—so much so that she had to struggle to read a line, much less a page. And she did so love to read.

She was becoming a nocturnal creature because she had so much trouble sleeping. She had always been able to get by on four or five hours of sleep a night. Lately, though, since Bob had died, she would feel lucky if she got half that amount. He'd been the only person she had ever truly respected, and in her way, she had loved him. She would always be beholden to him because he had saved her from living a very different life from the one he had provided for her.

She was lucky it had been he who came into the Yellow Dog Saloon that night twenty years ago. Kate had never known her pa, and her ma had died when she was twelve. She had found work at the saloon, scrubbing and cleaning rooms for a place to sleep behind the stairs. And that was how she had lived until one night when Patty, one of the saloon girls, had run away with a buffalo hunter. Kate had certainly never been a beauty. But it hadn't mattered, because the owner had been short one girl, and it had been payday for the wranglers of the nearby ranches. He had ordered her to change into Patty's costume and to be nice to the men, or he'd throw her out on the street.

Bob Reynolds had been the first to buy her a drink and to take her to the room upstairs. Bob, who had seen her tears and listened to the story of her life—Bob, who had taken her away with him that very night. They had not made love then or anytime since. He had made her a vow that he would never lay a hand on her, that he would see she was always safe. He had kept his promise and built her this house.

There had been lovers—mostly some of the cowhands who worked at the ranch. Bob had had his women, but the two of them had never been together that way. Their feelings went much deeper than lust—they were the very best of friends. They had been sympathetic to each other in troubled times, and they had laughed together in happy times. And now he was gone, and she was left behind to mourn him.

She had never felt she had given Bob as much as he had given her, but now she would repay him by looking after his kin. He had talked about his only sister's children a lot. Although he had never seen them, they had corresponded with him regularly.

When the soft rap came on the door, she expected it to be one of the Hamiltons. She was surprised when she found out who her visitor was.

"Well, as I live and breathe, can it really be you, Gabriel? Come on in and set yourself down."

"I wouldn't have disturbed you this late, Kate, but I saw your light."

She gave him a wide grin and patted his shoulder, drawing him into the house and closing the door behind him. He had removed his hat, but he was still so tall that he'd had to duck under the door frame.

Gabe knew that Bob Reynolds had built this house especially for Kate, and since she was so petite, everything seemed to be in miniature. It was like an oversize dollhouse. He, like many other people, had speculated about Kate's relationship with the old man, but no one really knew for sure.

"I never mind being disturbed by a handsome man. Make yourself to home. Do you want some coffee—or maybe you'd like something stronger? I don't have any of the good stuff, but I have a jug that'll knock your boots off."

Gabe shook his head. "Thanks, but no. I need to know about the people who claim to own the Spanish Spur. What happened to Bob?"

"He up and died of the lung sickness—he went fast, and I wasn't expecting it. The people you're asking 'bout are the Hamiltons."

"Are they related to Bob Reynolds?"

"Yeah, they are. None of them are much more'n young'uns. They can't make it out here with Cyrus wanting to get his hands on the place—you know it, and I know it—but there ain't nobody gonna make that pretty little gal believe it."

She watched his silver eyes flash in the flickering lamplight. If anyone wanted to get Gabe riled, all that was necessary was to mention Cyrus.

"They can't go up against him and live to tell about it, Kate. And no one from around here is going to help them. Everyone's too afraid of Cyrus."

"He ain't gonna be happy 'bout them being here—and when he ain't happy, people die."

"I know."

Gabe stood up slowly and stretched his tall frame. Kate was nearing her sixtieth birthday, but the sight of that gorgeous man made her eyes widen.

"It's none of my affair. The woman's husband should take them back where they came from."

"Husband? There ain't no husband. There's just Casey and her brother, Sam, and the little one, Jenny."

"Then what in the hell are they doing here?" He started pacing. "Cyrus won't care that they're young, or even that two of them are female; he'll only care that they are standing in the way of something he wants."

Kate shook her head. "I wouldn't want to see anything happen to them. Hell, if Cyrus could just wait a month or so, they'd probably be happy to sell the Spanish Spur to him. They came here all the way from Virginia, burying their pa along the way. Now, you know and I know"—she glanced up at him expectantly—"they can't last out here without help."

"Then the woman is a widow?"

"She never had no husband. What makes you think such a thing?"

He had assumed the little girl was her daughter. "Then the child—"

"Is her sister."

Gabe settled into a cane-bottom chair and stared at the lamp, which was running out of oil and needed the wick trimmed.

"You've been away since the war; I didn't even know you were back till now."

"I had planned to leave for El Paso tomorrow, and I didn't expect to see anyone I knew. I left Texas in 'sixty-three, swearing I would never come back. After the war I bummed around, and I don't know why I ended up back here. I certainly didn't intend to."

"Have you seen Cyrus?"

"No. Why should I? We have nothing to say to each other. We never have."

He leaned his head back and took in a deep breath before looking at Kate. "I thought I could ride through and no one would be the wiser. Now I've become embroiled in the Hamiltons' troubles. It kind of muddies the water, so to speak."

Kate's laughter cackled out. "You're going to stay and help 'em, ain't you?"

"I don't have any choice. Cyrus already has the blood of too many innocents on his hands. I can't let him have these three to add to his tally."

"I didn't think you could."

He was quiet for a moment. "Kate, I'd appreciate it if you didn't mention my last name to the Hamiltons."

"I can see how you'd feel that way. Things should start getting interesting 'round here in a few days. You and Cyrus was bound to butt heads sooner or later. I knew the day would come when you'd return and fight him. I guess you chose the Spanish Spur as your battleground."

He made no reply, but she saw a muscle clench in his jaw, and his hands slid into fists.

"Yeah, it's definitely going to get mighty interesting 'round here, Gabriel."

At the moment, all Gabe could think about was the beautiful young woman, so courageous and strong, thinking she didn't have a friend in the world. He couldn't just ride away and leave her at Cyrus's mercy.

* * *

Casey still could not sleep. She sighed, remembering that her father had once told her that troubles always seemed darker at night, but brightened in the light of day. She doubted that the problems that faced her family would look any better at sunrise.

It was still dark when she dressed and climbed out of the wagon, taking care not to disturb Sam and Jenny. She reasoned that if she couldn't sleep, she might as well get busy cleaning the house. She lit a lantern and made her way to the well; tossing the wooden bucket over the side, she heard it splash below. Hand over hand, she tugged the rope upward, then cupped her hands and drew water up to her mouth.

Cautiously, she took a sip, then smiled. There was nothing to worry about; it tasted as sweet as springwater.

Half an hour later Casey had gathered a cleaning bucket, lye soap, and a brush, and went down on her knees to clean the kitchen floor. Soap suds swirled out about her as her scrub brush dug into the wooden floor, washing away two years of neglect. Ignoring the stabbing pain in her shoulder, she dipped her scrub brush back into the water and sloshed it across the floor. Her heart stopped when she watched water splash across the toe of a black boot. Her gaze followed the line up the long leg to the face of the man she had expected never to see again.

"Didn't you see that the floor is wet?" she asked,

blowing a tangled red-gold curl out of her face. She dabbed at the toe of his boot with a wet cloth, but her action only made the suds worse.

He took a step away from her. "Is it your habit to scrub floors before the sun comes up?"

She bristled. "Is it your habit to go skulking about whenever and wherever it pleases you?"

She watched his mouth turn up into a grin. "Skulking about—is that what I'm doing?"

"That is what it seems like to me. You were here last night and now first thing this morning." She glared at him and asked suspiciously, "Just why are you here again?"

Ignoring her question, he knelt down and stared at her for a moment. "I might have known you would be a redhead," he remarked, and for some reason he did not understand, he wanted to brush the unruly red-gold curls off her cheek. "You certainly have a temper to match the color. And," he said with irony in his tone, "for some reason, you always seem to be having some kind of mishap with water."

He was too close to her, and she couldn't breathe as she looked into those silver eyes. She had intended to get to her feet so she could put some distance between them, but her hand slipped on the wet floor and, to her horror and dismay, her face landed in the bucket of water. She sputtered and tried to wipe the soap out of her stinging eyes.

Casey felt strong hands grip hers, and the man

lifted her to her feet. She grabbed his arm in an attempt to steady herself, trying to hang on to as much dignity as she could with water streaming down her face.

She felt his muscles flex beneath her fingers. This was not a man to be trifled with, and she feared the way he looked at her. What was the look; what did it mean?

She managed to move away from him so she could dab at her eyes with her apron. It didn't help much, though; her eyes still stung. "You never did answer me—why did you return?"

"I took the liberty of sleeping in your barn last night, so I never actually left."

Casey stopped dabbing at her eyes and stared at him. "You stayed here last night?"

"I hope you don't mind."

She was struck by his audacity. Why would he have done such a thing? She certainly would not have slept at all if she had known he was so nearby.

"You should have asked me if I minded before you did it."

He leaned against the door frame and watched her just as the rooster crowed, announcing sunup. "Do you mind?"

"I . . . do not feel comfortable with strangers."

He held up his hand and laughed. "I know. You don't like strangers skulking about. And you're right—I should have asked you." He watched her face carefully. "I'm sorry. You see, I had nowhere else to sleep."

She dabbed at her hair with her apron. "Look, whoever you are, I have troubles of my own, and I don't need to take on any more."

"I was wondering if you had any work for me." He gestured outside and shrugged his broad shoulders. "It looks to me like you could use some help."

By now her eyes had stopped burning a bit, and it was light enough for her to get a good look at him. He wasn't wearing his gun this morning, but he still looked dangerous to her. His eyes, which had appeared to be a flat slate color a moment ago, seemed now to swirl with silver light. He filled the doorway with his size, and she assessed his features. He had the kind of handsomeness that would draw her attention even if he were in a room with other men. His dark brows arched above those glorious eyes; his nose was in harmony with his other features. His mouth was what drew and held her attention. What would it feel like to have it pressed against hers? She went weak all over at that thought, and scolded herself for even entertaining such fantasies.

"I doubt that you know anything about ranching," he said, breaking into her thoughts. "I could teach your brother some things he needs to know, and I do need the work."

He needed a shave, and his hair was too long, but judging by the rich material of his trousers and the fine blue shirt he wore, he didn't look like he needed money.

"You don't seem to be down on your luck to me," she quickly pointed out.

He gave her that devastatingly masculine smile that tightened her insides. "You never can tell; maybe I'm just a supporter of lost causes."

"We aren't lost, mister. You are the one who seems to be wandering around aimlessly."

"I would make you a good hand," he said, as if she had not spoken. "I work hard and don't eat much."

She didn't want him around, and yet she could not stand the thought of never seeing him again. Where had that thought come from? "I don't know anything about you," she stated firmly.

"Kate knows me. She'll vouch for my honesty."

Casey was torn. She didn't want to admit to him that she didn't have the money to pay him; it would be too humiliating. So she chose another method to turn him away. "I have been warned that there is a powerful neighbor to the south of us who is likely to cause trouble. I'm afraid that anyone I hire would be considered his enemy. I can't do that to you."

His eyes turned glacier cold, and he stared at her so hard, she took a step back. She managed to say without hesitation, "I don't want to be responsible for you if trouble comes."

"I know who you are talking about." There was a sharp edge to his voice, a coldness, and she imagined it was the tone he might use before he drew his gun on someone. "I'm not afraid of Cyrus Slaughter."

"From what Kate tells me, you should be." She stared down at the hem of her soaked gown, unable to look at him any longer. "I think it would be better if you rode on."

When she glanced back up, he was watching her. "I really do need the work."

She took a steadying breath and dived in. "The truth is, I can't pay you wages. We don't have much money and—"

"I'll work for a bed and grub. Later we can talk about wages."

"I don't know. It doesn't seem—"

"I'd like a place to settle for a while. You'd be doing me a favor."

She didn't believe him. He had a motive for wanting to work for her, but she didn't know what it could be. "I don't even know your name."

"I am called Gabe, Miss Hamilton."

She wiped her wet hands on her apron. "I suppose you have a last name."

"Just Gabe."

Casey didn't completely trust him. But it was true that she and Sam just didn't know how to run a ranch the size of this one.

"We *could* use the help," she admitted. "As you said, you could show Sam a few things, since the ranch will one day belong to him."

Gabe digested that bit of information and nodded. "It's settled then. If it's all right with you, I'll start rounding up what cattle you still have."

"I will want my brother to learn how to work on this ranch. Do you want Sam to go with you?"

"Not today. It looks to me like you need him to help around here."

Without another word, he turned and walked away, leaving Casey wondering how he had gotten her to agree to hire him—she hadn't meant to. He had a persuasive way about him, and a gift for turning a situation to his advantage. He was the last person she had wanted on the Spanish Spur, and yet she had just agreed to let him stay.

Suddenly a calmness settled over her, something she had not felt since her father's death. She was living in the midst of a swirling storm, and the man called Gabe had just become her anchor. Where had that feeling come from? She hardly knew him, and there was certainly no reason to trust him. She wanted to ask Kate if she had done the right thing in hiring him.

Chapter Six

Sam had nailed down the loose steps, removed the front door so he could repair the broken hinges, then hung it back in place. After he had repaired the fence that enclosed the chicken coop, he and a delighted Jenny herded the wayward chickens into the enclosure and locked the gate.

Jenny had objected when Casey informed her that the chickens would not be coming back into the house.

After the kitchen was cleaned to Casey's satisfaction, she turned her attention to the front room. She and Sam made many trips to the well for clean water so she could scrub the walls and floors. Sam had insisted on cleaning the loft, since he intended to take it for his bedroom. It was almost dark when Casey swished her drying cloth over the last window, satisfied that it was clean enough for her to see her reflection.

The house had been scrubbed and aired, and it now had the fresh smell of lemon oil. It occurred to her that she had been so busy she had not yet asked Kate about Gabe.

Sam stood in the doorway with a wide grin on his face, amazed at the change. "We have a home, now that we've wrestled it away from the chickens."

Casey slid her arm around his waist, and he lifted Jenny in his arms. The floors were quite beautiful since the grime had been scrubbed away and the wood had been polished. The three of them stared at what they had accomplished, and it was a poignant moment for them all. If only their father could have been there to share the triumph with them.

Casey smiled, feeling hope for the first time since their father had died. "We don't have a stick of furniture, and I'm not sure where our next meal is coming from, but we have a home."

"Your next meal is gonna be with me," Kate said, coming up behind them and staring about her. "This looks good—you did a lot of work."

"Thank you," Casey said, smiling at the older woman. "I don't believe I could lift a pan to cook tonight."

"Did I forget to mention that I did all the cookin' for your uncle's cowhands? There used to be anywhere from twelve to twenty wranglers at any given time. Nary a one of them complained of my cookin'."

"I wanted to ask you about someone I hired. He calls himself Gabe, and he said you knew him." She searched Kate's eyes when she asked, "Did I do right in giving him a job?"

Kate was happy Gabe had agreed to help them. "Shoot, yes, I know Gabe real well. If you have him on your side, you don't need much else. You can't do better than to have him riding for you." Kate felt a prickle of guilt because she knew more than she was telling. "He'll make you a good hand."

Casey felt relief. "I wasn't sure."

Kate walked through the three rooms and came back smiling. "Tomorrow I'll take you to the shed so you can see what furniture is left for you to use." She lifted Jenny out of Sam's arms and started off in the direction of her house. "You'd better come on if you want to eat dinner while it's hot. Gabe just rode in, and he's washing up."

They were all seated around Kate's table when Gabe entered. Casey hadn't realized how tall he was until she saw him standing in Kate's kitchen doorway. He was clean shaven, and his black hair glistened in the lamplight as if he had just washed it and it was still wet. He had rolled his shirtsleeves up to his elbows, and she could see the black hair on his tanned arms.

Casey had always noticed people's hands. Her father's hands had been those of a gentleman, easy to blister when doing the work required on the wagon train. Kate's were work-worn and calused, showing signs of age. There was strength in Gabe's hands; his fingers were long and tapered, beautiful but masculine at the same time. She wondered what it would feel like to have them brush against her skin.

She quickly glanced down at her plate, her cheeks flushed. Why did she always have to think about him in that way? It was disturbing to have him look at her with those beautiful, wolfish silver eyes.

"Looks like you've gone and got yourself hired here at the Spanish Spur," Kate said to Gabe.

"I wish you would tell Miss Hamilton that I'm respectable," he said, smiling at Casey. "I wouldn't be surprised if she's afraid I'll run off with her cattle. I didn't make a very good first impression on her, did I, Miss Hamilton?"

"You did help us get our wagon out of the river," she reminded him.

Kate saw the blush on Casey's cheeks and smiled to herself. No female was immune to that handsome devil's charms. "I never knowed him to steal cattle, but there's many a young lady whose hearts he's stole."

Gabe made no comment as he took the empty chair beside Kate, but he gave her a sharp glance. "Something smells mighty good," he said, changing the subject.

"Tastes good, too," Kate remarked without modesty. She looked at Sam. "Your uncle Bob used to say I was the best cook in Texas, and that's saying a lot."

Sam was staring with hungry eyes at the bowl of mashed potatoes heaped high and fluffy. "My sister's a good cook," he said loyally. "She can cook about anything."

Casey met Gabe's gaze. "Did you have a productive day, sir?"

He liked the sound of her soft Southern accent. He liked the way her red-gold hair curled about her face. He liked the blue of her eyes; he was certain that he could spend hours looking into them. This was the first time he had seen her in good light, and he was particularly fond of the soft sprinkle of freckles across her nose. If there was a more beautiful female in this world, he had never met her. Her lips were pink and full, just right for a man to kiss.

"Yes, ma'am, I did," he said, turning away from dangerous thoughts. "I rounded up about twenty strays and herded them into the east pasture. There may be about a hundred head yet to round up. I'm going to have to have help with them."

Casey shook her head. "I can't hire anyone else. You know that."

Kate passed Gabe the platter of meat. "There ain't no one going to work for the Spanish Spur, and you know it."

He met Casey's blue-eyed gaze. "I know of two men who would be willing to work for you with the understanding that they wouldn't be paid until you sell the cattle."

"How much is cattle going for now, Gabe?" Kate wanted to know.

"Four dollars a head if we sell them here in Texas—thirty dollars a head if we drive them to the railhead. Of course, we would have to have at least five hundred head to make a drive pay, and you don't have near that many." He looked at Casey. "I can't very well round them up alone. And Sam is too inexperienced to be much help until I can teach him what to do."

"You mentioned two men who would be willing to work for us," she said, feeling overwhelmed by their situation. "Will you ask them to come to the Spanish Spur so I can talk to them?"

"Miss Hamilton, there is one fact I forgot to mention. You may not want to hire them when I tell you that they are Comanche."

She stared at him in disbelief and uncertainty. "Indians!"

Sam grinned. "I've never been close to an Indian before. When we were on the trail, I caught a glimpse of some on a hill, but they never came where I could see them up close."

Casey laid her fork aside and placed her hands in her lap so no one would see them tremble. "Aren't they dangerous?"

Gabe's gaze dropped to his plate so she could not see his expression. "If they were, I wouldn't be recommending them to you."

Casey glanced at her brother. The thought of having Indians on the ranch frightened her, but she decided to let her brother make the decision, since he was trying so hard to be a man. "What do you think, Sam?"

His brow furrowed. "Papa always said the only yardstick to measure a man's worth was integrity." He spoke directly to Gabe. "Do these men have integrity?"

"I would have to say they do." He looked as if he would have said more, but he shook his head. "I would, and have, trusted them with my life. Yes, I would say they have integrity."

"It's your decision, Sam," Casey told him.

"We need help, and if Gabe says they are all right, then that's good enough for me."

Gabe saw the uncertainty in Casey's eyes, and he expected her to object. "And what about you, Miss Hamilton?"

"My brother has already made the decision. He is head of our family."

Gabe's lips met in a firm line. He knew she made all the important decisions, but she was trying to give Sam confidence, and he admired her for that. "I'll send word to them in the morning. It'll take a couple of weeks for them to get here."

Casey looked into Gabe's eyes, and then hurriedly lowered her gaze. He was the most disturbing man she had ever been around. "My family would like to thank you . . . for everything."

"You are welcome, Miss Hamilton," he said, taking the platter of meat Kate had been holding for him. "Sam, how would you like to ride out with me tomorrow?"

"I would, sir. I really would." His voice deepened with excitement, and he glanced at Casey for permission. "Is it all right with you if I go?"

"Yes. Of course." She frowned thoughtfully. "We have only the team horses, and they have never had a saddle on them."

"When I was rounding up strays, I found three horses with the Spanish Spur brand on them. I would imagine they are workhorses. But Sam can ride my horse, and I'll ride one of the others, since they may be a bit wild from running free for so long."

Excitement flushed Sam's face as Gabe handed him the platter of meat. "I love fried chicken, Miss Kate. It's my favorite!"

A sudden whimper came from Jenny, and she scooted off her chair and threw herself into Casey's arms. "My chicken, she cooked my chicken!" the child cried, burying her face against her sister's chest.

Casey looked apologetically at Kate as she hugged the child to her. "Chickens are raised for their eggs and to eat, Jenny—they can't be pets."

The child only sobbed harder. Casey stood up with her sister in her arms and moved back from the table. "I am so sorry, but she's really upset. If you will excuse me, I need to explain this to her so she will understand. Please eat without us."

Kate nodded, looking distressed. "I should have knowed that child was attached to those chickens. I'm real sorry."

Gabe watched Casey walk away, speaking quietly to her sister. Something caught in his throat and twisted in his belly. It was clear to him that Casey was the one who kept the family together and kept their spirits up. But in the dark of night, when Casey was alone, who was there to comfort her? He had realized last night when he found her at the house that she was deeply distressed about their situation. And she had reason to be. It wouldn't be long before Cyrus came calling, and then she would know what real trouble was.

Although Sam wanted to eat the chicken, it seemed to stick in his throat. "I'd better go help my sister. Jenny can be a problem sometimes."

Gabe stood up, suddenly losing his appetite. "Excuse me, Kate. I think I may know how to settle this."

Kate blinked her eyes and shook her head. "I can't eat that fried chicken, either."

Chapter Seven

Casey sat on Kate's porch step and pushed the hair out of Jenny's face. "Chickens don't make good pets, sweetheart. They can't love you back. Remember how you and Sam had to chase them this afternoon, and how they tried to avoid you? They don't want to be your friend."

The child laid her head against her sister's shoulder and wiped her eyes. "I wanted them to like me."

Sam stood on the step, feeling helpless but wanting to help Casey. "She's right about them, Jenny. They don't make good pets. They're raised for food."

His comment brought a fresh burst of tears from Jenny.

Gabe moved off the porch and knelt down beside them. "Do you like dogs, Jenny?"

The child raised her head, her little face creased in a frown. "I never had one. But Mr.

Fletcher back in Virginia had one, and he'd let me pet it sometimes. And Letty Marton had one on the wagon train, but she wouldn't let me pet it at all."

"Let's ask your sister if you can have a dog. And if you can, I'll see if I can find one for you. Would you like that?"

Gabe was taken totally by surprise when the child propelled herself into his arms. "I want a puppy of my very own. Can you get it now?"

Casey smiled at Gabe, who looked like he didn't know quite what to do with the bundle of energy that hung around his neck. He smiled when she planted a kiss on his cheek. Casey wished at that moment that she were in Jenny's place. She would love to— She dipped her head and blushed.

"I like you so very much, Gabe. Really I do." She pulled back and frowned. "Even if you wouldn't let me put a flower in your hair that day when I got lost."

Laughter rolled out of Gabe. This child was enchanting, and he had never known anyone as precocious as she was. She made such outlandish statements, and she made him smile. "What do you say, Casey—can Jenny have a pup if I find her one?"

Casey's heart softened at the sight of her sister in Gabe's arms. When his gaze met hers, she was hit by a sensation that felt something like falling over a cliff. "I think that would be very nice, Mr. . . . Gabe."

"No. Not mister—just Gabe," he reminded her.

Jenny leaped out of Gabe's arms and ran into the house so she could tell Kate about her good fortune, and Sam trailed along after her, glad about her happier mood.

Gabe stood and leaned against the porch post. "Do you think she will ever eat fried chicken again?"

"Knowing my sister like I do, I doubt she will." She gave a deep sigh. "Jenny can sometimes be a real trial."

"I imagine you were much like her as a child."

"Papa said I was very much like her." She clasped her hands in her lap. "Jenny never knew our mother, since she died the night Jenny was born. So I probably indulge her more than I should. But Papa said you can't spoil a child with love."

"That's probably true. And then you have Sam, who wants to be a man so he can take care of both of you."

"Yes." She glanced up at him with a worried frown. "He's just a boy, and yet he has so much to worry about."

He had never known a woman like Casey. She was soft and gentle with her family, but she could turn into a raging storm if she thought her brother or sister was threatened in any way. She had something that he had never seen in a woman—she had forbearance and patience. "And you guide both Samuel and Jenny in the right direction."

She was quiet for a moment, pondering her answer. "I do try, but sometimes . . ." She fell into silence and met his gaze. He was so near she could see the pores in his skin, feel the heat of his body. His broad shoulders looked inviting, and she wanted to lay her head there and have him make her troubles go away.

"Most of the time I don't even know what *I'm* doing, so it's difficult to guide my brother and sister."

He offered her his hand. She hesitated only for a moment before she allowed him to draw her up beside him. Her breath caught in her throat, and her heart pounded erratically. Something was happening to her, and she didn't know what it was. There had been beaux who had come calling back in Virginia, and one of them had even stolen a quick kiss, but none of them had stirred her as deeply as this man did when he merely touched her.

"Thank you," she said, withdrawing her hand from his and rushing up the steps and into the house.

Gabe stood there in the darkness for a long moment, the soft, sweet scent of her still lingering in the air. He was treading ground that he had never trodden before, and that little gal was beginning to get under his skin. He watched a shadow move across the moon like a bad omen. Casey was going to need him in the days to come.

Gabe had been away from the ranch most of the morning. He dismounted, struggling with a wiggly white pup that was trying to climb up his shoulder and lick his face. He smiled as he carried it into the barn, threw a blanket down in the tack room, placed the pup on it, and partially closed the door so the little scamp wouldn't escape.

When Gabe walked to the ranch house, he heard voices coming from the backyard. He went around the corner to find Sam sitting in a chair while Casey trimmed his hair. Since they hadn't noticed him, he was able to observe them in a private moment. He heard the loving exchange between brother and sister and became more aware of the closeness they shared.

He found himself wishing he could be a part of this family. But that was not possible.

His gaze, as always, went to Casey. She wore a yellow print gown that made the red of her hair seem alive. Her scissors snipped at the hair over Sam's ear while Jenny sat on an overturned bucket with a book on her lap.

"Now, Jenny," Casey urged, "read me the next page. And don't skip any words, because I'll know if you do."

The little imp traced her small finger across the page. " 'The . . . boy . . . ran to . . .' " She glanced up. "Casey, I can't read this. It's too hard."

"Go back to the beginning of the page and try again. We don't give up when things are difficult, Jenny. We try harder."

The child nodded and started over again. " 'The boy . . . ran to his h . . . house.' "

"That's enough. You can read two pages tomorrow."

"Why do I have to read? It's hard, and I like it better when you read to me. Besides, Milly, on the wagon train, said I'm too young to be reading."

Casey turned her attention to her sister. "You did start reading young, but you were ready to learn. And Sam and I don't want you to grow up without an education."

"Who made you and Sam read?"

"We went to school. But they don't have a school here. I already asked Kate. So you will have to be satisfied with me as your teacher."

"You'd better listen to her," Sam said, adding his support to Casey.

"If your hair had gotten any longer, I could have braided it, Sam," Casey remarked, putting the comb in her mouth and holding up a long strand. With a last snip, she nodded in satisfaction. "Now you look presentable again." She tilted his chin up and smiled. "You are very handsome, Samuel. When you grow up all the girls are going to come after you."

He actually blushed. "Aw, Casey, don't say things like that. I'm not handsome."

She turned and winked at Jenny. "We certainly think he is, don't we?"

"I want my hair cut like Sam's," the child stated, putting her book aside and sliding into the chair that Sam had just vacated. "I don't like long hair."

At that moment Casey realized they were not alone. Her gaze collided with a silver one, and she stared at him for a moment before saying, "You're next, Gabe."

He walked toward her like a marauding tiger, and the thought of actually touching his hair was very provocative. She shook herself. If she thought that way, she'd never be able to cut his hair.

"What do you mean, I'm next?"

She lifted Jenny off the chair. "You need a haircut."

A slow smile curved his mouth. "And you are going to give me one?"

"There's no one else here who can."

He bent down to Jenny and touched a soft curl. "Is your sister always like this?"

Jenny's eyes widened and tears gathered in them. "She won't let me have short hair like Sam's. And she makes me read."

Gabe smiled and placed his hand on her head. "Jenny, your hair is too pretty to be cut."

"That's what Sam said." She looked pensive for a moment and then grinned up at him. "Do you want to marry me so I can have my mother's Spode dishes?"

He was startled and looked toward Casey for help, but she was shaking with laughter, giving him a look that said he had gotten himself into the situation, and she wasn't going to help him get out of it.

"Uh, I would, but you're too old for me, Jenny."

She shook her head, and her curls danced around her charming face. "I'm not old—Casey's old. Some men back in Virginia wanted to marry her, but she just wouldn't do it."

Gabe looked back at Casey and smiled at her discomfort. "Why do you suppose she turned them all down?"

Jenny frowned thoughtfully. "I don't know. Why didn't you marry them, Casey?"

"That's enough, Jenny." Casey pointed to the chair. "Sit here, Gabe."

He grinned, feeling somehow lighthearted. When he sat down, he felt Casey's hand fall on his shoulder. "Jenny, if you will go look in the tack room in the barn, you'll find someone waiting to meet you."

"For me!"

"That's right."

Sam took his young sister's hand. "Let's go see who it is."

As the two of them hurried away, Casey asked, "Did you get her a pup?"

"Ned Holston at the feed store was giving them away. He said they were weaned two weeks ago. I picked out the friskiest one so it could keep up with Jenny."

She paused with the comb in her hand. "Thank you. Jenny gets so lonely with no one her age to play with."

The comb ran through his hair, and she touched the back of his neck. He closed his eyes as her hand lingered there. She could not know where his thoughts were taking him as she gathered the hair at his crown.

Gabe hadn't known that a haircut could be so sensuous. He had the strongest urge to turn around, take her onto his lap, and hold her next to his heart. He wanted to cherish her and make all her troubles his. How much more could he take, he wondered, as her fingers traveled gently through his hair, stirring his blood.

Not realizing what she was doing, Casey caressed the nape of his neck. She felt the now-familiar ache start in her stomach and work its way up to her breast. It was hard to breathe, and she had to drag air into her lungs.

Gabe sat there so straight and tall, seemingly unaware of what was happening to her. The scissors trembled in her hand when she snipped the hair at the nape of his neck. She forced herself to concentrate on what she was doing and finally finished the back of his hair and moved to the front.

Hesitantly, she lifted his chin so she could see where she needed to cut, and she stopped dead in her tracks. There was no mistaking the look he gave her—it was raw and hard, burning with desire.

Not knowing what to do, she said hurriedly. "I . . . will soon be finished."

"Just do it," he said in an impatient tone.

Her hand was really trembling as she snipped about his face. She tried not to look at him, but her gaze was drawn to his lips.

"Dammit," he said, rising to his feet and jerking her against him. "Do you have any idea what you're doing to me?"

In confusion she could only shake her head.

Gabe gathered Casey close, pressing her against him. "I have wanted to hold you like this almost from the beginning, even when I thought you had a husband."

She went weak, and her head dropped against his broad chest. "I don't understand any of this," she said, drawing back and looking at him. "I don't know why I feel this way."

"Don't you? Think about it, and the answer will come to you," he demanded roughly.

Casey shook her head. She had never seen such deep torment in anyone's eyes as she saw in Gabe's. She wondered what secrets he kept hidden. She wished he would share them with her, so she could help him.

"This has never happened to me before," she admitted, more confused than ever.

His lips feathered softly across her cheek. He

was trembling when he realized her mouth was just a breath away from his. Sweet torment tore at him, and he felt like a man dying of thirst.

He had to have her, all of her, or he would drift forever with nothing to live for. He could feel her body soften against his, and he knew she wanted him too. His mouth touched the edge of her full lips, and they trembled against his.

Casey felt his breath on her mouth, and an incredible sweetness touched her heart. He hadn't kissed her yet, but merely brushed his lips across hers.

What would she do if he actually kissed her?

Gabe's arms tightened around her shoulders so he could bring her closer, and she cried out, moving quickly away from him. He realized he had frightened her with his unleashed passion.

What he didn't know was that Casey's shoulder hurt so badly she couldn't speak for a moment. Once the pain subsided, she bit her lip and rubbed her shoulder. "I didn't—"

"I know. I stepped over the line, and I'm sorry." He looked down at the ground for a moment and took a deep breath. "It won't happen again." When he gazed back at her, there was no sign of desire in his eyes. His expression was flat and cold. "I ask your pardon."

The last thing Casey wanted was for him to be sorry he had taken her into his arms. She wanted to be near him, to feel the hardness of his body, and his kiss upon her lips. She stooped to retrieve the scissors where she had dropped them, trying to hide the fact that her shoulder still hurt. She actually welcomed the pain, because it gave her something to think about other than the way her heart was slamming against her chest.

"Do you want me to finish your hair? I just need to take a little off the top."

He pushed his hand through his midnight-colored hair. "No. That's what got me in trouble in the first place." He stared at her for a moment, trying to find the softness he had felt in her moments ago, but she was solemn, her eyes clear, and she had distanced herself from him.

Without another word, he turned and walked away. She listened to the faint sound of his boot steps, and then there was only silence.

Casey dropped onto the chair, wishing her shoulder would stop hurting. He had probably thought she had pushed him away because she didn't want him to kiss her. He didn't know about the pain in her shoulder.

Casey sensed such a loneliness in him. She wondered who had hurt him so badly.

She heard Jenny laughing with joy as she ran toward her, so she stood, forcing a smile onto her face.

"Look what Gabe gave me. It's my very own puppy!"

Chapter Eight

Casey was relieved.

They had been living on the Spanish Spur for three weeks, and so far there had been no real trouble. In fact, she was beginning to feel encouraged because everything seemed to be going so well.

The house felt like home to them—especially now that Sam had built two wide wall shelves so they could display their mother's china.

It was nice to go to bed at night without having to move out the next morning with the wagon train.

She stood in the doorway, her eyes going to the loft. Kate had given her some goose feathers and ticking and had helped her make a mattress for Sam. Gabe had helped her brother put up a dividing wall so Sam could have privacy.

The only furniture in the front room was a swaybacked settee and a straight-backed chair.

Casey and Jenny shared the bedroom, but they still slept on pallets. Kate was helping her make a mattress for Jenny and herself.

The days were full, and there was so much to do there was very little time to be idle. Most days Sam rode out with Gabe, and he would come home in the late afternoon excited about what Gabe had taught him that day.

Gabe was acting differently toward her since the day she had cut his hair. He was distant and formal when he spoke to her, and it seemed to Casey that he avoided her whenever he could. She wondered what he could be thinking; he must have thought she had been too forward when she insisted on cutting his hair, and then she had practically thrown herself in his arms.

He probably thought she acted that way with every man she met.

She gave her head a small shake and glanced at the barn, which still needed extensive repairs. At least the broken boards on the corral had been replaced, and the three horses that Gabe had rounded up were now enclosed there.

She watched the wind stir the leaves on the elm tree near the porch. It was a mild October day with clear skies and only an occasional breeze blowing from the south. She had chosen today to clean the bunkhouse, and she had gathered her broom and mop as soon as she had seen Gabe ride away. Luckily, the bunkhouse was in good repair—it was just dusty from not being used for so long.

Four cots were lined up against the north wall, and there was a potbellied stove at each end of the room to keep it warm in the winter. The structure seemed sound enough, and she glanced up at the ceiling. Since there was no sign of a leak, she knew that the roof was sound.

She had just finished scrubbing the floor and was standing to flex her sore muscles when pain stabbed through her like a knife. By now her shoulder should be getting better, but it wasn't. She didn't know how much longer she could go on this way, because sometimes the pain was unbearable.

She had made up three of the beds, two for the Indians Gabe had sent for. She had just spread a clean blanket across Gabe's bed, and she paused to stare at the pillow where he would lay his head tonight. She could almost imagine his long, lean body lying there, his dark hair contrasting with the whiteness of the pillowcase. She ran her hand across the wool blanket and closed her eyes, wondering what it would feel like to lie beside him and have him take her in his arms. Her heart throbbed, and her breath caught.

When she thought of him, her body always betrayed her. Why these feelings for him, and why now?

Disgusted with herself for allowing such erotic flights of fancy, she placed the jar of wildflowers she had brought with her on the window ledge, then gathered her broom and mop and left. Tomorrow she intended to go to Mariposa Springs to meet with the attorney, Bartholomew J. Murdock.

Jenny was playing in the front yard, the new pup bouncing around her, while she patted out mud pies. Her little face was so muddy, all Casey could see was the blue of her eyes. She was grateful to Gabe for giving Jenny the dog, because she played with it all day, and it even slept at the foot of her pallet at night.

"You have to come in soon, Jenny. You'll need a bath before you can eat."

Her sister's bottom lip slid into a familiar pout. "I don't like baths. I like to live in the mud—all the time."

"Nonetheless, I am going to heat water for the tub, and you will have a bath. Come on into the kitchen after you have put your toys away."

Moments later Jenny stomped into the kitchen, displeasure sparkling in her eyes. "You don't love me, Casey. If you did, you wouldn't always make me take a bath."

Casey took her hand and then stripped the muddy clothes off her, dropping them beside the door. Lifting Jenny into the tub, she smiled at her. "It's because I love you that I want to see that sweet face of yours. Right now I can't see it for the mud."

Jenny glanced up at her. "You like my face?"

"I love that face."

She considered for a moment. "I'll take a bath."

It was late afternoon by the time Casey had finished her household chores and was able to feed and water the horses. She gave a carrot to the chestnut gelding that always came to the fence to nudge her hand. She had already decided she would make him her horse.

When they had lived in the big house in Charlottesville, she had ridden almost daily, and she had been considered quite an accomplished horsewoman. But when the Union soldiers had ridden through town, they had confiscated all the horses for their troops. Her family had lost so much because of the war.

But time passed, and they had a new life now. Absently, she gave the gelding a pat.

She was not concerned when she heard a rider approaching; she expected it to be Sam or Gabe. She placed her hand above her eyes to shade them from the sunlight.

The rider's horse was completely white, definitely a thoroughbred. She couldn't see much of the man's face from this distance, but he was a stranger. He must have noticed her standing by the corral, because he rode in that direction. She watched him dismount and walk toward her.

He removed his hat with perfunctory politeness. "Ma'am," he said as though he were not sure she deserved the courtesy.

His hair was dark, speckled with gray, and she would place him somewhere in his fifties. He was a tall man with wide shoulders. His face might have been called handsome except that his eyes were cold and devoid of feeling—almost like dead eyes, and she found she could not look into them, so she turned her head away.

"Good afternoon," Casey answered, waiting for him to tell her his name and state his business.

"I'm your neighbor." His words were spoken softly, but they still sounded harsh and angry. "I heard in town that there were squatters on the Spanish Spur, and I came by to see for myself. You'll find we don't take kindly to people living where they don't belong. No one in town seems to know anything about your bunch, so why don't you just tell me what you're doing here?"

He went straight to the point, not bothering with niceties, and she answered him in the same manner. "Why don't you tell me who you are and what interest you have in the Spanish Spur? And then I'll tell you my name, and what I'm doing here."

His eyes hardened even more. "It's none of your business who I am, young woman. I'll give you until tomorrow to pack up and be gone. You'd better heed me well. If you aren't gone by sundown you'll regret it. And I'll be back to make sure you aren't still here."

Her anger hit a quick zenith. "You are the one who will leave and not come back. This ranch was left to my family by our uncle. And neither you nor anyone else is going to make us leave."

He digested that bit of news and nodded. "That figures—you got a Southern-like accent, and I knew Bob had kin in Virginia. I wrote to a man named Hamilton asking to buy the Spanish Spur, but he wrote back that the place belonged to his children, and he wasn't selling."

Her spine straightened, and her chin went up. "That would have been my father." Ordinarily she would have invited a stranger into the house and offered him refreshments, but this man deserved no such courtesy.

She stood her ground as if guarding her domain.

"I'm Cyrus Slaughter." He paused for effect, then said, "Maybe you've heard of me?"

Although she had already guessed who he was, she cringed inside at the mention of that name. She was afraid of him, but she wasn't about to let him know it. Casey met his angry gaze with a steadfast one of her own. "I have heard that you will probably cause my family problems. Are you here to make trouble for us, Mr. Slaughter?"

"Ma'am, you don't know what trouble is until you've crossed me. I want you to make sure to remember that we had this conversation."

She stepped backward, shocked at the venom in his tone. She was about to answer him when she saw Jenny come out the front door and run toward her. Casey shook her head and motioned for her sister to go back, but the child didn't stop until she could grab Casey's hand and glance inquisitively at the newcomer.

Jenny had a sunny disposition and treated no one like a stranger, but at the moment she was oddly silent, as if she recognized that this man was not a friend. She tugged on Casey's hand. "Let's go into the house."

Lifting Jenny in her arms, Casey battled between anger and fear; fear finally won. She just wanted to get Jenny safely away from Cyrus Slaughter. "If you will excuse me," she said, hearing the tremor in her own voice, "I have work to do."

He leaned against the corral and stared at her, long and hard. "Where's your pa or ma? You're too young to be the mother of that little gal."

"We don't have parents, Mr. Slaughter." She didn't want to explain that her mother and father were dead in front of Jenny. "Now if you will excuse me."

He moved so quickly that he was in front of her before she could react. "Who else is here with you?"

The man's eyes were so frightening that Casey shivered. She had never seen eyes so devoid of feeling. Kate was right about this man. He would brush aside anyone who stood in the way of what he wanted—and she had the feeling she was in his way.

"Kate is somewhere about," she said hurriedly, not wanting him to think they were alone. "And my brother and our hired hand will be riding in at any moment."

He smiled because he knew he had frightened her. He was accustomed to people fearing him, and that gave him power over them. "I don't know what you've heard about me, and I don't care. The only interest I have in you is your signature on a document that will make me the new owner of the Spanish Spur."

Casey could feel her face flush as anger flamed inside her. She quickly pushed her fear to the back of her mind. "We have no plans to sell the Spanish Spur to you or anyone else. So if you want to buy land, you might want to look elsewhere."

She watched his fists ball at his sides.

She didn't know what would have happened next if Kate hadn't come out of her house and seen Slaughter there. Kate came rushing toward them with her eyes flashing.

"Cyrus, you leave her alone. She's just getting settled in, and she don't need you here stirring up trouble."

He swung around to face the little woman. "Oh, I'll be stirring up trouble, all right, Kate. You can bet on that. Before long you'll be looking for a new home, because I'll be tearing your shack down." His glance went to the young woman. "I don't see anyone around here willing to help you except Kate, and she knows what happens to people who get in my way, don't you, Kate?" He adjusted his hat to an angle that satisfied him and dipped his head.

"Ladies. Until the next time."

"I'm not scared of you, Cyrus," Kate called after him as he walked toward his horse. She had planted her small body protectively in front of Casey and Jenny. "You may be able to bluff some people, but not me. Don't ever come back here."

Cyrus made no other comment as he mounted his horse.

"I'm afraid of him," Casey admitted as she watched him ride out of sight. "I have never met anyone like him before. He threatened us with such hatred, I could almost feel it in my heart. He is an evil man."

Kate caught Casey's trembling hand in hers. "He's as bad as they come. I didn't reckon on him riding in big as you please. He usually has someone else do his calling for him. He must have been real set on meeting your family."

"If today was the worst it gets, I can manage him. We had men like him in Virginia—we called them carpetbaggers. We dealt with them just fine."

"But you had your pa with you then, didn't you?"

Her heart sank. "Yes."

"Honey, what you witnessed here today was just Slaughter's way of leaving his calling card. He'll be back meaner and stronger than ever; you can be sure of that. And he aims to run you off this ranch."

"I don't understand why people let him get away with his meanness."

Kate watched Cyrus disappear over the rise. "Not everyone will. Gabe won't."

Chapter Nine

Sam had ridden in around sundown, exhausted but rambling excitedly about helping Gabe round up cattle and drive them into a pen. After he had eaten, he climbed to his loft and immediately fell asleep.

Jenny, however, had been another matter. Casey had read her an entire chapter in her favorite book before the child finally nodded off to sleep. Casey herself was wide-awake.

She couldn't get the threats Mr. Slaughter had made out of her mind.

She covered Jenny and left the bedroom, walking outside into the fresh air. A cloud crept across the moon, shrouding the landscape in shadows, but it was still light enough for her to make her way to the corral. Her shoulder was hurting so badly she wanted to cry.

She leaned against the fence post and ran her hand down the chestnut's glossy neck.

"I heard you had a visitor today."

She whirled around to find Gabe right behind her, and she wondered how long he had been standing there watching her. She glanced back at the gelding and patted his neck. "You moved so silently I didn't hear you."

He came up to the fence and propped a booted foot on one of the rungs. "I learned to move quietly when I was young."

She could not imagine him as a boy because he had such a commanding presence as a man.

He turned his head away as he said, "Tell me about your visitor today." He stared straight ahead. "Kate told me about it, but I want to hear it from you."

"There's not much to tell. Mr. Slaughter has the mistaken idea that he can scare us off our land."

"Did he make threats?"

"Veiled ones. Nothing I could accuse him of. But he threatened me all the same."

"Cyrus is a hard man, Miss Hamilton, and a dangerous one. He can and will use whatever means it takes to get his hands on this ranch. Are you willing to fight him, or do you want to sell to him?"

"I won't let him have the Spanish Spur."

His tone hardened. "Think carefully before you answer, because if you decide to stay, there will be a war the likes of which you have never seen before."

"I didn't come all this way to Texas to give up at the first sign of trouble. And you are wrong: I have seen a war, and nothing can be more frightening than Yankees burning my father's bank and our home. My brother and sister have already lost too much. I will not see them put out of another home."

He was quiet for a moment. "Then it'll be a fight."

"I'm not leaving."

He reached out and softly touched her cheek with his knuckles. "I have seen grown men cringe before Cyrus Slaughter, and yet you, a little slip of a girl, are ready to take him on."

It took her a moment to speak because the look in his eyes was so tender. She could not be mistaken about that. "You will have to tell me what we must do, because I don't know."

"What you should do is leave."

She started to say something, and he held up his hand. "I know, I know. You won't sell to him, although it would be better for you if you did. If it's a fight he wants, then it's a fight we'll give him."

"Why would you do this for us?"

He couldn't tell her that when she was hurt, it tore into him, dragging him down into the depths of despair with her. He had never had such a protective instinct toward any other woman. The feeling was too new for him to know how to deal with it, and he didn't want to examine it too closely.

"Someday I may just tell you, when I have reasoned it out myself. Right now I'm warning you to be vigilant. Don't invite strangers into the house, and keep Jenny close to you at all times. I don't want you to go anywhere alone."

"But surely we are not in any physical danger. Mr. Slaughter wouldn't really hurt a woman or a child, would he?"

"You don't understand." He gazed into the distance as if his mind were taking him to another place and time. "Cyrus won't care who you are. If you don't give in to his demands, he sees you only as as an enemy."

"But I don't—"

"Let me tell you about Cyrus Slaughter so you can judge him for yourself. It's not a pretty story."

"I'm listening."

"Cyrus had a daughter by his first wife, who was a respectable woman. When she died, he took a second wife, whom he did not find respectable enough to bring to Casa Mesa. He set her up in a house miles from nowhere and visited her only when the notion struck him."

He paused for a moment, then went on. "Eventually Cyrus had a son by the second wife, and for years he saw the boy only on rare occasions. When the second wife died, she left a boy of thirteen—Sam's age. It seemed to give Cyrus some kind of sick pleasure to bring the boy to his home. You see, his son was wild, a little savage, and he knew nothing of the niceties of society. Cyrus set his boy down at the table with his daughter, Nora, who was seven years older. Folks who knew about it thought Cyrus was trying to humiliate his daughter."

He was quiet for a long time, and she waited for him to continue.

"As time passed Cyrus began to criticize everything Nora did, making her life very hard. She loved Frank Yates, a poor farmer her father didn't approve of. He wanted Nora to marry the man he had chosen for her—a man who was wealthy and would have added more land to Casa Mesa."

Casey frowned. "What happened?"

"The boy was rebellious because he hadn't wanted to come to the ranch, and it didn't take him long to realize his father had been using him to embarrass his half sister."

"Was she embarrassed?"

"No. Her father's actions had the opposite effect on Nora. I think you would have liked her; in some ways you remind me of her. She was sweet and soft-spoken, and everyone loved her. From the moment her half brother arrived, she treated him like her real brother. They would take long rides together, and she was responsible for any manners the boy had. She even taught him to read and write. They spent many hours reading to each other."

"I would like very much to meet her."

His eyes were almost colorless as he stared into the night. "The closeness of the brother and sister angered Cyrus. Everything came to a head the day the son came to the evening meal and displayed some semblance of civilized manners. Cyrus must have realized that his plan to humiliate Nora had failed. She told her father that night that nothing he could do would stop her from marrying Frank Yates. He became enraged, making all kinds of threats. At the time no one could have guessed the tragedy that would result from Cyrus's fury."

"Please don't tell me he did anything bad to the boy."

Gabe's eyes took on a sad expression. "Cyrus did something so deplorable, many of his neighbors still will not speak to him. His rage fell on Frank, the only person he could use to punish his daughter."

Gabe looked away as if it were difficult to go on. Casey held her breath, afraid to hear the rest of his story and yet needing to know.

"What did he do?"

"Nora and Frank had planned their wedding for the next week. Frank loved her and wanted to get her away from her father. No one had anticipated that Cyrus's retribution would be so swift and hard. He claimed that Frank had rustled Slaughter cattle. Of course, everyone knew that Frank was an honest man, so no one believed the accusations."

"Surely there was a trial, and Frank was cleared of the charges?"

Gabe threw his head back, and she saw the muscles throbbing in his throat. "Cyrus thought he was above the law. He rounded up all his hands, and they dragged Frank out of his house in the middle of the night. They hanged him from a tree in his front yard."

Casey gasped, feeling so sick she had to clamp her hand over her mouth. "Was he allowed to do such a thing? Did no one demand justice for . . . ?"

The hardness in his gaze stopped her. "No one would speak out against Cyrus. That very day Cyrus took Nora over to Frank's place and made her look at the man she loved hanging from a tree. She collapsed in a dead faint and had to be taken home. That same afternoon, she took her own life." He gripped the fence and lowered his head. "She shot herself."

Tears gathered in Casey's eyes, and she touched his sleeve. "You loved her, didn't you?"

He took a deep breath and let it out slowly. "Everyone loved Nora."

"What happened to the boy?"

"He was seventeen at that time. He joined the Confederate Army and went off to war, because he knew if he stayed in Texas, he'd kill Cyrus."

"Where is he now?"

"Some would say he died the day his sister killed herself; others believe he was killed in the war. Personally, I believe he is trying to forget the sight of his sister's body lying in a pool of blood on her bedroom floor."

Casey again covered her hand with her mouth. "Oh. How can that be?"

"It happened just the way I told you."

"I would like to think that the boy has found peace."

"Would you?"

"If what you say is true, he is the tragic figure in all this. His sister is beyond caring, and Mr. Slaughter probably felt no remorse for destroying his own son and daughter. The son, if he is alive, must be devastated by what happened."

He moved some distance from her. "The reason I told you about this was so you would know what you are up against. Cyrus is dangerous when anyone defies him."

"I admit I am afraid of him, even more so since you told me about his son and daughter. But you have to understand this about me—I will not cower in a corner just because everyone else is afraid to defy him."

He took a step toward her. "You don't understand—the lives of your brother and sister will mean nothing to him." He stopped so near her she could feel the heat of his body. "I don't want to see anything happen to the three of you."

He was so tall she had to tilt her head to look up at him. "I will not give in to him," she repeated decisively.

Gabe wondered what circumstances had honed Casey into the woman she had become. It was clear she had been raised in a genteel manner, but she was a scrapper who didn't run when life got hard. And lately her life had been very hard. He admired her more than he had ever admired anyone. He also couldn't be near her without wanting to take her in his arms. "Are you the one who put the wildflowers in the bunkhouse?"

"I thought they would brighten the place up." She stared into his eyes. "What I don't understand," she said, taking the conversation back to him, "is why you help us when you know of the danger involved."

"I have several reasons."

"What are they?"

He smiled as he tilted her chin up so he could see her face better. "Maybe it's because no one has ever given me flowers before." His voice deepened. "Maybe it's the little touches you add to everyone's life, the love and care you give your brother and sister. Shouldn't that inspire devotion in those around you?"

She was aware that his chest expanded when he took a breath. "I'm glad you see me that way." She lowered her lashes. "But I often stumble through life not knowing what I'm doing."

He reached across the fence and rubbed his hand against the horse's flanks. "You should be sleeping. You work hard and need your rest."

He was dismissing her, and she knew it. "I have to go into town tomorrow to see my uncle's attorney. Can you spare Sam to go with me?"

He turned to her, his gaze skimming her face.

He hadn't meant to, but he drew her slowly into his arms. He halfway expected her to resist, but she came to him, her eyes wide with uncertainty. He cradled her head against him, wishing she was his to hold forever, but knowing she would never belong to him. He dipped his head, breathing in her sweetness. His lips brushed her hair, and his hand moved up her ribs just inches away from the tempting swell of her breasts.

Realizing what he was doing, Gabe released her so quickly she almost stumbled until he steadied her.

He had left so much unsaid between them, but it was the only way. "You need to get an early start for town in the morning. Take Sam and Kate with you. She's a good shot, and not many people want to get in her way when she's riled."

Casey nodded, trying to hide her disappointment. She had wanted him to kiss her. How brazen she had become since meeting Gabe. "I will."

When he walked toward the bunkhouse, she was reluctant to have him leave, so she called out to him, "Could you tell me where I could purchase a milk cow?" It appeared she would try anything to keep him near her.

He paused and turned back to her. "A what?"

"Sam and Jenny need milk. We were able to buy milk from the Fromes on the wagon train, but the children have been without milk ever since we started out on our own."

He was quiet for a long moment, as if he were

pondering her words. At last he said, "I'll see what I can do."

She raised her gaze to his, looking embarrassed. "I . . . Can you tell me how much a cow will cost?"

"Not nearly so much as beef cattle. I can probably get you one for four or five dollars."

He saw the relief on her face. Someone needed to take care of her, but it wouldn't be him. Someday a nice young man from her own class would make her his wife. For all he knew she might have someone back in Virginia whom she loved. Besides, he had no time for settling down, and even if he did, he was not the kind of man she needed. She was innocent and . . . "Night, Miss Hamilton."

With a heavy sigh, she walked toward the house. Tomorrow Sam and she would have to hear what the attorney had to say. She had little doubt that there would be debts to pay, and she didn't know where they would get the money.

Chapter Ten

Sam had discovered their uncle Bob's buckboard stored in the barn. After he had cleaned and oiled it, he was relieved to find it sturdy and reliable.

On the way to Mariposa Springs, Casey sat in the back with Jenny while Sam drove, and Kate sat beside him, her rifle resting across her lap.

When they reached town, Sam slowed the team to the same pace as the other wagons. Jenny was chattering away, while Kate slid her rifle under the seat.

Casey looked about her and quickly concluded that the town was nothing like Charlottesville; in fact, it was nothing like any town she had ever seen. The dirt road was muddy from the rain that had fallen during the early-morning hours, and the wooden buildings all looked alike, or so it seemed to Casey. The bank was small, and she could see through the window that the walls were a drab brown. There was a general store and a barbershop. They rode past a saloon, where a man had just stumbled out the door with his arms around a scantily clad woman. Casey quickly distracted Jenny by directing her attention to the bolt of material that was displayed in the window of the dry-goods store.

"Wouldn't you like to have a new yellow gown? That material is just right for you."

"I don't want to see it right now," the child said, struggling to turn around and watch the drunk. "I want to see if that man is going to kiss that woman."

Casey placed her hands on both sides of her sister's face. "That is none of our business, Jenny. Now, how about that yellow material?"

"I'll let you make me a dress out of it if you'll put all the sparklies on it like that woman has on her gown."

Kate chuckled as she pointed out the attorney's office. "You got your hands full with her. Land of mercy, that child makes me laugh."

Sam halted beneath the sign that swayed overhead: BARTHOLOMEW J. MURDOCK, ATTORNEY-AT-LAW. He handed Kate the reins and hopped to the ground, then took Jenny in his arms and helped Casey disembark.

"I'll meet you over to the general store when you've finished up here," Kate stated, still grinning at Jenny's antics.

Casey was worried about the meeting with Mr. Murdock. Most likely he would have grim news for them. "Let's get this over with," she said, moving toward the door. "If he has bad news for us, we may as well know it right now."

The bell above the door tinkled when they entered. The office was sparsely furnished with only a desk and three chairs. No one was in the outer office, but they heard someone shuffling through papers in the next room. They waited for several moments before a man finally appeared in the doorway.

He smiled and nodded. "Good afternoon, ladies, gentleman. How can I help you?"

To Casey's way of thinking, the man looked very much the way she had pictured him: he was small and wiry with thinning brown hair, a pair of glasses perched on his nose, and a studious expression on his face.

"Are you Mr. Murdock?" she asked.

"Yes, madam, I am." His smile was genuine. "What can I do for you, young lady?"

"Sir, I am Cassandra Hamilton. This is my brother, Sam, and our younger sister, Jenny. You wrote us a letter about our uncle's death."

He looked surprised for a moment but quickly recovered and flashed her a grin. "I had the understanding that your father would be with you. Did he not come into town today?"

Sam glanced at Jenny and lowered his voice. "Papa died before we reached Texas, Mr. Murdock."

He heard the pain in the boy's voice and saw

the deep sadness in his eyes. "A tragedy. Please accept my sympathy. And please draw up chairs and be seated. I've been expecting you for some time."

It took him some moments of fumbling in his desk drawer before he came up with the correct papers. He glanced up at the three of them with a smile. "Your uncle was a good man. Since he had no family of his own, he kept in touch with your mother until her death. After that, he corresponded with you and your father so he would not lose touch with you. He often told me that he wanted you to come to Texas while he was alive, but, of course, that did not happen. He wanted you to get to know Texas, since this is where your mother was born and grew up. He told me about your losing your house; he wanted the Spanish Spur to become your home."

Casey folded her hands in her lap. "My mother had great affection for her brother. And I want to assure you that my brother and I intend to pay any debts he might have left behind—if his creditors will only be patient with us. We have no money to speak of at the moment."

Murdock looked amazed. "Debts? My dear young woman, your uncle owed no man. The Spanish Spur is clear of debt." He shifted the papers around and looked at the three of them in turn. "But let me read you the will."

Jenny became bored by the attorney's talk and squirmed off Sam's lap. She peeked under the desk but found nothing interesting there, so she moved across the room, where she pressed her nose against the window to look outside.

The attorney cleared his throat. "Your uncle's will includes Cassandra Jane Hamilton, Samuel Trace Hamilton, and Jennifer Sue Hamilton. There is a small bequest for another person, which I will speak to you about later. For now, I'll skip the preliminaries about Bob Reynolds being of sound mind and so on, and get right to the meat of the matter. Your uncle was a frugal man, and as I said, he left this world without owing anyone anything. He bequeathed the Spanish Spur and everything he owned to the three of you, free and clear, with the exception of one piece of property."

He pushed a sheet of paper toward Casey for her inspection. "These are your uncle's investments and bank statements showing the net worth of his estate. It isn't a fortune, but many folks have a lot less. There are six hundred head of prime cattle roaming the range, and at today's prices, that'll give you a substantial amount of money."

"There aren't nearly that many cattle now, Mr. Murdock," Sam told him.

The attorney glanced over his bifocals at the boy. "Are you sure?"

Sam nodded. "As far as we can tell, there's a little more than a hundred head."

"The foreman took off right after your uncle's death. I tried to keep someone out there to look after things, but no one would stay for long. The cattle probably strayed, or someone could have even rustled them. There's just no way to know for sure."

Casey was staring at the paper in front of her. She swallowed a lump in her throat as the column of figures danced before her eyes. Holding her breath, she handed the paper to Sam.

"Is that . . . Does that mean Uncle Bob has nineteen thousand dollars in the bank?" Sam asked, going pale. It sounded like a lot of money to him, since Casey had given Kate most of their money to buy the supplies they needed.

"That's right, young Samuel. As I said, it's not a great deal of money, but it'll get you started." He was gratified by the look of relief on the boy's face. Murdock had always prided himself on being an honest and fair man, and he respected that trait in others. The young people had come to him today prepared to make arrangements to pay off any debts their uncle might have incurred, and that said a lot about their character.

"I am stunned," Casey stated, wishing she had known their benefactor better. Her uncle Bob had once written them that he might come to Virginia to visit, but he never had.

Murdock flipped through other papers and tucked some away in a drawer. "Your uncle would often tell me incidents about your lives. He knew when Jenny took her first step; he knew that you, Cassandra, were going to a ball with a handsome young cavalry officer. And, Samuel, he was proud that you made such good marks in school."

Casey suddenly wished she had known her uncle better. She had grieved when they had received Mr. Murdock's letter informing them that their uncle had died, but she had no face to put on her mother's brother. It amazed her that he had followed their lives so closely. "If only we had come while he was still alive," she said.

"Yes, well, that can't be helped now. Let me say that the three of you are the beneficiaries of his generosity, because the plum in all this is the Spanish Spur—nine thousand acres of prime ranch land. Of course, your uncle had expected that if you came to Texas your father would be with you."

"We wish he were," Sam said.

Murdock frowned as if struggling for words. "If Bob Reynolds were here today, he might well advise you to sell the Spanish Spur." He looked into Casey's eyes. "If you haven't met Cyrus Slaughter, you will. He's had his eye on the property for many years. Your uncle was the one man who didn't bow down to Slaughter. But I have to warn you that Cyrus is a very dangerous adversary."

Casey had to agree with him on that. "I have seen that for myself."

"My sister's already met him," Sam remarked. "He came to see us and said he wanted to buy the ranch. Then he made some threats to my sister. I won't let him come on our land again, and I won't let him hurt my family."

Murdock could have pointed out to the boy that he'd be no match for Slaughter, but the lad wanted to protect his sisters, and the attorney found that admirable. "Your uncle was afraid Cyrus might try to push you into selling the ranch. Now, with the three of you having no one to look after you, I'd advise you to consider any reasonable offer."

"Do you think that is really what our uncle Bob would have wanted us to do?" Casey asked pointedly.

The attorney glanced down at the will without seeing it. "No. Bob Reynolds was a fighter. He withstood Slaughter for many years, but he had twenty cowhands working for him, and he was a man who could stand toe-to-toe with Slaughter. I've heard that Slaughter spread the word around that anyone who agrees to work for you, or tries to help you in any way, will be considered his enemy. No one around here will be willing to go against him. I don't know how you'll make it without good hands to work the place and to help guard against Slaughter and his men."

Casey looked at her brother. "The way I see it—and I think my brother feels the same way—our uncle entrusted the Spanish Spur to us, and I say we keep it. What do you say, Sam?"

"Mr. Murdock, my sister's right. We are not going to sell to Slaughter or anyone else."

The attorney looked worried. "It is my place to warn you that you're facing terrible odds."

Sam didn't hesitate before he remarked, "We are prepared to do whatever we must, Mr. Murdock."

In that moment, Murdock wished Reynolds could have lived to meet his kin, because he would have been proud of them, but he would also have worried about what Slaughter would do to them. "Then that's the way it'll be. If you don't have any objections, your uncle wanted me to guide you financially."

"Yes, please," Casey said. "Our uncle trusted you, and so do we."

"I'll introduce you around town today. I'll take you first to Finnegan's General Store so you can set up credit. Since you are the oldest, Cassandra, I'll make arrangements for you to have access to the bank account. I'm sure there are many things you need." He cleared his throat. "I have just one other matter concerning the will. Your uncle has asked that you allow Kathryn Eldridge to live out her days in comfort in the house he had built for her."

Casey and Sam smiled at each other. "I don't know what we would have done without Kate. I'm glad my uncle left her the house," Casey said. "And I want to tell you," she added, "just so you won't worry so much about us, Mr. Murdock, that we've hired a man to help us. And he isn't the only help we have. There will be two more arriving any day now."

Murdock was suddenly suspicious. He wouldn't put it past Slaughter to plant some of his own cowhands on the Spanish Spur so he could keep an eye on the Hamiltons. "Do you know anything about the man you hired? Maybe I need to ride out to the ranch and meet him for myself."

"Kate says we should trust him, although he didn't give us his last name. He goes by the name Gabe. Do you know him?" She looked into his clear brown eyes expectantly.

Murdock frowned and rubbed his chin. "This Gabe you speak of wouldn't tell you his last name?"

"No, sir," Sam said. "I don't think he has one."

"Then tell me this—the men he has coming to help you . . . would they, by chance, be Indians?"

Sam shifted in his seat so he could keep an eye on Jenny. "Yes, sir, they are."

"Did he happen to mention whether the Indians were Comanche?"

"Yes, they are," Casey said. "Is it usual in Texas to hire Indians to help out on a ranch?"

Murdock glanced down at his desk as he digested the information. "No, not usual at all. There's only one man I know of who could entice an Indian to work for white folk. If it's who I think it is, I wonder what he's doing back here? I haven't seen him since he left several years ago."

Casey leaned forward and folded her hands on his desk. "Then you know him?"

"I think so. I haven't seen him in years." He looked thoughtful and then met her gaze. If Gabe wanted to keep silent about his past, then Murdock would honor his wishes until he did some checking around. "He was only a young man the last time I saw him. He'd be full-grown now."

"And the Indians are harmless?"

Murdock checked his pocket watch. "They will be to you. What better watchdogs could you have than the Comanche? They can be fearsome warriors if the need arises. Now," he said, standing, "I have just enough time to introduce you around before my next appointment arrives."

Casey took Jenny's hand, and they walked out into the sunshine. There had been a lot of sadness in their lives lately, but because of their uncle Bob's generous nature, they would get by just fine. Things might be hard for a while, but they were Hamiltons, and they would come through this as they had so many other difficulties in their lives.

At least they had a home that was free of debt, and to Casey's way of thinking, they had a lot of money.

Sam touched her shoulder; he knew she was still worried about Cyrus Slaughter, especially since Mr. Murdock had warned them against him. "It's better than we expected, Casey."

"Yes," she said, her mind on Gabe. "Much better."

Chapter Eleven

Gabe dismounted with a sick feeling in his gut because he already knew what he would find. He had followed the circling buzzards to the place where he and Sam had driven fifty head of cattle only yesterday. When he dismounted, he swore under his breath. They were all dead but one—a newborn calf stumbled about, trying to rise on wobbly knees.

"Dammit," he said, opening the gate and stepping inside. It had been a mistake to pen the cattle so far from the house, but this was the only pen large enough to hold them until they could be branded.

He looked at the gruesome sight and smelled the unmistakable stench of rotting flesh.

Taking a cleansing breath, he removed the bandanna from his neck and tied it so it would cover his nose. He had to get close enough to the cattle so he could determine what had killed them.

Opening the gate, he moved to the closest carcass and knelt down beside it. The belly was bloated, and there was foam around the mouth. He examined another animal and found it had died with the same symptoms.

Standing up, Gabe felt rage coil inside him at the senseless destruction. Some person with a twisted mind had ordered this carnage. The condition of the carcasses told its own tale—the cattle had probably been poisoned, and he had to find out how.

Removing his bandanna and tying it back around his neck, he walked to the drinking trough and scooped water into his cupped hand. It certainly smelled pure enough—he brought it to his mouth and touched his tongue to it and found that there was no bitter taste. If these cattle had been poisoned, it certainly hadn't been from the water.

Puzzled, he examined another body. The cows had most certainly not died of natural causes; their deaths had been deliberate. His jaw tightened when his searching gaze fell on a strange-looking plant near the fence. He stooped to pick it up and recognized what it was at once.

Careless weed!

The plant was a rancher's worst nightmare. The strange thing about the weed was that if it was eaten green, it was harmless; but eaten dry, it released a noxious poison. Careless weed did not grow in this part of Texas, so someone had brought it there.

He glanced around and saw several other clumps of the dried weed. Whoever had done this knew exactly what he was doing. And Gabe knew without a doubt who that someone was. Cyrus would not have dirtied his hands with the poisoning, but the orders would have come from him all the same. The deed had probably been carried out by the foreman of the Casa Mesa ranch, Ira Teague; that coldhearted bastard would follow Cyrus's orders without question.

Gabe watched a buzzard tear at the flesh of one of the animals—the bird would probably die from eating the poisoned flesh, but no one mourned the death of a scavenger. In his own way Cyrus was a scavenger who existed on other people's misery.

Gabe knew just how Cyrus would go about getting rid of his adversaries—he would start small, pick at them and feed on their wretchedness—then he would apply more pressure and torment them. The more his enemy suffered, the more pressure Cyrus would apply, and the more pleasure he would derive from it. Cyrus was the only person Gabe knew who possessed no redeeming qualities whatsoever.

"So it's begun," he said, picking up the newborn calf and mounting his horse.

Cyrus had struck sooner than he had expected.

It was time for Gabe to pay him a visit at Casa Mesa.

Kate was instructing the store's handyman how to load supplies in the wagon when Casey and Jenny approached. "Where's Sam?" she asked, fitting a crate of apples under the spring seat.

"He's talking to the blacksmith about shoeing one of the mares. Jenny is hungry, so I think I'd better find her something to eat."

Kate hopped down from the wagon and nodded at the man. "Keep an eye on our supplies, and when a young man named Sam comes along asking for us, direct him to Betsy's Tearoom."

The tearoom turned out to be something of a surprise to Casey. She hadn't seen the building when they came into town because it was located behind the bank. It was white with green shutters, and had window boxes with some kind of plant with purple flowers.

Casey found the inside to be just as cheery as the outside. There were six tables with red-and-white gingham tablecloths, with fresh flowers in the center of each.

The woman who greeted them could have come straight from the pages of one of Jenny's fairytale books. She was blond and petite with blue eyes and dimples. She wore a blue-checked gown and a crisp, ruffled apron.

When she spoke, her voice was soft. "Kate, what

a pleasure to see you again. And who are your friends?" She smiled at Casey. "You must be new in this part of Texas."

Jenny slid her hand out of Casey's and climbed up on a chair, dipping her head so she could smell the flowers.

"This here's the Hamiltons," Kate said. "The little one there is Jenny, and this is Casey. They're the new owners of the Spanish Spur. Casey, this here's Betsy Turner."

"It's just delightful to meet you, Mrs. Hamilton. Your daughter looks just like you."

Jenny, never one to let an opportunity pass without having her say, remarked, "I don't have a mama anymore—Casey is my sister, and she's much prettier than you are."

Casey glared at her sister. "That's enough, Jenny. Apologize at once."

"But, Casey," the child reasoned, "you always said I was to tell the truth."

Betsy looked shocked at Jenny's statement, while Kate turned away to hide her smile.

"You must forgive my sister," Casey said hurriedly, giving Jenny a look that warned the child she was going to be in trouble later on. "She will say what she wants, and there doesn't seem to be much I can do about it."

"Perhaps," Betsy suggested, her voice no longer soft, "you might spank her when she misbehaves. Children should never be allowed to speak their mind so freely."

Kate stopped Casey from answering by picking Jenny up in her arms. "No one is going to spank this adorable little angel—not as long as ol' Kate's 'round."

Casey flashed Kate a grateful smile as she watched Sam cross the street toward them. Jenny sometimes needed a stern hand, but Casey had never hit her; she cringed at the very thought. But Jenny would have to be punished for her rudeness, and that punishment would come in the form of being denied a slice of the custard pie Casey intended to bake the next day. Custard pie was Jenny's favorite dessert.

Sam joined them at the table. After they had ordered, he asked Casey, "Have you told her the good news?"

Casey shook her head and nodded at Betsy, who was slicing bread for their sandwiches; it was apparent that she was listening to their conversation. "We'll talk about it on the way home," she told him.

Betsy set a plate of assorted sandwiches on the table, but her attention was on Kate. "I heard a rumor that Gabe was back in the area. Have you seen him, Kate? Can it be true?"

"I'm sure if Gabe had come back, you'd have seen him," Kate said. Her gaze met Casey's, and she gave a slight shake of her head.

Jenny frowned. "He is—"

Casey interrupted her sister, because it was apparent Kate did not want the woman to know that

Gabe was working at the Spanish Spur. "Jenny, eat your sandwich."

The child took a bite and mumbled.

"And, Jenny, don't talk with your mouth full," Casey scolded her.

It was late in the afternoon when they finally started back to the ranch. This time Kate was driving, and Casey was seated up front beside her. Sam was sitting in back with a sleeping Jenny curled up on his lap.

"How was your meeting with Murdock?" Kate asked, slowing the horses on a steep incline.

"Oh, Kate, I couldn't wait to tell you the news." Casey was still dazed by the meeting with the attorney, and it was difficult to accept that they no longer had to worry about money. "Uncle Bob didn't owe anyone anything. And he left us with a good deal of money—at least, I think it's a great deal."

Kate grinned. "I thought he might have some money, 'cause he never spent much. I 'spect he was saving it for you kids. That's the kind of man he was. I never knew a better one."

"Kate, he left you the house you live in."

At first it didn't appear that Kate had heard what Casey said, because she gazed into the distance. After she could speak, her eyes shimmered with tears. "That old man was determined to have the last word." She dabbed at her eyes. "I didn't reckon on him doing that." She paused another moment. "I do declare—he did that for me?"

Casey had already begun to love the small woman who watched over them so faithfully. "You will always have a home with us. Even if our uncle hadn't left you the house, we would not have let you leave us. You were our first friend here in Texas, maybe our only friend."

"I feel like you're family. But you are wrong when you say I'm your only friend. Gabe will stand by you in any trouble that comes your way."

"I think so, too. And so did Mr. Murdock."

"Hmm. Did the attorney say anything else about Gabe?"

"No. He hadn't seen him in several years and didn't know Gabe had returned to Mariposa Springs." Casey sighed. "Mr. Murdock warned us about Mr. Slaughter."

"Don't you fret none, honey. You have Gabe looking after you. And that's a powerful lot."

"I don't know why he's helping us, but I'm glad he is."

" 'Cause that's the kind of man he is."

"You like him, don't you?"

"Yeah. I like him and respect him." She grinned. "I wish I was as beautiful as you are and as young, so I could go after him." She chuckled. "He'd be the man for me."

Casey studied her with a serious expression. "I got the feeling you didn't want Miss Turner to know that Gabe was at the Spanish Spur."

"If he wants her to know he's back, he can do

the telling. Time was when people thought those two would one day marry. At least, that's what Betsy was telling 'round. Course, Gabe may have had other ideas, 'cause he never went near her much. She's never married, and it's almost like she's been just waiting for Gabe to come back." Kate met Casey's gaze. "Course, I could be all wrong, but that's the way I see it."

Casey felt a prickle of jealousy that she didn't have any right to feel. "She's very pretty."

"Um-hmm. Like one of those dolls I once saw in a store window in San Antone. And with about as much emotion, the way I see it."

Casey watched the setting sun as they pulled through the gates of the Spanish Spur. It felt like coming home. And Gabe would be there. She wondered how it would feel to be loved by a man like him?

He was dangerous—she could see that by the hard look in his silver eyes—but she was no longer afraid of him. She had begun to depend on him for so much. Casey also wondered what she would do when he left. There was a restlessness in him, and she knew he would one day move on.

How would she survive when that day came?

Chapter Twelve

Gabe was waiting for them when Kate halted the buckboard in front of the house.

Casey watched him walk toward them, and her heart did a somersault. He was so handsome, tall, lean. He was everything she had ever dreamed of in a man.

He approached Casey's side of the wagon with a grim expression on his face. "Miss Hamilton, Sam, I need to talk to the two of you."

Kate took a sleeping Jenny in her arms. "I'll just put this little one to bed for you."

"Sam," Gabe began, "the cattle we drove into the pen yesterday are all dead." He looked from Sam to Casey. "The deed was done deliberately, and you can pretty well guess Cyrus was behind it."

Sam was stunned and angry at the same time. "They're all dead?"

"Just a newborn calf survived. I put it in one of

the stalls in the barn and bottle-fed it, but I don't think it'll live."

Sam looked from his sister to Gabe. "We should ride into town and tell the sheriff what's happened. Surely he will do something about this."

"I wouldn't look for help in that direction. Sheriff Burford owes his job to Cyrus. He might as well be working for him, because he won't do anything that goes against him. Besides, we have no proof."

"Then what can we do?" Casey asked in frustration, feeling sick inside.

"There is nothing we can do tonight," Gabe told them. "Let's get some sleep, and we'll talk about it tomorrow."

Sam shook his head. "I want to ride over to Casa Mesa right now and confront that man. He has no right to kill our cattle!"

Casey laid her hand on her brother's shoulder. "That's exactly what we shouldn't do, because it's probably what Mr. Slaughter will expect." She glanced up at Gabe for verification. "Am I right about that?"

Gabe liked the way Casey gently nudged her brother in the right direction. Once again he was reminded of her strength and courage. And he could see the tired lines around her eyes and knew that worrying was taking a lot out of her. He already knew she didn't get enough sleep. He wanted to draw her to him and make everything all right in her life. "You're exactly right."

"I don't want him to get away with this," Sam stated with anger. "There has to be something we can do."

"Slaughter won't get away with it, Sam," Casey assured him. "But we can't do anything about it tonight, so start unloading the wagon. I want to speak to Gabe."

Sam looked like he wanted to object, but she watched him walk to the back of the wagon, lift a twenty-pound bag of flour on his back, and head toward the house.

When she glanced back at Gabe, he could see the uncertainty in her eyes. "I wish I could protect Sam from this kind of worry. He's so young to face such a bad situation."

Gabe's voice was deep with concern. "And you? What about you?"

She smiled shyly at him. "In case you hadn't noticed, we Hamilton women are a stubborn lot. Surely you have noticed this trait in Jenny."

He wanted to tell her that she was the one who had the strength. It was she who held the family together against impossible odds. He wanted to make her heart and spirit his. "I have noticed that trait in both of you."

Sam had returned for another load, and they both watched him shoulder a bag of potatoes. Casey was so aware of Gabe standing close to her that if she followed her heart, she would reach out and touch him. She could hear his intake of breath, and she closed her eyes for a moment to marshal her thoughts in a different, safer direction.

"Gabe, you knew we had gone into Mariposa Springs to see my uncle's attorney."

He watched as a slight breeze drifted through her long, silken hair, rippling it at her shoulders. He had to fight the urge to reach out and take a handful of the soft curls and bury his face in them. He was close enough to smell the sweet scent she wore. He hadn't known women could be soft and sweet, yet still strong. "You did mention that to me."

"My brother and I were stunned by what Mr. Murdock told us." She glanced into his eyes. "My uncle left us enough money to pay your salary and hire other men to help you. I have talked this over with Sam, and we both agreed that we would like you to stay on as foreman of the Spanish Spur. Later we can work out the details of your wages." She looked uncertain as he propped his booted foot on the wagon wheel. "Do you find that acceptable?"

"It's never been about the money—I think you know that."

Casey heard the warmth in his voice, and she tried to think why else he would stay on at a ranch that was the target of Mr. Slaughter's greed. "My family will always be indebted to you for offering to stay on without pay. But we don't like to owe anyone. Now, because of my uncle's generosity, we can repay you for your kindness."

For a reason he didn't understand, Gabe suddenly felt anger boiling inside him. He wasn't sure what he wanted from her, but it sure wasn't her money. "Go on in the house and get some rest. I'll help Sam unload the wagon."

"And you will consider staying on as foreman?"

"We'll speak of that another time."

She heard the anger in his voice and wondered at the reason for it. What had she said wrong? "I know I've already said this, but my family is indebted to you."

"Don't be," he said bitingly. "I have reasons of my own for helping you."

Casey had drifted off to sleep, but she awoke when a sharp pain shot through her shoulder. She sat up in bed, wanting to cry, it hurt so badly. Quietly she got up and went into the kitchen so she could get a carrot. She then headed for the horse paddock, a habit she had developed since coming here. The chestnut gelding came over to her and accepted his reward. She ran her hand across the horse's sleek neck, and tried to forget that her shoulder was bothering her.

Tonight her mind was particularly troubled about the cattle that had been poisoned. And the cattle that were missing, if what Mr. Murdock said was true. What kind of man would do such a thing? She shuddered.

What kind, indeed?

She absently ran her hand across the horse's

mane. If she were looking for the silver lining in their situation, as her father had always advised her to do, she must be grateful that they had a home, and that their uncle had left them money.

But money wouldn't help them in the situation they faced. Mr. Slaughter was the most vicious man she had ever known. When she thought of how he had treated his own son and daughter, it made her sick inside. The daughter was dead, and the son probably was too—at least Gabe had indicated that he might be.

How could her family survive in the face of such evil? What would they do when Mr. Slaughter came calling a second time?

Gabe stood in the shadows of the bunkhouse watching Casey. He knew she came there almost every night, and he found himself waiting for her to appear. There was a part of him that wanted to approach her, take her in his arms, and hold her against his body. But the time would come when she would discover who he was, and then she would probably despise him.

He watched her lay her face against the horse's neck. Then he heard her cry out in pain when the horse made a sudden move that twisted her body.

Casey leaned her head against the fence, not allowing herself to cry. She could tell her shoulder was getting worse; she should have asked Kate today if there was a doctor in town who could take a look at it.

"What's wrong with your shoulder?"

She lifted her head and found Gabe standing beside her. "I . . . It's nothing. I injured it that day our wagon got stuck in the Brazos. I thought it would have healed by now, but it still bothers me sometimes."

"And you haven't said anything about it before now?"

"I didn't want to worry anyone."

"Is it getting worse?"

"I . . . Yes."

"Come with me." He left no room for argument. "I'll need to have a look at it in the light."

She started to follow him before she realized he was heading toward the bunkhouse. "I can't go in there with you."

He turned to her, took her hand, and urged her forward. "Getting that shoulder tended to is more important than your modesty, Miss Hamilton."

Hesitantly she took a step. "It isn't proper."

His clasp on her hand wasn't tight, but it was firm, and he brought her forward. In that moment she had a feeling he could right every wrong in her life if she would only allow it. She stepped onto the porch, and he held the door for her to go inside. She hadn't been there since the day she'd cleaned it. In the soft lamplight, she noticed that Gabe had neat habits.

His clothing was hung on pegs, and two pairs of boots were lined up along the wall. He didn't seem to have many possessions, and that made her sad. Did he have so little that he could fit it all into a saddlebag?

He led her closer to the lamp before he relinquished her hand. "Since you are so modest, just turn your back to me and unbutton your gown enough to slip it down so I can get a look at your shoulder."

She backed away from him, shaking her head. "I can't do that!"

He took her arm and gently pulled her forward. "How else can I look at your shoulder?"

"I—"

"If it isn't healing, you may need a doctor to look at it, but I won't know until I see for myself. Would you like me to unbutton your gown?" His gaze dipped to the swell of her breasts and then he met her gaze. "Would you?"

"No." She turned her back to the lamp and unbuttoned two buttons. She felt his hand on her shoulder and felt her stomach tighten, not in fear, but with something else—a need to feel him touch her all over. She swallowed as he slid the edge of the dress off her shoulder.

"You will have to unbutton more buttons. I can't see all of the injury."

With trembling fingers, she undid two more buttons, then reluctantly a third.

His hands were gentle as he slid her gown down

further. She closed her eyes when his hand paused at the strap of her chemise; then he pushed it down as well. He was silent as he looked at her wound.

"Dammit, Casey, there's a deep cut here, and there's bruising around it as well. Why didn't you at least have Kate look at it before now?"

It was the first time he had spoken her name, and she liked the way he pronounced it. "I really thought it would get better on its own."

"I know you by now—you didn't want your brother or sister to know you'd been hurt," he said with certainty. "Didn't it occur to you that it might get infected if it wasn't treated?"

"I hoped it wouldn't."

She looked delicate and soft, but anyone who took that for a sign of weakness in her would be wrong. Pulling his mind back to her injury, he probed around the wound, trying not to notice that her skin was every bit as smooth as he'd thought it would be. The arch of her neck invited his touch, and he ached to do just that. He breathed deeply and tore his gaze away from the creamy slope of her back. He slid his hand along her shoulder blade and felt a tightening in his gut.

"Does that hurt?"

She nodded. "Not so very much."

"I think it hurts like hell." His gaze went back to her graceful neck, and he saw the blush that tinted her cheek. He swore under his breath, knowing he was causing her embarrassment, and he was about to cause her pain. "At least you didn't dislocate your shoulder. But the wound is deep, and I'm going to have to clean it."

"Will it be bad?"

"I won't lie to you. It'll hurt like hell."

He felt her tremble. "Just do it quickly."

He eased her down on the edge of his cot and felt her body stiffen. If he didn't handle this right, she would surely take flight. He attempted to put her at ease by distracting her. "I found you a milk cow at the Bolson farm. I put her in the barn, in the second stall. Now you can stop worrying that your brother and sister don't have milk to drink."

She smiled slightly. "Once again, I am in your debt."

He had never wanted to kiss a woman as badly as he wanted to kiss her at that moment. He could only imagine how soft her lips would be beneath his seeking mouth. "Just sit still," he said gruffly, "while I gather what I need."

She glanced up at him while attempting to pull the front of her gown together. "I will."

He would have liked nothing better at that moment than to lay her down on his bed and cover her body with his. He felt himself swell and harden, and he cursed under his breath.

Gabe managed to drag his attention back to her injury. In the not-too-distant future their lives would take a different turn, and he would have to leave. He knew if he kissed her, he would never be able to ride away when that time came.

After he had gathered everything he needed, he knelt down beside her, his feelings raw and close to the surface. "First," he told her, "I am going to cleanse the wound. That's the part that'll hurt the most. Hold still." He dabbed at the wound, wishing he did not have to cause her more pain.

She sucked in her breath, and tears gathered in her eyes as the wound burned painfully. She relaxed a bit when he applied soothing ointment, then winced when he taped the bandage in place.

Gabe was reluctant to move away from her, but after he had eased her gown back onto her shoulder, he could think of no excuse to linger.

"You should have Kate look at this tomorrow."

His thigh brushed against her leg when he stood, and she felt a shock go through her whole body. She quickly buttoned her gown. When he held out his hand, she allowed him to help her stand.

"Thank you."

He smiled down at her and reached out to untangle a curl from the back of her gown. "Anytime, boss lady."

Casey edged toward the door and rushed outside. He stood for a long time without moving.

He couldn't remember when he had wanted a woman so much. He'd been with a few, but they had disappeared from his thoughts as soon as he left them. He had a feeling he would remember this one a long time after he'd left the Spanish Spur.

Casey slowed her steps when she reached the house. Her heart was beating so fast she could hardly catch her breath. She could still feel the touch of his hand on her skin. When he had knelt beside her, they had been so close she could see the stubble where he needed to shave.

When he'd glanced up at her, Casey had lowered her gaze. But no matter what she tried, her gaze went back to him. He must have just bathed, because his hair had still been wet, and she had wanted to push her fingers through the dampness. She wanted desperately to touch him, to lay her head against his shoulder and cry out all the pain that had been building inside her since her father's death.

She quietly opened the door and went inside the dark house. It was stuffy in the room she shared with Jenny. She opened the window and stared out into the night while she flexed her shoulder. It could have been her imagination, but it seemed to feel better already.

She lay down beside her sister, wondering how she could get Gabe out of her thoughts. He was a man, and she was a woman, and he had awakened her to that fact almost from their first meeting.

Why did she feel so empty inside? Why did she want to run back to the bunkhouse and throw herself into Gabe's arms? She wanted him to hold her tightly against him. She closed her eyes and felt a light breeze cool her body.

She had to think of something else. She closed her eyes, and weariness soon overcame her resistance and she fell asleep.

Chapter Thirteen

Saddle leather creaked as Gabe dismounted and walked up the steps of the house that he had sworn never again to enter. He stood before the massive wooden door, hesitant, knowing once he stepped inside he would start something that probably wouldn't stop until either he or Cyrus was dead.

He was suddenly struck by memories of when he'd first been brought to Casa Mesa. At that time he had still been grieving for his mother, who had just died. He had been placed under the care of a father he had hardly known, who had taken him away from everything familiar in his life.

As a young boy he had lived through anguish in this house. Cyrus had been cruel and demanding, and he seemed to derive some kind of sick pleasure from humiliating those around him. But Gabe had found an unexpected ally in his half sister, Nora, who had become a wonderful companion. It wasn't until a few years had passed that Gabe understood why Cyrus had brought him to the house. It hadn't been out of any fatherly affection.

Looking back, he wondered if there could have been a way to prevent the tragedy that had befallen Nora, but no one had known the extent to which Cyrus would go to get his own way.

Gabe placed his hand on the doorknob, feeling the cold brass beneath his fingers. He had been the one who'd found Nora's body, and the scene kept playing over in his mind. He would sometimes awake during the night drenched in sweat, trying to forget the awful sight of her lying in a pool of her own blood. The rage he had tried to suppress for so long now reared up inside him, almost choking him. He remembered how his father had stood in the doorway of Nora's room, unwilling to go near her lifeless body, cursing her for a weakling.

He had even refused to attend her funeral.

Cyrus was twisted, cruel, and cunning, and he had now cast his greedy eyes on the Spanish Spur. Gabe had to stop him. There were not many men Gabe could call on to help, because everyone was afraid of Cyrus; that fear allowed him to ride roughshod over anyone who got in his way.

Gabe stepped inside the door and looked about the main room—it was just the way he remembered it. It was large with overstuffed leather furniture that had been made in Italy especially to

Cyrus's specifications—a fact that his father repeated to everyone who admired the furnishings.

The wooden floors were beautiful and unique, made with wide planks that had come from California cypress trees. Gabe remembered the large kitchen with its open hearth and many copper pans hanging from racks.

He wondered if the cook, Juanita, was still around. He had loved the plump little woman as a boy. She had often made him special desserts that Cyrus never knew about.

He glanced at the dark mahogany staircase that curved upward in two different directions and led to five bedrooms. The one room he knew the least about was his father's study, since he had been in it only one time: the day he had told his father that he had joined the army, and he wouldn't be coming back.

Memories of the past walked beside him as he moved down the long hallway that led to the study. He took a deep breath and stopped at the doorway. He was there for a purpose, and he wouldn't leave until he faced his father.

Gabe's footsteps were silent as he stepped into the room. There behind the desk, with his head bent over paperwork, was the man Gabe despised most in the world.

Cyrus didn't even look up when he spoke. "I've been expecting you, Gabe. Come in and sit down. I'm just finishing up here. I'll be with you shortly."

"Thank you, I'll stand. What I have to say to you won't take long. I know you're the one responsible for poisoning the cattle on the Spanish Spur. And I came to warn you to stay away from the Hamiltons. They are under my protection."

Cyrus shoved his papers aside and glanced at Gabe. "Is that right?" There was utter contempt in Cyrus's voice, and a coldness in his eyes that chilled to the bone. "So the boy thinks he's become a man and thinks he can take on his father?"

"I am a man, and I will stop you. No one knows you like I do. You won't quit until you get what you want." Gabe leaned against the door and crossed his arms over his chest. "You aren't going to win this time, Cyrus."

For the first time Cyrus really looked at his son; Gabe had become a man in the years he'd been away. He favored his mother in many ways, but there was plenty of evidence that Gabe was his son, too. They were about the same height and their eye color was the same. Over the years Cyrus had grown accustomed to people either avoiding his gaze or looking into his eyes with fear. There was no fear in his son's eyes, and it gave him a certain feeling of pride, but that pride would not stop him from bringing Gabe down and crushing him beneath his boots.

Gabe noticed the changes in his father. There was gray at his temples and a slight stoop to his shoulders. The lines were deeper along his mouth. He had aged more than Gabe had expected. His eyes were just as hard and cold, but now his brows were dusted with gray and not stark black, as they had been the last time he'd seen him.

"And you think you will be the one to stop me?" Cyrus asked, his eyes marble-hard and cold.

"Yes, I will. I've watched you destroy lives with the same dispassion you would feel if you swatted a mosquito. You are responsible for my sister's death as surely as if you had pulled the trigger yourself."

His father shot to his feet, rage twisting his features. "I did nothing but try to give her some backbone, but she was a weakling like her mother. She latched on to that bastard Yates, thinking she loved him. She should've known I'd never let her marry a man like him. But you are not here to talk about Nora, and I don't want to hear anything more about her. As far as I'm concerned, I never had a daughter, and I certainly don't have a son."

Gabe noticed that his father was breathing heavily, and he had paled. He had struck a nerve by bringing up Nora's death. Cyrus had been more affected by his daughter's death than he would have anyone believe.

"My sister deserved better than you gave her. She deserved a better life than the one you provided. But you're the one I pity the most. You destroyed everything that was good in your life because of greed."

Cyrus stormed around the desk and planted himself directly in front of his son. "Pity me? The bastard I brought into my home and sat at my table! Pity me!"

Gabe's gaze did not waver. "A bastard, no. You did marry my mother, although I never could figure out what she saw in you."

"I'll just tell you about your mother. She was the most beautiful woman I'd ever seen, with her long black hair and doelike eyes that could look right into a man's soul."

"You have no soul."

Cyrus went on as if Gabe hadn't spoken. "I wanted her, but she wouldn't have me without marriage, so I obliged her with a proper ceremony. But if she thought I was going to parade her before my friends and introduce her as my wife, she was disappointed, wasn't she?"

"My mother loved you until the day she died, even though you moved her to a small cabin miles from nowhere, and then neglected her. But I'm not here to talk about my mother. I'm here to warn you to stay away from the Hamilton family. I will do whatever it takes to keep you from destroying another life. Nora's spirit demands that of me."

Cyrus's eyes dimmed, and his eyebrows met in a frown across the bridge of his nose. "Don't do it, Gabe. Come home to me and we'll build an empire together, something that will last long after we're both gone."

Gabe was shocked by his father's words. Before now, he had not been invited to be a real son. But it was too late now; he didn't want what Cyrus offered. "If you want to build an empire, you'll have to do it without me. I never realized it before this, but you have no family, no friends. No one to care if you live or die. You have only the men you pay to be loyal to you, and many of them have left out of fear. That can't give you much comfort in the dead of night."

"Know this and remember it—I'll kill you if you get in my way, Gabe!"

"I have no doubt you'll try. Consider yourself warned. Stay away from the Spanish Spur," Gabe said as he turned and walked out of the room.

Cyrus shouted after him, "Come back here and you can have all this! Don't you walk away from me!"

Gabe kept walking. He didn't see the dark look on Cyrus's face, or the fists that had balled at his sides.

"No one talks to me that way," the old man said to himself. "No one!"

Chapter Fourteen

It was late when Gabe arrived back at the Spanish Spur. His gaze automatically went to the main house, and in his imagination he could envision Casey curled up, soft and asleep. But he wouldn't allow his mind to go any further than that.

He had been caught by her smile and captured by the golden laughter that spilled out of her mouth. That mouth he wanted to take with his. As he wanted to take her tempting body.

He noticed that Kate's house was dark, and she was usually up at this hour.

Loneliness weighed heavily on his shoulders, a feeling so dark and deep it was almost like a physical pain. It had been difficult to face his father, but he had learned something important today. There had been fear in Cyrus's eyes, and something else Gabe could not define.

As he dismounted and led his horse to the corral, he noticed that there was a faint light coming from one of the stalls in the barn. He closed the gate and moved silently toward the light. A lantern hung from a hook, and he made his way toward it. He was surprised to see Casey sitting on scattered hay with the newborn calf he had rescued.

She had no idea he was watching her, and he felt a little like he was invading her privacy. He would have made her aware of his presence except that he was mesmerized by the sight of her trying to entice the calf to drink from the bottle. Gabe had a feeling that he was looking into Casey's soul as her delicate hand swept up and down the calf's neck, and tears glistened in her eyes.

"Come on," she whispered, rubbing the nipple across the animal's mouth. "You have to drink, or you will die."

Gabe watched as her red-gold hair came alive under the glow of the lantern and framed her beautiful face. He felt a tight clenching inside his heart. He was in awe of Casey's gentleness and her love for a helpless animal. The sudden outpouring of emotion rocked his world. When he had held her and kissed her, he had trembled for an hour afterward. What he felt for her was pure and deep.

Casey had not heard a sound, but she glanced up to find Gabe watching her. His silver eyes were shining, and he had the softest expression on his face.

It took her a moment to find her voice. "Gabe, I'm so glad you're here. Jenny tried to feed this calf several times today, and it wouldn't eat." There was panic in her voice. "I don't know what Jenny will do if this animal dies. Can you help me?"

He sat down beside her and took the bottle from her hand. "You know, Casey, most of the time newborns die when they have no mother."

"This one can't!"

He slowly began to tease the animal's mouth with the nipple. "She isn't going to take this."

"Please try a little longer," she implored him.

He would have done anything she asked. In that moment he wanted nothing more than for the animal to latch on to the bottle. Casey held her breath as the animal's tongue lapped out and touched the nipple. She smiled and glanced up at Gabe when the calf took it in her mouth.

"You did it, Gabe!"

He felt ten feet tall. He wished he could solve all her problems as easily. Soon the bottle was drained, and the animal closed its eyes to sleep. Casey gave the calf a soft pat and stood up beside Gabe.

"I was so afraid it was going to die, and I'd have to explain to my sister what happened. Sam had to take her to the house and put her to bed because she wanted to stay with the calf all night. She's lost so many things in her young life. The death of this calf would have been devastating for her. She takes everything so hard."

"What about you?"

She smiled mischievously. "I have a sinister side to my character. You see, I love fried chicken, and I would have eaten it with no guilt involved."

He grinned. "So you're not an angel. You can be tempted by fried chicken?"

"As I said, I love fried chicken."

His gaze swept across her face, and he reached out to take a sprig of hay from her hair. His hand lingered, touching, sifting the softness between his fingers. Then he dropped his hand while she stood there, trembling inside.

When Gabe touched her like that, didn't he know what it did to her? But she had reached a place where his touch was not enough. She wanted so much more, even though she didn't know exactly what it was. Her face flushed, and she wondered if Gabe could guess her thoughts.

He brushed against her arm as he stood. Then he clasped her hand, bringing her up beside him, taking care not to hurt her injury.

"How is your shoulder?"

She was reluctant for him to move away. "It hardly hurts at all."

He grinned down at her. "Maybe I'm a better doctor than I thought."

"I took your advice and had Kate look at it. She says it's healing nicely."

"Did you tell her who dressed the wound?"

She smiled up at him. "Yes."

"And what did she say to that?"

Casey laughed. "She said she was going to go out and hurt her shoulder so you could tend her, too."

He placed his hand over hers, wanting to touch her, hold her, be near her. "Kate is like no one else."

Gabe was speaking words, but Casey couldn't quite catch their meaning because she was thinking about the hand that touched hers with such gentleness. She met his gaze and felt as if a swirling tide were washing toward her.

His silver eyes were drawing her in. She was not even aware that she had moved closer to him. He clasped her hand against his chest. "Do you feel my heart beating?"

She did. It was thundering beneath her fingertips. Her gaze went to his beautiful mouth, and she wanted to feel it pressed against hers.

As if he could read her thoughts, Gabe brought her closer, raising her chin and slowly lowering his head. His lips were soft as they skimmed over the fullness of her mouth, savoring the caress, drawing out their mutual need. "Do you want me to stop?" he asked.

Her arms slid around his shoulders in answer. He drew her closer, pressing her against him, his lips settling firmly against hers.

The soft touch of his mouth made her insides quiver, and she pressed tightly against his thighs.

He accommodated her by fitting her against his hard swell.

Gabe had a deep need for Casey, but he wanted their loving to be right; he wanted to tell her everything about himself, or it wouldn't be fair to her. He raised his head and looked into her shimmering eyes. His gaze dipped to the gentle swell of breasts that begged to be cupped in his hand.

He touched their softness in wonder and watched her eyes widen and then drift shut. He had half expected her to protest, and when she didn't, he dipped his head to touch his lips to one tempting point that pressed against the material of her gown.

Gabe heard her sigh when he cupped the fullness of her breast in his hand and gently traced the nipple; the sound filled him with the sweetest sensation. Need, want, desire tore through him, but he kept his feelings under control. He could touch her only in this way, and only this one time, and then he had to let her go.

Casey hadn't known the sweep of a man's hand could bring such pleasure. When he touched her like this, she wanted more. His hand drifted up her back to settle near her throat, bringing her unbelievable joy. She thought she would die if he didn't satisfy the aching need that was building inside her as he deepened the kiss. She trembled, and her knees almost buckled when his tongue parted her lips and darted inside.

Gabe realized that Casey trusted him as his

mouth explored the silken curve of her neck. He could tell she was inexperienced, but she wanted him as much as he wanted her. He drew back so he could look into her eyes, and he saw total surrender in the blue depths.

He needed her to fill the empty void inside him. No woman had ever touched the part of his heart that she had taken as her own. Gabe had a feeling that when he left her, he would leave behind everything that was good in him. No woman but Casey would ever satisfy the hungry need that gnawed at him.

He also knew that he should stop before he had gone too far to turn back. It would be wrong for him to take what she offered. Her life was complicated enough without him making it worse. He was a breath away from heaven's gate, but he could not enter. He had to let her go.

"You have never been touched this way by a man, have you?"

Her eyes shimmered. "No. James Udall kissed me once after a ball, but it was nothing like this."

He pressed his cheek to hers, wanting to hold her for a moment longer. "It's lucky for Mr. Udall that he isn't here right now. I'm afraid I'd have to take his head off for touching your lips." He dipped his head and pressed his mouth against hers, fitting her against his hardness. "Feel what you do to me."

"Yes," she said, burying her face against his chest. "I do feel it."

"Have I erased Mr. Udall's memory from your mind?" he asked in a husky voice.

She smiled. "His kiss was nothing."

He tilted her chin up so she had to look into his eyes. "Casey, I know what you are feeling, because I feel it too. But I was wrong to take it this far. I have more experience than you, and I took unfair advantage of your innocence."

His words were like a dash of cold water in her face, and she drew back from him. "You didn't take advantage of me. I knew what I was doing."

He cupped her face in his hands. He had hurt her, and the knowledge was like a knife in his heart. "Sweet Casey, I would gladly pick you up and carry you to my bed, but it isn't the right thing for you—you know that."

She closed her eyes, wondering if he just didn't want her, or if he thought her too forward. "I'm sorry if I did something wrong." She wedged her elbow between them, attempting to shove him away and refusing to give in to the tears gathered behind her eyelids. "I have to go now."

"No, no, Casey, don't go like this." He held her firmly in his arms. "You don't understand what I am saying. I want you so badly I almost forgot you have troubles enough without me complicating your life."

She saw pain and devastation in his eyes. "What do you feel for me?"

His breath came out in a great rush. "What do I feel for you? I have walked in darkness for so long, I want to bask in the light of your smile. Until I met you, my life was the same from one day to the next. Now the simple touch of your hand can get me through a whole day. There is not an hour that passes without me thinking of you. That's how I feel about you."

"You probably think I'm too young to know what I feel, but I'm not. I want to . . . I . . . think I love you."

His breath hissed out, and he pressed his face into her hair, his body trembling and quaking. Those were the sweetest words he'd ever heard, and they pushed away his loneliness like the sun breaking through the darkest clouds. But still, he had to do what was best for her. "Sweetheart. If you only knew the truth about me, you would despise me."

She pulled away from him, wondering what he meant. He had not said he loved her; he'd said only that he needed her. "Nothing you could do would make me despise you. You are a good and honorable man. Don't you think I know that? I couldn't feel about you the way I do if that weren't true."

"The time will come when you will regret what you've said here tonight."

"Gabe, what are you talking about? I know there's something in your past that's bothering you. Why don't you tell me about it? It won't matter. I trust you more than I trust any man."

He saw the confusion in her eyes and thought

about admitting the whole truth. But he couldn't say the words. When she heard them, she would probably order him off the place, and he needed to stay close to her to protect her from Cyrus—especially after today.

"I'm just an ordinary man. I have no criminal past, and I have killed no man except faceless enemies in the war." He touched his mouth to her cheek and closed his eyes. "I want nothing more than to hold you like this forever." He pressed his face against hers. "I know just how to touch you and make you need me—I know the words to say that will make you fall willingly into my bed, but I won't. Do you understand that?"

Casey didn't understand at all. She only knew that he was rejecting her, and that hurt so badly.

"I'm sorry, Gabe, about the way I threw myself at you. I should never have behaved in such an unladylike manner. I don't know what I was thinking."

He knew it was better to hurt her a little now rather than to destroy her completely by taking all she had to give. "I have never allowed any woman to get as close to me as you have. I never needed anyone—I still don't."

"I see." And she did see what he was trying to do. He was trying to do the honorable thing by her. But she believed he needed her, whether he would admit it or not. "I understand what you are doing better than you think. It's all right to put your past behind you and start a new life."

He felt a gut-wrenching twist in his heart, and it left him breathless. She had reached inside him and found a tenderness that he hadn't known existed. He had lain awake many nights trying to imagine what it would feel like to be a part of her family.

Casey saw pain and indecision in his eyes, and she thought she might know him better than he knew himself. What set of events had made him such a loner? Gabe's strength and endurance had been apparent from the first day she'd met him, but there was a part of him that cried out for something—she wasn't quite sure what.

"You have no family, have you, Gabe?" She stepped closer to him and touched his cheek, feeling the stubble of his beard. "Has your life been so intolerable?"

He turned enough to touch his lips to her hand, and he knew this would be the perfect time to tell her about himself. But he let the moment pass and said, "I had not given my life much thought until I met you."

"Are you saying you love me?"

Love . . . he certainly had never given that emotion much thought, either; he wasn't sure he knew what it meant. He had seen what love had done to his mother. Her whole world had been wrapped around the husband who so rarely came to see her. He remembered her standing at the door for hours watching for Cyrus. Most of the time, she'd been disappointed. His mother had died without her husband beside her, and she had been buried without him to mourn her.

"I don't want to need anyone, Casey. Don't look for feelings in me that I don't have." He stepped away from her. "I need to leave you now."

She looked at him solemnly, feeling heavy-hearted. He was so alone, and he didn't even know how to accept love or to give it. "I must go in myself. I wouldn't want Jenny to wake up and find me gone."

He watched her leave, knowing he could never have her. He was Cyrus's son, and she would never understand why he hadn't told her the truth from the beginning. Now things had gone too far for him to admit he had tainted blood in his veins.

With a last glance toward the house, he headed for the bunkhouse. He had to let Casey go. He had to concentrate on what his father's next move would be, and he had to be ready for it when it came.

Chapter Fifteen

Jenny was taking a nap, and the house was quiet, so Casey stepped outside to sweep the front porch. It must have been windy during the night, because autumn-colored elm leaves were scattered across the porch.

She had been restless all day. Gabe had been avoiding her for the last week, and she certainly wouldn't seek him out. She waited for him to come to her and explain some of the things he had said that night in the barn.

She heard the rider before she saw him. He didn't come by way of the main road to the house but from the little-used river road.

She gripped the broom as a stranger rode into view. He dismounted and approached with a rolling gait. His skin was dark and swarthy, his hair so blond it was almost white.

Silently she watched him climb the steps. He paused at the railing and looked at her for a moment. His eyes were so pale it was almost impossible to tell the whites from the irises. He was tall and beefy, and he was staring at her as if he knew what she was wearing beneath her gown.

She started to lean the broom against the porch railing but reconsidered—it wasn't much of a weapon, but it was better than nothing. Gabe had warned her not to be alone with strangers, but there was nothing she could do to avoid this man.

He shoved his hat farther back on his head and smiled, making his thin lips appear even thinner. He had managed to make his smile look like a threat.

"I suppose you're Miss Hamilton?"

Casey bristled. "In my family, a man introduces himself to a lady before she gives him her name—if she chooses to give him her name at all."

His jaw hardened, and although his voice was soft, it was no less menacing. "Name's Ira Teague, and I'm foreman over to the Casa Mesa ranch. I waited until everyone rode away so I could have a little talk with you, alone. Sort of a private talk to clear up some things for my boss." He ran his large hand across his chin. "I kinda like the thought of being alone with you."

Fear twisted inside her, and she had the strongest urge to dash into the house and bolt the door. But she had a feeling a locked door would not keep this man out of the house. At last she found her voice, and she hoped it didn't show how frightened she really was. "If you have business with this ranch, you can wait at the bunkhouse until the foreman gets back."

"I didn't come to talk to Gabe. The boss said I was to talk to you, and no one else."

"Your boss already had a talk with me, and I didn't much care for his topic of conversation."

"We don't have to talk. You're a pretty little gal—we could do other things. I could think of a few I'd like."

She almost stumbled over the broom in her haste to get farther away from him. There was a cruel twist to his mouth when he smiled at her. "Now you don't want to run from me, do you? I won't hurt you much."

She was never so brave as when her back was to the wall. "You can just leave now."

"Not yet," he said, taking a step toward her. "I'm not ready to go." He stopped right in front of her, his hand touching her sleeve and rubbing the material between his fingers.

She quickly jumped back and swatted his hand away. "Don't you dare touch me!"

His gaze swept her body. "I'll do more'n that. I ain't never had me a woman as pretty as you."

Casey knew she should run, but she didn't want to draw him into the house where Jenny was, and she knew that if she tried to dart around him, he would only catch her.

"Get off my land," she said in a voice that shook with emotion.

He took another step toward her, and she was

about to cry out when they heard the sound of riders. Casey feared it would be more of Mr. Slaughter's men arriving. She hoped it would be Sam and Kate returning.

Teague swung around to stare at the two riders, and so did Casey. Even though they wore white man's clothing, it was evident that they were Indians. As both of them scrutinized the situation, hope bloomed inside her. Were they the two Comanches Gabe had sent for?

"Flint, Omous," Teague said with contempt, "what're the two of you doing here?" His colorless eyes seemed to darken, and his fists tightened at his sides. "I guess wherever Gabe is, I'll always find the two of you somewhere near."

"It's good if you remember this, Teague," the older Indian remarked. "Our path is not for you to know. I do not answer to you."

He spoke English with an accent Casey had never heard before.

"Are you unharmed, miss?" There was concern in the Indian's dark eyes, as if he knew she had been threatened in some way.

She nodded her head, relieved that they were not with Teague. She was trembling so badly she hid her hands behind her back so no one could see them.

The younger Indian moved in her direction and stationed himself between her and Teague in a protective manner.

"Gabe would not want you to be near this

woman. If you are wise, you will leave now," the older Indian stated.

"It's always been the same, Omous. Whenever I see the two of you, I know Gabe isn't far behind. I'm sure the boss'll be mighty pleased to hear you've joined up with him."

"Your words have no meaning to me. I do not listen to the skunk that moves in the night."

Teague merely grinned. "I'll be leaving now, but I'll be back." He looked pointedly at Casey and winked. "You and I have unfinished business together, pretty gal."

Casey's legs went so weak, she leaned against the porch railing for support. "I am so glad you came when you did," she said to the young Indian. She watched Teague ride away, even now fearing he might come back. "I was afraid."

"I am Flint," the younger Indian said, then glanced at her. "If you are Gabriel's woman, you have nothing to fear from that man. He will not let anyone harm you, and neither will my father or me."

She shook her head. "I am not Gabriel's woman. I am no one's woman."

He looked puzzled. Why would Gabe go to so much trouble to keep this woman safe if she was not his? "I am sorry if I mistakenly spoke of something I know nothing about," he said apologetically.

He had a better command of the English language than the older man did, and she thought he might have been educated in school. She was surprised that she felt no fear of them; in fact, she sensed only concern for her safety. It was fortunate for her that they had come along when they had. They were of the same height, each tall, each with a leather band around his forehead and long hair that came past his shoulders.

Omous must have been somewhere in his forties, or maybe even fifty; it was difficult to tell. His features were sharp, his nose was prominent, and his dark eyes were alert as he stared after Teague, making sure he didn't double back.

Flint was younger, perhaps in his late twenties or early thirties. She could see his resemblance to his father.

"Gabriel is not here?" Omous asked.

"He rode out early this morning, and I don't know when he'll be home." She pointed to the bunkhouse. "You can stow your belongings there, and if you are hungry, I have stew on the stove."

"We will just wait for Gabriel," Omous told her.

Flint's smile was gentle. "You have nothing to fear from that man. We will be watching over you until Gabriel returns."

Casey had always imagined that all Indians were fierce, people to be feared. She now realized that bringing the Comanches to the Spanish Spur was Gabe's way of protecting her family when he wasn't there.

* * *

Gabe walked the length of the bunkhouse and back again. "You are saying Teague threatened her?"

Omous nodded. "Yes. And she was frightened. I believe it is good that we came along when we did. Why did you leave your woman unprotected?"

Gabe frowned. "Miss Hamilton is not my woman."

Omous smiled. "She said that also. But you must say this to someone who has not held you when you took your first breath. My son and I thought because of the urgent message you sent to us that this woman is important to you."

"You see things that are not there."

Flint chuckled. "She is unusually fair. If she smiled at me, I know I could not resist her."

Gabriel swung around to face Flint, whom he had played with as a boy and who had always been his best friend. "You will not go near enough to her to see her smile."

Omous shook his head and smiled at his son. "It is much worse than I thought. If he is jealous of you, he is in a bad way."

Gabe waved Omous aside, unwilling to speak of his feelings for Casey. "I can't let Teague get away with threatening her. This insult must not go unanswered."

"You know they will be expecting you," the Comanche warned him.

Gabe looked at the two men he trusted above

all others. Whenever he had been in trouble, they had always come to him. Flint was a year older than Gabe, but they had been like brothers.

"You taught me to move silently, Omous. I will be in Teague's face before he sees me coming."

"Then we must go tonight."

Gabe nodded. "My father will stop at nothing to get his hands on this ranch. But at the moment he's more interested in catching me in a trap than obtaining the Spanish Spur."

Flint grinned. "Then we must not disappoint him."

Chapter Sixteen

Dark clouds covered the moon, casting the night in darkness, and Gabe knew that was to his advantage. He had left Omous with the horses some distance from the ranch house, while he and Flint cautiously approached the bunkhouse.

There were no lamps burning, but they both knew they were expected. Silently they crept in the shadows to an open window.

"They will expect us to go in through here," Flint whispered.

"Then we go in by the door, which they won't be expecting."

"That would be wise."

"You stay low and go to your left, and I will go to the right," Gabe instructed him.

"I understand."

The door opened easily, too easily. Still, Gabe stepped inside and flattened his back against the wall, knowing Flint, crouched down behind him, was sliding in the opposite direction.

It was suspiciously quiet. At this time of night everyone should be sleeping, and someone would be snoring. Gabe knew only too well how the room was arranged, since he had once lived on the ranch. He also knew the black heart of the man who waited inside that room to spring a trap.

Someone struck a match, and someone else lit a lamp. There were only three men present, and Gabe knew them all. Richard Bates was always ready to do whatever Teague wanted him to do. Charley Latter was nearly as mean as Teague, but not quite.

Apparently none of them had seen Flint, who had hunkered down behind a cot.

"We've been waiting for you," Teague said with a sly smile. "You might like to know you've got friends here, 'cause none of the others had the stomach for what I'm going to do to you." The lines around his mouth deepened. "You have been stuck in my craw for years, and I'm about to spit you out."

Teague motioned for the others to come forward. "Take him! Drag him to me, and don't be too gentle about it."

Flint stood up, cocked his rifle, and aimed it at Teague's heart. "If any one of your men steps in to help, I will shoot you." His voice was cold, his words decisive. "Do not try to help," he said to the others, "or the foreman dies."

"Take him at his word," Gabe said, remembering the hell the foreman had made of his life as a child. "This fight is between you and me, Teague. It always has been."

Teague smiled slowly as he took a step toward Gabe. "That's just the way I like it. The boss will thank me for what I'm about to do to you. How does it feel to know your pa don't care what happens to you?"

They circled each other while everyone else watched. Their gazes locked as they each looked for the first opening.

"I feel only contempt for him. You're the one who always licks his boots."

"You bastard."

"Are you going to talk me to death, Teague?"

The older man's face reddened. "I gave you a beating once. I can do it again."

"That's right, you did—but I was a boy at the time. I'm a man now. The odds are in my favor this time. I'm younger than you by at least ten years," Gabe taunted.

"That's to my advantage. Because I'm thirty pounds heavier than you are," Teague retaliated.

Gabe's contemptuous glance showed what he thought of the extra weight Teague carried. "How are you when you face a man instead of a young boy, or a woman, foreman?"

Teague was the first to strike, and he was lightning quick. Gabe didn't see it coming, and his knees buckled when Teague's fist connected with his midsection.

Teague thought he'd take advantage of Gabe while he was hunched over, heaving for breath. He dived at Gabe, but Gabe was ready for him this time, and he rolled to the side, grabbing Teague's leg and taking him to the floor.

Latter moved to help the foreman, but Flint aimed the rifle at him. "Do not do it, white man. You have my promise you will be dead before you hit the floor."

That stopped Latter in his tracks and made him reconsider. There was a hard look in the Indian's dark eyes, and that was a mean-looking Winchester pointed at him.

Meanwhile, Gabe and Teague were wrestling on the floor. Gabe's fist crashed into the foreman's jaw.

"That one was for Miss Hamilton." Gabe rolled to his feet and brought the man up with him. He drove his fists so hard into Teague's stomach that the man cried out.

Another punch to the stomach brought Teague to his knees. He looked stunned when Gabe hit him in the jaw again. He seemed to crumple and then fell backward—out cold.

Gabe turned to the other two. "Do either of you want to take me on?"

Bates was studying the toes of his boots, and Latter was sullenly silent.

"In that case, give Teague a message for me. I

hadn't figured he'd pass out this fast, or I would have told him myself. Tell him if he ever sets foot on the Spanish Spur, or approaches Miss Hamilton in any manner, he will curse the day he was born."

Latter gave Gabe a disgruntled look. "I'm not your messenger. Do it yourself."

Flint bent over Teague and looked up at Gabe. "He will live, but he's going to be sore for a long time."

Gabe glanced back at the other two men. "Then give this message to Cyrus—tell him not to stir up trouble he can't finish. Remind him that I meant what I told him the other day, and that he shouldn't send Teague or any of you to the Spanish Spur because we'll be waiting for you."

"I'll be glad to tell him that," Bates spoke up. "You're already a walking dead man."

"If there's any more trouble, and I find either of you is part of it, you'll curse the day your mother gave birth to you." Gabe spoke quietly, but the threat was there all the same.

He picked his hat up off the floor, and he and Flint backed to the door, watching the two men. "Think twice before you ride against the Spanish Spur."

Someone tapped Gabe on the shoulder, and he spun around, ready to fight.

The tall, lanky cowboy smiled at him. "Settle down, Gabe. I ain't here to fight you. Fact is, I made money on you tonight. Some of the men bet their month's pay that Teague would be the one left standing, but I knew better."

Gabe had always liked Will Fletcher, who had taught him most of what he knew about ranching. He hadn't seen the cowpoke in seven years, and the man hadn't been young then. Now his hair was mostly gray, but there was still a bounce in his step.

"I have a warning for you, Fletcher, and any of the others who might think they can ride onto the Spanish Spur and stir up trouble. I won't allow anything to happen to the Hamiltons. Anyone meaning them harm will have to go through me to get to them."

Fletcher chuckled. "I have been thinking 'bout moving on myself. You got any use for a broken-down ol' cowhand?"

Gabe thought for a moment. He had wanted someone always at the house to watch over Casey. Could he trust Fletcher? "I do need someone I can depend on when I turn my back."

"Then I'm your man. I always was partial to you when you was a boy—and I had a soft spot in my heart for the boss's daughter, too. Some of us took it real hard the way she died. I know several others who would come work for you and stand by you in a fight against Slaughter."

"Just tell them not to get in my way. I trust you, but not the others. I can't be sure they won't go running back to Cyrus."

Fletcher nodded. "I'll just pack my gear and

head on over your way tonight. I don't want to be here when Teague comes 'round. He's going to be awfully mean."

"We are tightening the perimeters around the house; make yourself known when you ride in or someone might shoot first and ask questions later."

Gabe and Flint melted into the darkness without a sound; it was as if they had never been there.

Fletcher shook his head in amazement. He'd never known how some men, mostly Indians, could move so quietly and swiftly, taking a body by complete surprise.

He'd felt sorry for Gabe when he'd been a young boy. Being Cyrus's son had been hard at Casa Mesa.

The thing was, the boss had seen his son getting batted around, and he'd even laughed when Gabe had tried unsuccessfully to fight back against the larger men. Teague had encouraged the men's hatred toward the boy, and he had always hit the boy the hardest and the most often. It seemed like Gabe had grown into a fine man, regardless of the way he'd been treated as a boy.

There was real trouble coming. Slaughter would not like what had happened tonight. It was a fight that was long in coming—the older Slaughter against the younger.

Fletcher's money was on Gabe.

Chapter Seventeen

A blaze of color had just touched the horizon when Kate moved determinedly toward the bunkhouse and shoved the door open. Her eyes blazing, her chin at an obstinate tilt, she walked right past Omous and Flint without blinking an eye.

It didn't matter to her that Gabe had just stepped out of the tub and had only a towel draped about him.

"Well, Gabriel, just what in the hell do you think you're doing now?"

"Well, until a moment ago, I was taking a bath." He grinned. "I'm now standing here half-naked, dripping wet, with a woman who doesn't even notice."

"Don't play the fool with me, Gabriel. You know very well what I'm talking about."

He reached around her to grab his trousers off the cot. "I haven't got a notion why you came storming in here. You're pretty scary when you're mad, Kate."

She watched him juggle the towel and his trousers, trying to get dressed.

"I don't suppose you'd turn your head?" he asked with a touch of humor.

She stared at him for a moment as if she'd just realized what an awkward time she had chosen to approach him. But it didn't bother her. She was too mad to care. "What are you doing taking a bath before sunup?"

"I didn't realize there was a set time that a person could take a bath. But if you must know, I have something important to do this morning." He slid into his trousers and draped the towel around his neck. "Do you want to tell me what this is all about?"

"I don't mind if I do. I went into the barn this morning, thinking I'd milk the cow for Casey, since she's got so much work on her hands, and who do you think I ran into?"

"You tell me."

"Will Fletcher, bigger than life. I asked him what he was doing here, and he said you let him come on over. Now I know you know he works for Slaughter. A man can't ride two horses at the same time."

"I trust Fletcher, Kate. He may have worked for Cyrus, but he will be loyal to the Spanish Spur."

"What if he runs straight to Slaughter and tells him we don't have enough men to protect this ranch? Had you even thought of that?"

"He won't. I trust Fletcher enough to put him to guard the family. And, Kate, there's going to be trouble here. I don't know just when, but when it comes, we'll need every man we can get to come over to our side."

She digested that bit of information and said reluctantly, "If you trust Fletcher, I guess that's good enough for me. But mind you, I'll be watching him all the same."

She stared at him and then reached out and touched his bruised jaw. She noticed several cuts and scrapes as well. "You look like you been in a fight."

"You might call it that. I had a run-in with Ira Teague last night."

She nodded. "That figures. And it explains what Fletcher's doing here." She nodded toward the Indians. "I ain't never been good at figures, but even I can add a bit—with you and the Comanches and Will Fletcher, that still makes only four. Slaughter has an army of men on his side."

"I've never been interested in numbers. I know the loyalty of the men at my back. Cyrus can't say the same."

"You're up against trouble, but you know that. I've said my piece."

He reached for his shirt and held it in front of him. "In that case, will you leave so I can get dressed, Kate?"

She grinned at him and winked. "Don't think I

was so taken up with what I was saying that I didn't notice some things. With a body like yours, I don't know why some woman hasn't already snapped you up."

His gorgeous mouth slid into a grin. "Are you proposing to me, Kate?"

"Nope. You may end up dead, and I'm too young to be a widow. But you might want to cast your eyes on the lady in the main house."

His irises dilated just a bit. "Then you're matchmaking?"

"You're a handsome devil and don't need the likes of me to do your courting for you. But if you wait much longer, there'll be other bees sniffing around the honeypot. I seen the looks Casey got from the menfolk when we was in town the other day. She's a real looker, in case you ain't noticed."

He pulled his shirt on and buttoned it, then tucked it into his pants. "I noticed."

Cyrus Slaughter shoved Teague aside and seated himself on the edge of his desk. "You let him come here, catch you unaware, and you did nothing to stop him."

"He had the Indian with him."

"And you had forty-three men to call on."

"He took me by surprise."

"You knew he'd come if you baited the woman. Why weren't you ready for him? No, don't answer that—I'll answer it for you. Gabe took you because he's smarter than you are."

Anger flushed Teague's ruddy face. "He caught me off guard, boss, and he was stronger than I thought he'd be. I could have took him if—"

"That's not the way I heard it told. I heard you were ready for him. I heard he just plain outfought you."

Teague looked away from the piercing silver gaze. "If you want Gabe dead, I can do it for you."

"If I'd wanted him dead, I wouldn't have asked you to do it. I just wanted him roughed up a bit, and it looks like you're the one who got roughed up."

"I'll get him next time."

"Looks like you got what you dished out for a change."

"I don't know what you mean."

"It's like this, Teague. When my son was young you made life hard for him, you taunted him, hit him. Tonight he had the satisfaction of settling an old score."

Cyrus nodded toward the door. "I only allow a man one mistake, and you've had yours. Pack up your belongings and get out."

There was a look of disbelief on Teague's face. He'd ridden for the Slaughter brand for over twenty-five years, and he'd been the foreman for fifteen of those years. He had done unspeakable things on Slaughter's orders. He had never hesitated, never thought about it or felt guilty later on. "You can't mean that, boss. I can still get him for you."

"I don't usually have to say things more than once." There was coldness in his tone, and an uncompromising glare reflected in his eyes. "Draw your pay and don't let the sun go down on you while you're still on my land."

Teague was barely able to control his anger. He'd always fancied himself a kind of son to Cyrus, like family. He had resented Gabe from the first day he'd came to live at Casa Mesa. As Cyrus's natural son, Gabe had lived with the family.

Gabe had it all—the old man's name and a soft bed at the big house. It wasn't right that he should be thrown off Casa Mesa after being loyal for so many years.

Without a word, he turned on his heel and walked out of the house.

Anger guided Ira Teague's footsteps to the bunkhouse, where he threw his belongings into a saddlebag. He was halfway to town before he realized he had not drawn his pay.

Chapter Eighteen

It was a cool, crisp afternoon without a cloud in the sky and only a slight breeze blowing from the south. Jenny had gone to Kate's house after waking from her afternoon nap.

Kate liked to have Jenny read to her, and it was only a week ago that Kate had admitted to Casey that she couldn't see well enough to read her own books.

On one of Sam's last trips into town, Casey had asked him to go by Finnegan's store and order a pair of bifocals for Kate. He and Flint had ridden into town today, and Casey hoped the glasses had arrived by now, and he could bring them home.

She smiled when she thought of Sam. He had become fast friends with Omous and Flint, and they were teaching him the skills a young Comanche boy would learn. Flint was showing him how to track, and Omous was teaching him how to survive in the wilds with just a knife. It was a great opportunity for Sam to gain knowledge of the Comanche way.

Casey's life had settled into a comfortable routine, and so far there had been no more trouble from the Casa Mesa ranch. She hoped that Cyrus Slaughter had finally lost interest in the Spanish Spur.

Today was the first afternoon she had nothing to do. She was very aware that Gabe had set Fletcher to watch over her, and she knew it was for her own safety, but she wanted to get away for a while to be by herself.

Casey had no mirror, so she wasn't sure how well her old blue riding habit fit; it had been years since she had worn it. She was relieved to find it still fit around the waist, but it was just a bit too short.

She smiled as she tied her hair back with a matching blue ribbon.

Straightening her blouse, she gave a satisfied nod. She left the house and walked toward the corral to saddle the chestnut.

When she approached the horse, she smiled in anticipation. From the first day Casey had set eyes on the gelding, she had been wanting to ride him. But until today there had been little opportunity; her days had been too busy. Now that the house was in order, she had time to ride.

She lifted a saddle onto the horse's back, and it took her several tries to fasten the cinch.

Kate had found the saddle that had belonged

to Casey's mother in the tack room; it had been abandoned and suffered from neglect since her mother left Texas. Sam had polished the leather and replaced a buckle and a strap.

Casey liked the thought of using something that had belonged to her mother; it made her feel closer to her somehow. Of course, it was a western saddle, and Casey had ridden only sidesaddle, so that might be a problem for her.

Casey had half expected Fletcher to be in the barn, but the place was deserted. Hoping to get away before he returned, she tentatively slid her foot into the stirrup and awkwardly hoisted herself onto the saddle. At first it felt strange to her, but she thought she could get used to it with practice.

The chestnut tossed his mane as if he were ready to run. Sam had ridden the horse several times and found him to be a good mount, so she didn't expect to have any trouble from him.

She let her breath out as she settled her gown about her legs in an attempt to cover her petticoats.

The horse bounded forward in reaction to her command. In no time at all, she was riding across the pasture, toward the river.

Her spirits soared!

She had not ridden in so long, and she was glad to see she could still stay in the saddle. Her cares blew away with the gentle breeze that touched her cheeks. For this one afternoon, she was not going to think of anything unpleasant.

The gelding had great stamina, and he ran full-out until she slowed him to a lope. She found herself laughing out loud as her spirits soared even higher. It had been a long time since she had felt so lighthearted.

When she dismounted near the river, she stood on the bank, remembering that this was where she had first seen Gabe. Thinking of him brought her mind back to the present. If only there were a way she could get past the barrier he had erected around himself. She had often seen raw pain in his eyes, and it tore at her heart. He might not know it yet, but he needed someone to love and take care of him.

He needed her.

Casey turned away from the river and watched the chestnut grazing nearby. When she looked downstream and saw a boulder overhanging the river, she removed her book from the saddlebag, thinking it would be the perfect place to read for a while. When she climbed to the top of the boulder, she was amazed by her lofty vantage point. She could see for miles in every direction.

She was beginning to love Texas and the Spanish Spur. There was a beauty here, a quiet serenity, if you didn't think about Cyrus Slaughter.

After a moment of musing, she sat down with her book on her lap. The sun felt good on her skin, and she found her eyes drifting shut. She lay back, cushioning her head on her arm, thinking she would close her eyes for just a moment.

She smiled to herself, remembering other times when she had ridden with her friends back in Virginia before the war had changed everything. Virginia no longer felt like home to her. This was the land of her mother's birth, the land that had given life to Gabe.

This land spoke to her heart.

She tried to read a page in her book, but her eyelids were heavy, and she laid her book aside and soon drifted off to sleep.

Gabe had just ridden in when Fletcher hobbled out of the barn toward him, shaking his head. "Did you take the chestnut gelding somewhere today?" he asked in a puzzled tone.

Gabe swung out of the saddle. "No. Why?"

"It's missing. I know Kate ain't took it, and Sam went to town with Omous and Flint. If you ain't got him, who does?"

Gabe glanced toward the house, suspicion growing in his mind. "Have you seen Miss Hamilton this afternoon?"

"No, I ain't." He scratched his head. "You don't think she'da took the horse and rode off by herself, do you?"

"You're supposed to be watching her," Gabe said in a hard voice, and with long strides hurried toward the house. He took the porch steps two at a time and rapped on the door. "Casey, are you in there?"

When there was no answer, he opened the door and went inside. He looked in every room and found them all empty. Panic took over his reasoning, and he ran back outside to find Fletcher still waiting for him.

"Are you sure she isn't with Kate?"

"She ain't. I just got back from having coffee with Kate. She's got the little one with her, but not Miss Casey."

"Dammit, Fletcher, you should have at least heard Casey ride away."

"I didn't think she'd go off somewhere without telling any of us."

There wasn't a doubt in Gabe's mind that Casey had ridden out alone, even though he'd told her not to. He walked to the barn and studied the hoofprints—there were just too many to separate the gelding's from all the others. If Flint had only been there, he could have tracked her easily.

"Fletcher, saddle up and ride toward town. I'll search down by the river. If you meet up with Omous and Flint, send them to me there. Do not alarm Sam."

Fletcher nodded, feeling bad for letting Gabe down. He'd trusted him to watch the woman. "I'll saddle up to meet them right now."

Gabe had never felt such a deep foreboding. He knew that Cyrus had someone watching the house, and he didn't want to think about what might happen to Casey if one of his father's spies found her alone and unprotected.

He kicked his horse in the flanks and rode full-out toward the river.

When he reached the Brazos, he galloped along the bank, looking for signs of hoof marks. He felt his heart skip a beat when he saw the riderless chestnut.

Dismounting, he glanced in every direction to see if Casey was lying injured somewhere.

He squinted against the setting sun, and his gaze ran along the cliffs. He saw a flash of blue material blowing over the side of a boulder.

Gabe raced up the hill and stopped when he saw Casey lying so still upon the boulder.

When he bent down beside her, he saw the rise and fall of her breast and was overcome with relief—she was all right, merely sleeping.

He wanted to shake her for scaring him the way she had. If anything happened to her, he wouldn't know what to do. He needed to see her every day as much as he needed the air he breathed.

His anger slowly melted away when he looked upon her face. The sight of her gentle beauty cut right through his heart. This moment belonged to him because he had her all to himself, and she would never know it.

He lightly touched a red-gold curl while he watched the way her long lashes lay against her pale cheeks.

His gaze moved across her full mouth, down her slender neck to the swell of her breasts. He didn't allow his eyes to linger there because he didn't want to think about the satiny flesh that lay beneath her gown.

He stared at her tiny waist, which he was sure he could span with his two hands. She was so defenseless out here alone, and anyone could have happened upon her while she slept.

He touched her cheek, swamped with aching need. He allowed his fingers to drift tenderly down her face. Realizing his thoughts were going in a dangerous direction, he pulled his hand back.

"Casey, wake up." He gently touched her arm and shook it. "Casey."

Chapter Nineteen

Casey's lashes fluttered open, and the blue of her eyes was so dark, Gabe felt as if he were falling into them. She smiled, and her whole heart was in that smile.

"I was just dreaming about you," she said, stretching her arms over her head and sending his heart pounding when the gesture pushed her breasts tightly against the cloth of her gown.

She sat up, looking puzzled, then touched his arm. "How did you find me?"

"I thought I told you not to leave the house unless someone accompanied you." His anger had returned, and there was a bite in his tone.

She reached for his hand and laced her fingers through it in an intimate gesture that seemed natural to her, but sent a shock through him.

"Don't be angry," she cajoled, moving forward to look into his eyes. "Nothing happened to me."

He was staring at her mouth, wanting desperately to kiss her. "You have to listen to me, Casey. It's dangerous for you to go anywhere alone."

"You were worried, weren't you?"

"Hell, yes." He hadn't meant to, but he raised her hand to his lips, his mouth lingering on her knuckles. "Don't ever do anything like this again!"

She moved forward and pressed her head against his shoulder. "I was in no danger."

He jerked her chin up so she was forced to look at him. "You will be in danger until Cyrus is no longer a threat. Why can't I make you understand that?"

She tossed her head and gave him a provocative smile. Now he wanted to shake her for an entirely different reason. "Don't look at me like that."

"Why not?"

"Because—just don't do it."

She was suddenly armed with the knowledge a woman gleaned from a man's reactions to her: he felt the same emptiness and need she felt. "How can I be in any danger when I have you looking out for me?"

He stood and raised her up beside him, then released her hand immediately. Her lighthearted flirtation made him swell with desire. Casey didn't know she was playing with fire. If she but knew it, she was in far more danger from him, at the moment, than from anyone else.

"We need to get back to the house. Everyone is looking for you, and the sun is going down."

She slid her hand around his waist and stared

into his eyes. "Can't we stay here awhile longer?"

He moved her hands away from him, resisting the urge to take her down on the boulder, tear her gown off, and touch every part of her, to appease the ache inside him. "No. We have to go now."

"Why can't we just—"

He turned his back and took a step off the boulder, offering her his hand. "Let's go."

She retrieved her book and put her hand in his, allowing him to assist her down to the riverbank.

The sun hung like a huge red ball on the western horizon, and it painted the countryside with a soft vermilion glow.

Casey knew Gabe was trying to avoid touching her when he dropped her hand and moved away. She decided it was time to make her feelings known to him and to let him know that he wasn't alone in the world. She wanted him to know he had a family. There wasn't a doubt in her mind that he loved her; he just hadn't yet admitted it to himself.

Gabe was taken off guard when Casey propelled herself into his arms, crushing her mouth against his and sending them both backward. He couldn't concentrate on keeping his balance, because his mind was more on the lips that felt like silk on his, and the soft body that was pressed against him.

A deep groan took him to his knees, and she was carried with him. He let his mouth plunder hers, flicking her lips open with his tongue and driving deep inside her sweet mouth. She was his; all he had to do was take what she so willingly offered. He was like a drowning man going under for the third time. He felt her hand at his shirt, unbuttoning it and softly touching his skin.

He tore his mouth away from hers. "No. Don't. You don't know what you're doing."

Her eyes shimmered softly, and she smiled slightly.

"You're wrong. I do know what I'm doing. I've thought about it for a long time."

Her hand moved across his taut chest, and he swelled painfully, tightly against his trousers. He took her wrists and pulled her hand away from his chest.

His voice was harsh, his eyes hard. "Don't tempt me. I'm on the brink now, and if you touch me again, I may not be able to stop."

The pain in Gabe's eyes was so deep and disturbing that Casey wanted to comfort him. She reached up and touched his cheek, allowing her fingers to drift down to his mouth. "I don't want you to stop."

"Casey," he warned, catching her hand. "You're so dammed innocent you don't know what you're doing. Dammit, stop!"

He was trying to put that barrier up between them again, only this time she wasn't about to let him. "I don't know much about the intimacy between a man and a woman, but I do know that I was born to be with you. Don't you feel that way, too, Gabe?"

She felt his whole body tremble when she pressed a kiss on his cheek. She drew back and looked into his sliver eyes and saw the battle he was waging to resist her. She knew the very moment Gabe lost that battle, because his expression softened, and his eyes came alive with fire in them.

He jerked her into his arms. "I don't have the right to tell you this, but I want your smile reserved for me alone. I want only my hands to touch you." He leaned in closer, his breath touching her mouth. "I want your lips on mine and no one else's. Do you understand that?"

"I do understand. Because it's the same way I feel about you."

His gaze was burning into her eyes with the intensity of his desire. "Don't do this, Casey."

She unbuttoned another button on his shirt. "Don't do what?" she asked, pressing her lips to the pulse beating in his throat.

His will was broken; his restraint snapped. His gaze swept to the laces at the neck of her gown. Slowly, as if he were fighting against the urge to tear the gown off her, he undid the first tie. His hand was trembling so badly he could hardly unlace the next one, so she reached up and did it for him.

He swallowed painfully as she pushed the gown off her shoulders. "I know you need me, Gabe."

He groaned, gently shoving her gown lower. Since they were kneeling, it bunched at her waist and only her thin petticoat remained.

"Casey!" There was so much feeling in the way he said her name.

He reached up and undid the ribbon in her hair, and a mass of red-gold curls fell down her back. "How is the wound on your shoulder?" he asked, trying to clear the fog from his mind. "Does it still cause you pain?"

She shook her head. "The only pain I feel is the need to be with the man who was created for me. You know we are meant to be together, Gabe."

He yanked at the last bit of material that covered her, and her breasts were exposed to his hungry gaze. He shook and trembled inside as he touched their softness, traced a nipple with his finger, then dropped his head to take it into his mouth.

Casey threw back her head, feeling the warmth of his mouth stir an earthquake inside her. This was something she could give him, something he could take away with him when he left her. She could give him something to drive away the heavy sadness he carried inside him—her body was her gift to him.

Chapter Twenty

Gabe raised his head and stared at Casey. "Until you came along, I never knew a woman's smile could carry me through a whole day, or that a night could be so cold and empty because you weren't with me."

His words touched her heart, and she pressed her cheek to his, loving him so much it hurt. She spoke past the lump in her throat. "I have been yours from the beginning. How could you not know that?"

He whispered her name, lifting her up so he could remove her gown and undergarments. It amazed him that Casey felt no shyness with him, although he knew she had never allowed another man to go this far with her.

Casey was tenacious in her belief that they belonged together. But he knew her feelings for him would turn to disgust when she discovered the truth about him.

It was almost dark, and the countryside was awash in silvery moonlight. Gabe's hot gaze moved over the most perfect body he'd ever seen. She was soft, her waist small, her hips rounded. Her breasts seemed to beg for his touch, and he did touch them reverently. He didn't deserve her; he should walk away right now before he went too far, but he couldn't.

Gathering her close to him, he kissed her mouth until she was breathless. His hands moved over her hips, and he felt a stinging in his eyes from the raw emotions that tore at him.

"I can't wait any longer," he murmured, rushing to remove his own clothing. He tossed them aside, and somehow got out of his boots.

Casey had to admit she had fantasized about what Gabe would look like without his clothing, but nothing she had imagined could have prepared her for the beauty of his lean, hard body. He was strongly muscled, his wide shoulders tapering down to a tight stomach. Her knees almost gave way when she saw the huge swell of him, and she tried to imagine how they would—

He took her hand and drew her to him. "Sweetheart, don't you know you shouldn't look at a man like that?" His breath fanned her cheek, and he closed his eyes. "You are tearing me apart inside. I want to be patient, to take it slow, but I need to be inside you."

A sob escaped her lips, and she planted kisses across his mouth. "Gabe, I want to be right for you. Does it matter that I don't know what I'm supposed to do?"

His heart skipped a beat; then it skipped two beats. Gently he lifted her in his arms and laid her down on his shirt. "You'll know what to do. I will teach you." He closed his eyes. He wanted to drive into her, to reach as deeply as he could to put his brand on her, but he gentled his urge and lay down beside her.

Casey opened her mouth to his kiss, and she quivered when his hand swept across her breasts and then downward. She jerked upward when he spread her legs, his finger circling, then easing inside her.

She bit her lip as a flood of passion tore through her, and she pressed to get closer to the skillful hand that was doing such wonderful things to her.

His lips slid across hers, his hand edging ever deeper inside her, then withdrawing and easing forward once more.

"Gabe, I never knew—" A sob tore from deep inside her. "I never thought it would be like this."

He withdrew his finger from her and frowned. "Are you crying because I've hurt you?"

She shook her head and moved to touch his face. "You have not hurt me. It's just that . . ." She shook her head in frustration, trying to tell him how she felt. "I feel like I am a part of you. I never knew that was possible."

He closed his eyes and felt tears moisten them.

He couldn't remember a time when he had cried, not even when Nora had died, not even when he had stood beside his mother's grave.

"Casey . . . sweetheart!"

He could not say anything more because her hand had crept down and brushed against the swell of him. He gritted his teeth, and his body shook. Easing forward, he parted her legs. His head came down to her mouth, and he inched some of his length into her.

She was becoming frantic, pulling at him, grinding her mouth against his, trying to get closer to him, to take him farther into her body.

Her velvet tightness closed around him, and he almost lost it then and there. He felt the ground roll beneath them, and he hardened even more. Caught by her sweetness, he pushed deeper into her, past the barrier with half his length.

"Gabe," she whispered against his mouth. She arched her hips, and he went deeper, making a slow withdrawal, then easing in again.

He felt her body tremble, and he felt her warmth spill around him. He thrust deeper, pushing his full length, and she spilled her warmth again, calling his name as she was carried away by ecstasy.

Powerful tremors shook his body, shook his world to its foundation, and he gripped her to him until they both stopped trembling.

He kissed her tear-dampened cheek and brushed her hair away from her face so he could nuzzle her neck. "Sweetheart, what have you done to me?"

She closed her eyes, her hand sweeping up his back to slide into his midnight hair. "I have given myself into your keeping. I will always belong to you."

He ached to tell her how he felt about her, but he didn't have the words. He had never spoken words of love to any woman, and he couldn't say them now, when he wanted to the most. But he did make an attempt: "To think if I had never met you," he said, touching his mouth to hers, "I would never have felt this way."

"If I had known you could make me feel this way," she said, softly touching her lips to his shoulder, "I would have stripped my clothing off that first night you came to the house."

He laughed with warmth. "As I recall, you were not wearing much."

"No, I wasn't. And at first I was frightened of you." She traced her finger down his nose. "But I knew that night that something had happened between us. Did you feel it, too?"

"The feelings I had that night took me by surprise. And I even thought you had a husband at the time."

She nestled against him. "Let's just stay here for the rest of our lives and make love."

He touched his lips to an inviting nipple and then pulled away to ponder her words. "Life won't let us, Casey. It will soon intrude and carry us back to the real world."

Brazenly she dipped her head and kissed the pulse that beat at his throat, drawing a groan from his lips. She glanced up at him with a devilish grin. "What else can I do to torture you?"

His hands slid up her hips to her inner thigh, and he positioned her to receive him. "What would torture me is if I could never touch you like this again. You have given my life a . . . purpose. That's the only way I can explain it."

"Do you think you can trust me enough to tell me about your past?"

He held her hips while he eased into her softness. "I have no past—there is only now."

Omous topped the hill and quickly waved his son back.

"What is wrong, Father?" Flint asked, reining in his prancing mount.

"Gabe does not need us to help look for his woman. He has found her. Let us ride back to the others and tell them the woman is safe with him."

Flint nodded, understanding what his father was telling him. "She will help heal him."

"If he will allow it. Gabe has never taken the easy road. I fear more trouble awaits him."

Chapter Twenty-one

The moon was drifting high overhead, casting its silvery shadows over the land. Gabe held Casey in his arms, his hand spread out over her stomach.

"Are you all right, sweetheart?"

She smiled gently. "I have never been more all right in my life." She turned over and brushed his hair behind his ear. "You still need me to finish cutting your hair."

His fingers tangled in her curls, and he brought her face to his. "That day you tried to cut my hair, I wanted to pull you onto my lap and make love to you right then."

A teasing light came into her eyes as she displayed a mischievous side he had never seen. She smiled whimsically. "I wanted you to kiss me that day."

"Did you now?" His laughter was deep. "I think I knew that, and I also knew you weren't ready for me."

"What would have happened if you had not come upon us that day we were stuck in the river?"

He arched his brow. "You would still be stuck in the river."

She shook her head and grinned. "No, really, what would have happened?"

His reply was noncommittal. "Who can say? I am not good with words, Casey. I cannot always say what I feel, especially when the feelings are so new to me."

"What if we had never met?"

"Then I would have wandered aimlessly for the rest of my life, lost and alone."

Her hand caressed his jaw. "That's quite a statement for someone who says he has no way with words."

Giving herself to Gabe had not brought him the peace she had hoped it would. There were still tortured shadows in the depths of his eyes. "Tell me about your life," she urged, sensing he would never find real happiness until he put the past behind him.

He reluctantly sat up. "I guess this is where I ask you the big question," he said, changing the subject.

"What big question?"

He took her hand and stared at it for a long moment. "Will you have me for your husband?"

She sat up and laid her head on his shoulder. She knew he felt obligated to offer her marriage, and she could not accept until he admitted he loved her. "I don't think so, Gabe."

He frowned. "I thought you would . . ." He looked stunned. "I'm prepared to give you my name."

That was not what she had hoped for. She wanted more than anything to be his wife, but not this way, not until he could bring trust to a marriage.

"But, Gabe," she said, watching him closely. "You have no last name to give me."

He dropped her hand. "You do understand that I changed you tonight, that you can never be the same?"

"Yes," she said, trying to understand the sudden coldness in his voice. "And I hope I changed you a little as well."

He shook his head. "Casey, that's not what I mean, and you know it. When men make love they stay the same, but when it's the woman's first time, she is . . . different afterward."

"I know about that. I am no longer a virgin." She stood up, feeling the cool night air on her skin. She moved away from him and waded into the river, shivering as she splashed water over herself. When she glanced back at Gabe, he still stood where she'd left him, staring at her.

"You didn't really give me an answer to my question."

She waded out of the water and up the bank to him. "I know what we did changed me, Gabe. But that doesn't matter to me. And you don't have to marry me."

He pulled on his trousers as she walked dripping wet toward him. "You will be ruined for any other man."

He just didn't understand how she felt about him. No matter how many ways she said it, he didn't know how to take the love she offered him. "I was ruined for any other man the day you came into my life."

He couldn't bear to think that she might one day belong to another man. Then he could never have her again. "I see."

"I don't think you do." She pulled on her petticoats and struggled with her gown until Gabe turned her around and laced it for her.

"I have never understood women, and I understand you less than any of them."

"I hope the day will come when you will know what I want from you, Gabe. Telling you about it will not help—you have to find it out for yourself."

Casey was confusing him. What did she want from him? He had offered her marriage, and she said she didn't want to be his wife. He could understand that. She thought he was just a drifter. Reluctantly he said, "We should go home now." He brushed his hand through her hair, needing to touch her again. "Everyone will be wondering what's happened to us."

What had happened? Casey felt that she had

almost grasped happiness in her hand, and yet it was just out of her reach. The man she loved wanted to marry her out of obligation, not because he wanted to build a life with her, to father her children, to live with her until they grew old.

Yet he loved her; she couldn't be wrong about that.

"Yes, let's go home."

He watched her walk toward her horse and felt a coldness in his heart. He had never asked any other woman to be his wife.

Even now, the sight of her softly swaying hips sent blood surging to the lower part of his body. Now that he'd had her, how could he ever let her go? He could not imagine being around her and not wanting to make love to her.

He wanted to right now.

Gabe walked over to Casey and lifted her onto her horse, his hands lingering at her waistline. "I had to have you, Casey. You know it would have happened sooner or later."

He was still struggling with what he was trying to convey to her, and she couldn't help him.

"I do love you so, Gabe." She nudged her mount forward and rode away.

She was halfway up the hill before he mounted his horse and rode after her. They rode in silence until they reached the house.

Fletcher came ambling out of the barn and shook his head. "So you found her. Omous said you had, but when you didn't come back right away, I feared Cyrus might've come upon both of you. I was 'bout to go looking for you."

Gabe dismounted and helped Casey to the ground. "What makes you think Cyrus would find us, Fletcher?"

"Why, he came riding up here big as you please, asking after you. I can tell you he wasn't too happy to find me here."

Gabe wasn't aware his hand still rested on Casey's shoulder. "Did he say what he wanted?"

"Nope. You know him—he said he didn't squander his time talking to grunts like me."

"If the two of you will excuse me," Casey said, moving away, "I'm very tired."

Gabe watched her walk to the house, wondering what else she wanted from him. He led both horses to the barn to unsaddle them. He would talk to her tomorrow and maybe even tell her that Cyrus was his father.

Fletcher had trailed along behind Gabe. "It seemed to me your pa wanted to see you real bad."

"He has nothing to say to me that I want to hear."

"I 'spect he'll come back here if you won't go to him." Fletcher watched Casey enter the house. "There's something more. Ted Varnor came by tonight. Said he was heading out, but he wanted to warn me that Cyrus is planning something big and bad against the Spanish Spur."

"Hell." Gabe knew he had to get help, and he

wouldn't find anyone willing to stand up to Cyrus near Mariposa Springs. "I'll be leaving for Fort Worth tomorrow."

Fletcher nodded. "That's the way I figured it."

The night that had started out so promisingly had turned cold and bitter. Casey turned her face into her pillow, refusing to cry. She had thrown herself at Gabe, and he had accommodated her; what man wouldn't have under the circumstances? And because he was the kind of man he was, he had thought he should marry her. He'd been confused when she refused. He was an honest and honorable man, two traits she admired in anyone, but especially in him, because she had a feeling no one had ever believed in him the way she did.

Their lovemaking had touched him as deeply as it had her; she couldn't be wrong about that. She had the feel of him on her body, and the taste of him in her mouth.

She closed her eyes and prayed for sleep. Her hand went to her lips, which had known his passionate kisses. Even now she wanted to be in his arms.

One day this battle with Mr. Slaughter would be settled one way or another. On that day, Gabe might well ride out of her life forever.

Gabe stood in the dark, trying to remember at what point he had lost his ability to control his feelings. Ever since Casey had come along, she had turned him inside out. He couldn't think clearly when she was near him. Tonight there had been a while when she belonged to him alone. But tomorrow would rip her away from him.

He had no hope for their future together. He had only those few hours when he had forgotten his past.

"Casey," he whispered. "Dammit, Casey."

Chapter Twenty-two

"Wake up, Casey." Jenny was shaking her sister's arm. "I made you some breakfast. And guess what?" She didn't wait for Casey to answer. "Sam got Kate's glasses yesterday."

Casey blinked her eyes, a little confused by Jenny's chatter. It was already sunup, and she had overslept. She hoped Sam hadn't gone off without any breakfast. She blinked again and looked at Jenny holding a glass of milk and a cookie out to her.

"What have you there?" Casey asked, sitting up and pushing her hair out of her face.

"Since you didn't get up, I thought you might be sick, so I wanted to make you feel better."

Casey took the glass of milk and the cookie. "This is just what I need to make me feel better. Thank you so much for your thoughtfulness."

Casey and Kate had finished the mattress, so she and Jenny no longer had to sleep on the floor. The child jumped on the bed, then plopped down on her stomach with her chin propped on her hand. "You weren't here when I went to sleep last night. Where were you?"

"I rode down to the river."

"And Gabe found you. That's what Mr. Fletcher said."

Casey felt a slight ache in her lower extremities, a reminder that Gabe had, indeed, found her. She felt warm all over just thinking about his lovemaking. "That's right. He found me."

"Gabe came to the door this morning and asked for you. I told him you were sleeping, and he looked real worried."

Casey took a bite of the cookie, trying not to frown. She had never liked the taste of anything sweet for breakfast, but Jenny would be crushed if she didn't eat it.

"After I've finished breakfast," Casey said, pausing to swallow, "we'll get Sam and take Kate her spectacles." She had to take a quick drink of milk to wash the cookie down. "Do you think she will like that?"

"Miss Kate needs to see real bad. She told me the best thing she likes to do is read, but she can't. I didn't tell her about our surprise. Hurry and eat, Casey, so we can take them to her."

She took another bite of the cookie and forced a smile for Jenny's sake. "Umm. Good cookie."

"You won't ever let me eat good stuff for breakfast like cookies or pies. If I was older than you,

I'd give you good things to eat every day."

Casey raised her brow. "I'm sure you would. But I have to give you nourishing food that will help you grow up strong and healthy."

Jenny frowned and said, "I'm going to go find Sam now, so he can go with us."

With boundless energy she slid off the bed and ran out of the room.

Casey looked at the cookie and took another bite.

The three Hamiltons watched Kate withdraw her new glasses out of a decorative box Jenny had made for them.

"I do declare," Kate said, looking pleased. "As I live and breathe, spectacles."

"Try them on," Jenny said, grinning. "Casey says when you wear those, you can read all by yourself."

Casey hoped that would be the case. She knew that people had different sight problems. "Go ahead, Kate, try them."

The little woman slipped them on and blinked. "Everything's fuzzy."

Sam picked up the book that was lying on the end table. "Mr. Finnegan said they were just for reading. See if you can see the words on the page."

Kate took the book, and her head snapped back. "Lord o' mercy! Those words just jumped right off the page at me." She sat down and ran her hand over the page, then glanced up at the three of them. "I can't thank you enough. You've given me back my sight. I never thought I'd read another word."

Jenny scooted onto the chair beside Kate. "Read to me from your book."

Casey motioned for Sam to follow her outside. When they stood on Kate's porch, she said, "I heard Mr. Slaughter paid us a visit yesterday afternoon."

"He rode up just like he owned the place, demanding to see Gabe."

"I think it's time I put a stop to this." She stepped off the porch and walked toward the house. "It's time I paid a visit to Mr. Slaughter."

Sam walked along beside her. "You don't mean you're going to the Casa Mesa ranch?"

"That's exactly what I'm doing."

"I don't like the sound of that. And Gabe won't like you going over there either."

She turned to stare at her brother. "It's time we took matters into our own hands and stopped relying on Gabe."

Sam looked puzzled; he had never heard Casey speak that way about Gabe since he had come to work for them. "I'm going with you," he insisted.

She nodded. "This afternoon when everyone is busy elsewhere, hook up the buckboard." When they reached the house, her hand rested on the screen door. "Don't tell anyone, not even Will Fletcher, where we're going."

"Because you know they would try to stop you, and you know they'd be right."

"Ask Kate if she'll watch Jenny for us."

She went into the house, leaving Sam puzzled by her strange behavior.

Casey had just slid an apple pie into the oven when she heard a rap on the screen door. She knew it was Gabe before she looked up and saw him standing there.

"May I come in?"

The sound of his voice sent tremors through her, and she remembered the sensations she had felt when he'd made love to her the night before. Fearing he could read her thoughts, she blushed. She was determined to avoid those silver eyes that were so intently focused on her. She glanced up just high enough to concentrate on the top button of his green shirt. "Yes. Of course," she told him.

When he moved toward her, she backed up against a chair. "Jenny said you came by earlier."

Then she made the mistake of looking into his eyes. She couldn't speak, because she was remembering how he had held her in his arms so passionately. She wanted badly to rekindle the fire that had burned inside them both when they had made love.

"I just wanted to see if you were all right." His manner was terse, and there was no warmth in his eyes, no acknowledgment at all that they had been so close. He wouldn't even meet her gaze.

She lifted her chin, crushed by disappointment. "There is nothing wrong with me."

"I have to go away for a few days. I just wanted to tell you that what happened between us last night was a mistake—my mistake."

She wanted to cry; she wanted to beat against his chest until he admitted last night had meant something to him. "You don't have to worry, Gabe." She gripped the back of a chair, and her fingernails bit into the soft wood. "It won't happen again."

"Casey . . ." He took a step toward her. "It's not like that. I meant it was a mistake for you, not for me. What I did to you . . . I couldn't sleep last night for thinking about us."

"If there is nothing else you need, Gabe, I have housework to do."

He stood there, devastated because he had hurt her. He never knew what to say to her because he felt so much. His problem was expressing how deeply he felt. And he was afraid if he let down his defenses, he'd be swamped by his need for her.

He reached out and took her hand, rubbing his thumb across it. "I want to kiss you."

Casey's head went up, and her lips parted in invitation. He dragged her into his arms, clasping her close. Gabe's mouth hungrily covered hers, and he felt her soften all over. He guided her against the wall and pressed his hard body against her.

Even though she knew she should move away from him, Casey whimpered and ground her body against his. She could not deny her need for him.

He pulled back long enough to unbutton the front of her gown, shoving her petticoat aside so one of her breasts was exposed. His lips touched the nipple reverently, and then he took it into his mouth, swirling his tongue around it and feeling it swell.

She bit her lower lip and threw her head back, grabbing a handful of ebony hair to keep her earthbound.

Gabe raised his head, his heated gaze locked on her face. "I want you."

She nodded. "I know."

He shoved her gown up, his hand sliding up her leg and then moving to her thigh, his finger sliding into her warmth.

Casey couldn't breathe. Her head fell against his shoulder, and she started sobbing.

With a concerned frown, he withdrew his hand and straightened her gown. "Don't, sweetheart—don't. I can't stand to see you cry. I didn't mean for this to happen. I'm sorry."

"I want to be with you, but not like this."

"I know. It's just . . . when I'm near you, I have to touch you."

She wiped her tears on the back of her hand.

"When you decide where you want me in your life, I'll be waiting."

He stared at her for a long moment, as if he were memorizing her every feature. "I have to go now."

"Then go!"

"If this wasn't so important, I wouldn't leave you. We'll talk when I get back."

He had opened the door and started to leave when she said, "How long will you be gone?"

He stopped, turned, and stared at her as if he had wanted her to say something more. "At least two days, maybe three. But you needn't worry. Omous and Flint will be watching out for you while I'm gone."

"Have a safe journey."

"Casey, don't let your personal feelings for me get in the way of your family's safety. Let the men protect you."

She stared up at him. "Was there anything else you wanted to say to me—any other mistakes you made with me?"

He stepped back inside, allowing the door to slam behind him. "I have so much to say to you, it would take hours." He reached toward her, and when she pulled away he let his hand drop to his side.

She pulled the chair away from the table and sat down. "Last night I thought something special happened between us. Was I wrong?"

He started to speak and then shook his head as

if he were struggling for the right words. "Now is not the time to talk about that. I need to leave as soon as possible."

He knew the sheriff wouldn't do anything to stop Cyrus, so he was going to ride to Fort Worth and hope the state marshal would get involved. Someone had to stop his father before it was too late. "We'll talk when I return, Casey."

She watched him walk away with an ache in her heart. No matter what he said, last night had not been a mistake. She pressed her knuckles against her closed eyelids. She would not cry. She would not. She had cried too much since she had met Gabe.

What she *was* going to do was settle things with Mr. Slaughter once and for all. She was weary of living in fear of the man.

Casey stood on the front doorstep with Sam at her side and an apple pie in her hands. "This is really a grand house," Sam said. "It's much bigger than I thought. If he's this wealthy, why would he want the Spanish Spur?"

"I don't know," Casey admitted, wishing she hadn't decided to face Mr. Slaughter. Her hands were shaking, and she was afraid.

She nodded, and Sam knocked on the door. Moments later a woman, most probably the housekeeper, answered.

"My name is Cassandra Hamilton, and this is my brother, Sam. We have come to see Mr. Slaughter."

The woman nodded and opened the door wider. "He is in his office. I will take you there."

Casey and Sam exchanged worried glances. "Into the lion's den," Sam whispered.

The housekeeper announced them, and Casey walked right over to Mr. Slaughter's desk before he could even stand or acknowledge them. "This is my brother, Sam, and we have come to see if we can talk out our problem with you. I would much rather get along with my neighbors than battle with them."

"Would you now?" He nodded at Sam. "So this is your little brother."

"He's my younger brother," she corrected him.

"What have you there under the dish towel?" he asked, propping his elbows on the desk.

"It's an apple pie," she said, setting it on his desk and standing back. "It was my mother's recipe. I think you'll like it."

"You brought me an apple pie?" he said in amazement, momentarily surprised by her gesture. "I don't think anyone's ever done such a thing for me before."

"I hoped you would see it as a peace offering from us. We are neighbors, and we should get along. But let me repeat so there will be no misunderstanding—I will not sell the Spanish Spur to you or anyone else."

His brows furrowed, meeting across his nose. "And let me repeat so there will be no misunderstanding—I intend to water my herd on the river, and I intend to own all the land between here and the Brazos."

"Then I suppose we have nothing more to say to each other."

He leaned forward, smiling at her. It was the first time Casey had seen any softening in his expression. "I just bet my son can't keep his hands off of you."

She stared at him in total bewilderment. "Your son has come home? I thought he died in the war."

A look of amazement passed over his features. "He hasn't told you, has he?" He laughed in amusement. "You don't know, do you?"

She shook her head in confusion. "What?"

"My son, Gabe. He didn't tell you that I'm his father, did he?"

"That's imposs—" She looked into his silver eyes, and the truth hit her so hard, she felt herself reeling. "No," she admitted in a soft cry, feeling as if someone had just torn her heart out. "He . . . Gabe didn't tell me he was your son."

"That's not true," Sam said. "Gabe would never take your side against us."

Cyrus ignored Sam as if he hadn't even spoken. His target was the beautiful woman who was fighting against tears. He had her now. "Why do you suppose my son hasn't told you he's a Slaughter?"

The tears spilled down her face. "We both know why. You sent him to spy on us." She angrily brushed her tears away. "Both of you thought he could make me trust him so you could get your hands on the Spanish Spur. And you might be glad to know your plan worked very well, because I did trust him."

Sam stepped forward, his hand on Casey's arm. "Don't believe him. Gabe would never hurt us."

Cyrus smiled. Gabe had unwittingly played into his hands. Miss Hamilton would never listen to anything his son told her from this day on. "I can't believe Kate didn't tell you my son's name is Gabriel Slaughter."

"I thought he was . . . that he . . ."

"Was a bastard and didn't have a last name," Cyrus finished for her. "No. I was married to Gabe's mother. He is my true and legal son."

Casey wanted to run away as far and as fast as she could, but she stood her ground although her heart was broken. "You and your son were very clever. I should have known something wasn't right when he was so secretive. I knew there was something in his past he didn't want to talk about. I never imagined what it was."

A cunning look came into Cyrus's eyes. "You know how it is with a young man. He sees a pretty girl and wants to impress her." He was going to milk this situation for all it was worth. "You would never have let him anywhere near the place if you had known his real identity."

Casey gripped Sam's hand. "We will just be going now. I see that you are not willing to listen to reason."

Sam planted himself in front of Slaughter. "I think it's real mean what you and Gabe did. Don't think you can scare my family, because you can't. Take this as our last word—we aren't selling to you."

Slaughter laughed. "Run along home, boy, and play with toys. Leave the deal-making to the grown-ups."

Casey pulled her brother against her, insulted that Sam should be treated with such disrespect. "You will see just how grown-up he is if you come on our place again. You are a very rude man, Mr. Slaughter. We are sorry we took up so much of your time."

His laughter followed them to the door, and he called out to her, "I just think you ought to know—I don't like apple pie."

Chapter Twenty-three

Sam halted the horses just before they reached the house. He was worried because Casey hardly ever cried, and it hurt him to see her body shaking with such terrible sobs.

"Don't let what that man told us upset you, Casey," he said, running his hand up and down her arm. "He's just mean and tries to hurt people. I still believe in Gabe."

"Don't believe in him, Sam." She tried to stop crying, but it just hurt so badly to know that Gabe had deceived them. She had been the biggest fool of them all. She loved him and had wanted to help him.

"I want to believe him."

"He misled us, Sam."

"I can't believe Gabe is that man's son."

"I do. I now know the reason he tried to keep us away from the Casa Mesa ranch. He was afraid someone would tell us who he was. He brought

Indians to work for us, knowing they won't tell his secret, and then there is Fletcher, who came here from Casa Mesa. I don't know why I didn't suspect anything."

"But Fletcher's a good man," Sam said. "I couldn't be wrong about that."

"Most probably he was sent to the Spanish Spur to keep an eye on us."

"What about Kate?" Sam asked, not wanting to believe the little woman had been involved in trickery. "You know she wouldn't do anything to hurt us."

Casey didn't want to think the woman that they had all come to trust and to love as family would help the Slaughters against them. "She has to know who Gabe is—remember she told us to trust him. Why didn't she tell us who he really was?"

"You know Papa always said that if you sleep on a problem it won't seem quite so bad the next morning. Maybe we should try that."

She wiped her tears on the back of her hand. "But, Sam, Gabe will still be a Slaughter when you wake up in the morning. Nothing will change that."

She was trembling inside, but she had to stop crying, because her tears were hurting Sam. She hadn't known anyone could be as deceitful as Gabe. He'd taken her family's trust and ground it into the dirt. He must have laughed at her innocence last night when she'd told him she loved him.

No wonder he had acted so strangely. He had even offered to marry her. She clasped her hands tightly in her lap to stop their trembling. Did Mr. Slaughter covet the Spanish Spur so much that he would send his own his son to trap her into marriage? Why buy a ranch when his son could marry into it?

Sam looked worried as he picked up the reins. "What will we do now?"

"I am going to have a talk with Mr. Gabriel Slaughter, and then I'm going to order him off our ranch."

Sam bowed his head. "I liked Gabe a lot. After this, I'll never trust anyone again!"

She noticed the droop of her brother's shoulders. He still wanted to believe in Gabe, despite the evidence that had been thrown at them.

"Don't say you will never trust again, Sam. I don't want this experience to sour you on friendship. We know many good people. Not everyone is like the Slaughters."

Sam straightened his shoulders. "I'll be with you when you tell Gabe to get off our land."

The sun was going down when they reached home. Casey climbed out of the buckboard and headed straight to Kate's house to get Jenny while Sam unharnessed the horses.

Kate and Jenny were sitting on the porch while they both snapped green beans and dropped them into a bowl. Jenny's puppy, Lucy, was curled up beside her, often reaching out her tongue to give Jenny a lick.

"This here's the last of my garden," Kate said, dropping a handful of green beans in a bowl. "I'll cook a big pot, and we can all eat off it tomorrow."

"Jenny," Casey said, trying not to look at Kate because she didn't want Jenny to know how angry she was. "Go help Sam with the horses. Ask him to let you help water them."

Her sister's eyes lit up, and she scooted off the porch and ran in the direction of the barn with Lucy running at her heels. "I'll tell Sam that you said I could help him," the child called back over her shoulder.

When Jenny was out of hearing, Casey turned to the woman whose friendship she had treasured until today. "Why didn't you tell me that Gabe was a Slaughter? Worse still, why didn't you tell me he was Cyrus Slaughter's son?"

The older woman set her bowl down on the porch and turned to Casey. "I thought it was a mistake for him not to tell you who he was, but he asked me not to say anything, so I didn't."

Casey dropped down on the step and rubbed her temples. "You can't imagine what damage you have done to this family by keeping his secret."

"It weren't that way at all. Gabriel wanted to help you and the family, and he knowed you wouldn't let him if you found out who he was. It's that simple."

"There is never any reason to deceive a friend. We trusted you, thought of you as part of our family."

Kate put her hand on Casey's. "I'm still your friend, and you can still trust me. You can trust Gabe, too. He wouldn't do anything to hurt any of you."

Casey stood up straight. "You cannot imagine how much he has hurt me."

With her heart heavy, Kate watched the beautiful young girl walk toward the house. Cyrus would win if he came between those two. She was an old woman and had never had young love in her life, but she knew it when she saw it, and she had seen it between Gabe and Casey.

Hell, Gabriel was willing to put himself in danger just to keep her safe. Casey had been good for Gabe. Kate had seen that. When a man had never had love, he just didn't know how to reach for it, she supposed. Gabriel should have trusted Casey enough to tell her who he was.

"I should've told her from the first," the little woman said to herself, shoving the bowl of green beans so forcefully, they were scattered across the porch.

Sam hung the reins on a hook and spoke to Fletcher. "You'll want to stop at the house tomorrow and get your pay. You'll be leaving then."

Fletcher had been leading a horse into a stall. He closed the gate and gave his full attention to the boy. "I thought Gabe did the hiring and the firing 'round here."

"Gabe will be hot on your heels when you leave. I don't want either of you around here anymore."

"Now what bug's bit you, boy? Gabe's the only one keeping Cyrus from stealing this ranch."

"Gabe is Cyrus's son." Sam waited for Fletcher to deny it—wanted him to say it was a mistake.

"I figured you'd find out sooner or later. I 'spect all hell's done broke out now."

Sam picked up the dog and took Jenny's hand, nodding at Fletcher. "Just do like I said, and come by the house in the morning."

"If'n that's the way you want it, but you and your sister are making trouble for yourselves."

"You might want to tell Gabe to come to the house if he should get home tonight."

"He won't be back for days."

"Then we'll see him when he does get back."

Casey and Sam sat up long into the night, planning what they would do, while Jenny slept the sleep of innocence. Once again they faced trouble, and this time there didn't seem any way out of it.

Lucy bounced around, trying to get Sam's attention. When he opened the door, she ran out, did her business, and he let her back inside. Then the pup ran for the bedroom, where she would curl up beside Jenny.

Eventually Sam and Casey went to bed, but neither of them slept much. Sunrise found them both in the kitchen, with Casey pouring Sam his first cup of coffee.

He grimaced, shaking his head as he tasted the bitter brew. "Why would anyone want to drink this?"

"I'm not sure. I believe it helps you wake up in the mornings."

Sam took another sip. "I guess I'd better get used to the taste then."

It was difficult for Casey to give Fletcher his pay and send him on his way. But it had to be done. She had to get rid of all the men who had any connection to Gabe, and that meant his Indian friends as well.

It was late in the afternoon when Casey and Sam heard Omous and Flint ride toward the barn. She and her brother went out to them with a heavy heart. It was surprising to Casey how quickly they had become attached to the people who worked for them. But it had probably been part of Gabe's plan to get the family to trust his men.

Sam was the first one to speak. "We know all about Gabe; we know whose son he is. We don't want him here, and we want you to leave, too."

Casey could tell it had hurt Sam to send Omous and Flint away. He really liked them.

"We would like you to leave now," she said, avoiding their eyes.

"Miss Hamilton, you aren't safe here alone.

Gabe would not like us to leave before he returns. You need to talk to him."

"I will be talking to him. But only to tell him to leave as well."

She was finally able to meet Omous's gaze, and she saw sadness revealed there.

He shook his dark head. "Gabe has only your safety in mind, Miss Hamilton."

"We don't want his help," Sam said, his voice trembling.

There was nothing else Omous could say, so he nodded. "Young Samuel, you must look after your sisters. And we will be close by if you need us. There will be trouble, and I fear for your family."

Casey could almost believe him. She wanted to believe that he was a good man who was worried about her family's safety, but doubt crept into her mind, and she shook her head. "We will not need you. I'm going to put the word out that we are looking for hands, and someone will come to work for us."

Omous knew it would do no good to argue with her. Gabe had been wrong not to tell her the truth. Now he would suffer the consequences, and so would the Hamiltons.

By evening, Gabe still had not returned, and Casey slept badly, thinking about the situation they found themselves in. There would be no one left to work the ranch except her and Sam. Just to get by, they would have to rely on what Sam had already learned. She certainly knew nothing about cattle.

The following day, Casey found herself watching the road, waiting for Gabe to return. By the third day she had decided he might not return at all if he had been made aware that she knew he was a Slaughter.

It was early afternoon as Casey watched Jenny run into the barn with Lucy at her feet. She was glad they had been able to shield her sister from the problems they were facing. She wished in a way that she had the innocence of a child; then life would not be so difficult for her.

She glanced at Kate's cabin. The older woman had come to the ranch house door that morning, but Casey had not invited her in. They had talked for a while, but the conversation was awkward, and soon Kate left.

Casey felt they were living on the edge, that something terrible was about to happen. Maybe she should sell the ranch to Mr. Slaughter; then she and Jenny and Sam could go back to Virginia where they belonged. It was too hard for them here in Texas. Surely her father would have understood if she had to sell the Spanish Spur.

Suddenly she felt something strange, a slight tremor. Then the door shook and the windows rattled. There was a roar that grew progressively louder. Sam came out of the house, his gaze questioning.

Casey grabbed his hand. "I don't know what is happening." She flew down the steps to the ground, glancing toward the barn where Jenny was. Now the earth shook, and they saw a dust cloud.

"It's a stampede!" Sam cried, pointing to the mounted riders who were shooting their guns in the air to frighten the cattle. "Whoever it is, they are deliberately driving the cattle at us. There must be two hundred head or more."

"Jenny!" Casey cried. "She's in the barn!" The cattle were close enough now that she could actually see the markings on their faces. She started running toward the barn, frantic to get to her sister, but Sam was faster than she was. To Casey's horror, Jenny had just come out of the barn to see what the noise was.

"Jenny," she cried, fearing Sam would not reach their sister in time, "go back. Go back!"

Casey ran into the dust cloud, trying to get to her sister. The dust was so thick she couldn't see anything, and she soon lost her sense of direction. "Sam, Jenny, where are you?" she screamed, desperate to be heard over the deafening noise. One of the frightened animals brushed against her, and the impact took her to the ground. Dust and hooves were all about her, and she choked and gagged, trying to breathe. She tried to rise so she could get to Jenny and Sam, but she was struck again and blackness swallowed her.

* * *

Casey felt as if she were coming out of a fog. Her mouth was dry, and she licked her lips. She could see a faint light, and it grew brighter as her eyes focused more clearly. It took her a moment to realize that she was in her own bedroom.

What was she doing in bed? She didn't remember getting there.

Suddenly it all came back to her, and she whimpered, "Jenny, Sam, oh, God, where are you?"

Sam came rushing into the room and restrained her as she struggled to get up. He knelt down beside her, taking her hand. "Casey, we've been so worried about you."

She tried to sit up, but the room whirled, and she lay back against the pillow. "Jenny, I want to see Jenny."

"She's not hurt. She just has a scraped elbow. She's sleeping on a pallet in the living room because we didn't want her to disturb you."

"Are you sure she's all right? Are you telling me the truth?"

"I always tell you the truth. You know that." He glanced downward. "But, Casey, her pup . . . Lucy was trampled to death. Jenny took it real hard."

Tears seeped from the corners of Casey's eyes. "Oh, poor Jenny." She turned her head toward Sam. Now that the world had stopped spinning, she noticed that his arm was in a sling. "You were hurt!"

"It's just a sprain. The doctor said I was to wear the sling for a week; then my arm should feel much better." He touched her hair. "We were afraid, Casey, when the dust settled, and we saw you lying there. . . ." He wiped a tear away. "I thought you were dead. Kate went for the doctor, and I stayed right here with you, trying to console Jenny. This is the first I've left you, to tuck Jenny in. I couldn't have been gone for more than a minute."

She smiled. "As you see, I'm hard to kill, Sam."

"The doctor's in the kitchen with Kate. He wanted to know when you woke up."

"Oh, Sam. I thought you and Jenny were . . ." She tried to move and felt a heavy weight pressing her down.

"You have to be still, Casey," he warned. "You have a head wound."

Kate appeared in the doorway with a middle-aged man Casey assumed was the doctor. He had a shock of white hair, and he smiled softly down at her. When he touched her face, he had the gentle hands of a healer, warm and comforting.

"I'm Dr. Cahill." He lifted the lamp and handed it to Kate. "Hold it close so I can examine her."

He slid Casey's eyelids upward and studied her for a moment. When he confirmed that her pupils were a little less dilated, he nodded in satisfaction. "You've got a concussion, young lady. From what I've been told, you're lucky that's all you got. But you seem to be coming around just fine now."

"Tell me about my brother and sister," Casey

insisted, in spite of Sam's assurance that they were fine. "What is the extent of their injuries?"

"The little one has no more than a scratch on her elbow and face. Your brother's arm was sprained. You were hurt the worst." He touched her arm. "I want you to do exactly as I tell you."

She nodded in relief.

"Lift each leg one at a time, and then do the same with your arms.

"Good," he said as she followed his directions. "Good, that's excellent!"

When Sam still looked worried, the doctor said, "Your sister is going to be all right. A few scrapes and bruises, but they'll heal soon enough."

The day could have turned out so differently. Casey shivered and reached for Sam's hand, then closed her eyes, trembling. They had come close to being killed. And Jenny . . . how she must be grieving because of Lucy—she loved that puppy so.

Kate came up beside her. "I'll stay with her tonight, Doc. I won't leave her side."

Casey didn't bother to open her eyes—she was just too confused. Cyrus Slaughter had struck fast and hard, and he'd hit them where it hurt the most. She didn't know how much damage had been done to the ranch buildings, and at the moment she didn't care. She had been ready to give up and let Slaughter have the place, but after what had happened, she would give the ranch away to someone else before she'd let him have any part of it.

She heard Kate scoot a chair beside her bed, but she didn't say anything. She was thinking of Gabe. She wondered if he had been with the men who stampeded the cattle. No. She refused to believe that. He would never do anything that would hurt Jenny and Sam—would he?

Still, he was a deceiver and a liar. He could have ordered the stampede.

Chapter Twenty-four

It was late when Gabe arrived at the ranch. He had been in the saddle for most of the day and night, and he was weary. He glanced at the house as he always did and found it dark. There was a light on at Kate's cabin, so he dismounted and walked in that direction.

He didn't even have time to knock before the little woman opened the door and glared at him.

"Where've you been at? All hell's broke out while you went running off who knows where, doing who knows what!"

He shook his head tiredly. "I've been to Fort Worth. Fletcher must have told you that. Then rode on to San Angelo."

"Fletcher ain't here to tell me nothing."

He frowned. "You said everything was falling apart?" He went to the door and opened it, glancing toward the ranch house. "There is nothing wrong with Casey, is there?"

"You might say the bottom's fallen out of everything. Casey paid a visit to your pa."

"Ah, hell! What did she say?"

"Well, after running Fletcher, Omous, and Flint off, she didn't say much to me. She figures I'm in cahoots with you and Cyrus to steal the Spanish Spur from them."

"What?"

"Yeah. And that ain't the worst of it; if'n you'd ridden in daylight, you'd've seen the damage caused by the stampede—fences down, horses running free, the bunkhouse porch splintered."

"Dammit, Kate, quit beating around the bush and tell me—are Casey and the children all right? What stampede?"

"The one that Cyrus set up. His men were shootin' and hollering and driving the cattle right through the place. Casey was very nearly killed. She got knocked down, and it's a miracle she wasn't trampled to death. She has to stay in bed for a while."

"Is she going to be all right? Did you send for the doctor?"

"She's mending. But we could be attending a funeral. That's how close she was to being trampled to death."

He stepped out on the porch, and she followed him. "I should have been here," he said.

"Why weren't you? There wasn't any way I could get in touch with you."

Gabe paced back and forth, trying to think.

"This is all my fault. When I first came here, I only wanted to help the Hamiltons and then move on. It didn't matter about my name, except I thought they wouldn't trust me if I told them I was a Slaughter. But you already know that."

"They sure don't trust you now, and I can't say as I blame them."

He drew in his breath, trying to overcome his panic. "I need to see Casey right now!"

"You can't go busting in there in the middle of the night waking everyone up! Think of Jenny." She shook her head. "Speaking of Jenny, it's like the light went out behind her eyes. That pup you gave her got trampled right in front of her."

He leaned his head against the supporting post, feeling gut-wrenching pain in his heart. "In trying to help, I've only brought more trouble down on them. I should have figured that Cyrus would try to get to me through them. I don't know why I didn't think of that. He's played that game with people's lives before."

Gabe stepped off the porch. "I'm going to see Casey tonight if I have to wake up everyone in that house."

Kate didn't know what would happen when Gabe and Casey faced each other, but she didn't think anything good would come of it.

Gabe hurried toward the ranch house. He bounded up the porch steps and rapped softly on the door. It was a while before the door opened.

Sam's hair was mussed, and he blinked his eyes

sleepily. When he realized who was standing there, his hands formed into fists. "What do you want?"

"I've got to see Casey, Sam. Kate just told me what happened."

Sam stood taller, blocking the way. "You already know what happened. And you can't see Casey. She's been hurt, and she needs her sleep."

Gabe wrenched the door open; he knew it would be a waste of time to try to explain things to the boy. "I'm not leaving until I see her. If she's asleep, I won't wake her. I just need to know she's unhurt."

Sam stood his ground. "I'm not letting you by."

"Look, you can come with me. I just want to look at her. Then I'll leave and trouble you no more."

Sam stepped aside. Somehow he still trusted Gabe. And he had never known that Gabe cared this much about his sister. Now that he thought about it, he should have suspected something. Gabe was always watching Casey.

"You can see her, but you aren't to wake her up. And then I'll expect you to keep your word and leave us alone."

Gabe nodded. He followed Sam to the bedroom door. It took a moment for his eyes to adjust to the darkened room. He could make out Jenny curled up in her bed, and Casey in hers by the window. His footsteps were silent as he crossed the room. The lace curtain ruffled in the early-morning breeze, and soft moonlight fell on Casey's face. He bent down beside her so he could get a better look at the bandage on her forehead. Her breathing was even and steady. Her lips were slightly parted, and he ached to touch his mouth to them.

He stood up and left as silently as he had come, and Sam followed him to the door.

"You love my sister, don't you?"

Gabe didn't say anything, but the gentleness in his eyes revealed a truth that even Sam, at his young age, could understand.

"Then you wouldn't hurt her."

"I would die myself before I caused her pain."

Sam didn't know what to believe, but he knew what Casey believed. "You need to be gone when she wakes up in the morning. I'll give you what pay you think you have coming."

He studied the boy for a moment. If he had a son, he would like him to be like Sam. He would miss him, Jenny with her sunny personality, and Casey . . . What would he do without seeing the light playing across her hair, or her laughing blue eyes, enticing him to kiss her?

"Good night, Sam."

Casey awoke before sunup. She touched her head and found the bandage still in place. Jenny was still sleeping, and she assumed Sam was as well. She threw the covers back and slid her feet to the floor. She had no time to languish in bed.

She quietly dressed and went directly to the kitchen. She tied an apron about her waist and poured water into the coffeepot. Hearing a noise, she swung around to look out the door and found Gabe sitting on the steps, his hat pulled down over his face.

"What are you doing here?"

He rolled to his feet, opened the door, and came inside. "I had to learn everything from Kate; you fired everyone else."

"We gave them good wages first," she said, reaching for the skillet and banging it against the burner.

"How are you?"

She lit the fire and placed the coffeepot on the stove before she turned back to him. She couldn't let him know that just the sight of him left her weak and shaken. "I've been better."

"Sweetheart—"

"Don't call me that. I want you to leave right now."

"We have to talk, Casey."

"I don't want to hear anything you have to say." She turned her back to him. "Sam will give you the wages you've earned. Then we want you to go away."

He stepped closer to her. "Don't do this." Her coldness had wounded him deeply. "Just listen to what I have to say. There was a good reason I didn't tell you my name."

She angrily turned to face him. "Yes, there was,

and that reason is named Cyrus Slaughter." Tears were swimming in her eyes. "I'm such a gullible fool; you even warned me against your own father and convinced me I needed you to protect us from him."

She looked so fragile with the bandage on her forehead. He wanted to wrap her in his arms. He had done a lot of thinking while he'd been away. He didn't know what love was, but he knew what it felt like to have the memory of Casey's sweetness surrounding him. Just thinking about her made his heart overflow with joy—and he thought of her a lot. His body had ached and throbbed for her. He wanted to take care of her, to make love to her, long and slowly. He wanted her even now.

She turned away from him, unable to look at him any longer. But she felt the heat of Gabe's gaze, and she knew that he was willing her to look at him. She wouldn't let herself. "If I hadn't taken Mr. Slaughter an apple pie because I wanted to settle the misunderstanding between us, I would never have known you are his son." She spoke so softly he was barely able to catch her words. "He rejected the pie just as he rejected my offer of friendship. He said he didn't like apple pie."

"He's not a man you can reason with."

"You should know, since you are his son."

"Casey, don't do this. If you never believed anything I've said before, believe me now. You need me to protect you."

Her eyes blazed, and that stubborn chin came up in defiance. "Don't you dare say that to me! And from now on, you can refer to me as Miss Hamilton."

He knew her so well—she would not relent. To her he was the enemy, and nothing he could say would convince her otherwise. "The only lie I ever told you was a lie of omission when I didn't tell you my last name."

"You let me think you didn't have a last name."

"Yes. I did that."

He could only imagine what she was feeling. She had given herself to him and even admitted she loved him, only to discover what she thought was the ultimate betrayal. "Casey, I have seen my father only once since I came back to Texas, and that was to warn him to stay away from your family. The day I came upon you at the river, I had just come home."

"I don't believe you."

"I guess it's time for me to tell you all about myself."

"I asked you to tell me about your past the other night, and you refused, and now I know why. I don't care anymore."

He could hardly find his voice because she was looking at him with such contempt. "I did tell you that one day you would come to despise me, and you do."

Her head dropped just a bit, but she brought it up again. Standing there beside him, she still loved him; she still wanted him. She wanted to be in his arms right now. There were tired lines beneath his eyes, and he looked like he was suffering. But she told herself it was an act to gain her sympathy, and she would not fall for his trickery a second time.

"I don't feel anything for you." Now she was being untruthful; her need for him was stronger than it had ever been. "To love a man I must respect him, and he must be honest and honorable. You are neither."

He flinched as if she'd struck him. "I can see how you might feel that way."

"What did you expect?"

He pulled out a chair and sat down. "If that's fresh coffee on the back of the stove, I'd take a cup." He rubbed his eyes. "If you don't mind."

She poured him a steaming cup and set it before him. The longer he remained in her kitchen, the more her agony was prolonged. "Drink it fast."

He looked at her, wishing he dared reach out and take her hand, pull her onto his lap, and make her believe him. He took a sip of coffee and set the cup down. "I want to tell you about myself, Casey. It's not a pretty story, and you will probably be shocked." He raised his gaze to hers. "Another thing I haven't told you is about my mother. She was a full-blood Comanche. For the first thirteen years of my life I lived with her. I'm proud of the Comanche blood that flows in my veins, but I am ashamed of that part of me that came from Cyrus Slaughter."

She didn't believe him. He wasn't an Indian. "Don't, Gabe. I don't want to hear any more."

"Omous is my uncle, my mother's brother, and Flint is my cousin. My Comanche family is very devoted to me because of my mother, and they have always helped me when I asked it of them. They came here to help me protect your family."

Her gaze swept his face. What she had thought to be a dark tan could be the darker skin of an Indian. She knew he was waiting for her reaction. "Your eyes are like your father's," was all she could manage to say.

"No other comment—not how could I ever have kissed you when I am nothing but a half-breed?" He lowered his voice. "Or how did I dare touch you?"

She heard the defensiveness in his tone. What did he expect of her? "I am half English and half Scottish. What does that make me?"

"Fortunate. Everyone accepts you for what you are. Some people are not so fortunate."

Anger welled inside her. "How dare you say this to me? Do you think I care who your mother was? Although," she said, fighting for control, "I do have some objections as to who your father is. And I resent the fact that you brought Omous and Flint here to keep an eye on us when you couldn't."

When Gabe reached for her, she shook her

head and quickly stepped away from him. Heated words poured out of her. "Now that I think about it, their arrival was very timely. They appeared to rescue me the day Mr. Teague came here. You must have staged the whole thing just for my benefit."

"I know this has all been a shock to you, Casey. I never intended for you to learn that Cyrus is my father in this manner." He stood up, shaking his head. "There is nothing I can say that will change your mind. I'll do as you say and leave." He reached out and took her hand, raising it to his lips. "I missed you while I was away. I couldn't wait to get back here so I could see you."

She slid her hand out of his grasp. "I won't listen to any more. You should leave before Sam gets up. And we haven't told Jenny you are leaving. She . . . she liked you a lot."

"Casey." He shrugged, not knowing what to say. "Tell her I'll get her another dog."

"No, thank you. If Jenny gets another pet, Sam and I will give it to her."

His eyes closed for a moment. "It doesn't have to end like this, Casey."

She turned back to the stove, clutching the skillet to keep from falling into his arms. She heard the screen door open and close, and then his footsteps faded in the distance.

Jenny chose that moment to come into the kitchen, and Casey was glad. Otherwise she might very well have gone running after Gabe.

Chapter Twenty-five

Gabe rode down the deserted streets of San Bastion in a dark mood. He dismounted in front of the log cabin that served as the area's Texas Rangers headquarters. If he didn't get some satisfaction from the Rangers, he didn't know what he would do. He had nowhere else to turn.

When he entered the room, the man behind the desk glanced up at Gabe.

"Can I help you?"

Gabe sat down on a wooden chair and stared back at the ranger. "I hope so. I'm Gabe Slaughter from Mariposa Springs. The sheriff there won't help me, and neither will the marshals in Fort Worth or San Angelo. So I thought I'd try the Rangers."

"Since I am well acquainted with the sheriff in Mariposa Springs, I understand why you can't get help from him."

The man was of medium build with dark hair

and dark eyes. Gabe already knew him by reputation. He let nothing stand in the way of bringing in the bad guy. "Are you Ron Harwood?"

"Yes, I am. And I know who you are, Mr. Slaughter. I also know about your pa."

"Then you probably already know why I need your help."

The Ranger hooded his eyes but not quickly enough to hide a glint of suspicion. "You're a Slaughter, so I can't think why you would need our help. Your pa's got an army of his own."

"That's why I'm here. Someone needs to protect the family on the Spanish Spur. Cyrus has already caused them trouble, and there will be more. The family is named Hamilton—Casey Hamilton is the oldest; she takes care of her younger brother and sister."

"I already know about that family, and I know their situation. Bart Murdock asked me to send someone to look after them. He said there was a stampede on their place, and from what he said, it wasn't an accident."

Gabe rubbed his eyes, which felt gritty from his long ride. "Will you help them?"

"I can't figure you going up against your own pa."

"Let's just say that there is no love lost between my father and me."

Harwood nodded. "I do know about your situation. I've also been told how your sister, Nora, died."

Gabe leaned back in the chair. "Look, I'm not here to give you a history lesson on my family. I just want to know if you are going to help the Hamiltons."

Harwood glanced right into Gabe's eyes. "The reason I know so much about your family is because there have been complaints about your pa from other ranchers around Mariposa Springs. So many, in fact, it seemed reasonable to investigate him. I have someone watching him right now. And," he said, leaning back in his chair, "I mean to go down there myself and have a look around."

Gabe stuck his hand out, feeling relief. "Thank you, Mr. Harwood. The Hamilton family needs your help."

As Casey stepped out of Finnegan's General Store, a gust of wind tore her bonnet off and sent it sailing into the street. A man scooped it up and walked toward her, offering it to her on the tips of his fingers.

"You must be new to these parts or else you'd have had that bonnet tied on so it wouldn't blow away, ma'am."

She smiled and slipped it on her head, tying it beneath her chin. "I am fairly new here."

"My name's Ron Harwood. I just arrived here myself. I've been looking for work but haven't had much luck yet."

"What kind of work, Mr. Harwood?"

"Ranching mostly—cowherding. I'm not good at much else."

"I may be able to help you. But you will have to come with me to see the town attorney, Mr. Murdock. I want him to meet you before I agree to anything."

Gabe had followed Casey into town, staying a safe distance away so she wouldn't know he was there, but close enough to protect her if she ran into danger. He had held back when he saw her safely enter Mariposa Springs. He even circled town so he would enter it from a different direction than she. What he really wanted to do was demand that she not ride out alone, but she wouldn't listen to anything he told her.

When he spotted the ranger with Casey, he smiled. Harwood was a man of his word, and Gabe was relieved Harwood had taken the danger to the Hamiltons seriously.

Unknown to Casey, Fletcher and Omous had been camping out on the Brazos so they could watch for trouble. Gabe and Flint had set up camp closer to the ranch so they could ride in quickly if the need arose.

Sometimes at night, Gabe would visit Kate and just sit on her front porch, watching the house. He had even caught brief glimpses of Casey. Not enough to fill his need for her. But at least he knew she was safe.

He dismounted and met Harwood's gaze and

caught the slight shake of his head, indicating he didn't want to be recognized.

Casey stopped short when she saw him. "Good day, Mr. Slaughter," she said in a frosty tone. "If you will follow me, Mr. Harwood, I will lead you to Mr. Murdock's office."

The ranger smiled and touched his hat. "Excuse me," he said, stepping around Gabe.

Now what was that woman up to? Gabe wondered. And more than that, what was Harwood doing with her? He had asked him to watch her, not talk to her. The ranger was not a bad-looking sort. In fact, women might find him handsome.

For the first time in his life, Gabe was experiencing a new emotion: jealousy.

He had already made up his mind that he would visit the attorney later on and ask him why Casey had brought Harwood to his office.

Casey had given Mr. Harwood directions to the ranch after getting wholehearted approval from Mr. Murdock to hire him. It seemed the two men knew each other, and the attorney had a high regard for Mr. Harwood.

She crossed the street to Betsy's Tearoom. She had enjoyed the sandwich she'd eaten there the other time she had been in town.

Betsy gave her a cheery greeting.

"I remember you. I found out after you left the last time that you inherited the Spanish Spur from Bob Reynolds."

"That's right." Casey seated herself at a table. "I'd like a cup of tea and a sandwich, please."

Betsy set a cup of tea in front of Casey.

"I only have ham today."

"That sounds good."

As Betsy brought the sandwich, both women spotted the tall, handsome man crossing the street. Everywhere Casey looked, Gabe seemed to be there. Her heartbeat jumped at the sight of him. She wished he'd just go away.

"That's the man I'm going to marry," Betsy said, moving closer to the window. "I get these palpitations in my heart when he looks at me."

Casey took a sip of tea. Kate had said at one time that Betsy had planned to marry Gabe. There was a puzzle here she couldn't quite grasp. Kate had indicated that Gabe had not wanted the marriage. "Has he asked you?"

"No." Betsy sighed as Gabe rode away. "And he probably never will. I don't expect him to stay around very much longer. You see, he and his pa don't get on. They never have. I'm surprised Gabe came back at all. He took it hard when his sister, Nora, died. He blamed Cyrus for her death, and so do many of us."

Casey shook her head. "He's probably made up with his father."

"No. Pete Wilson, who works at the Case Mesa ranch, says there's trouble between them. It seems Cyrus wants this piece of property somewhere, and Gabe is determined he won't get it."

Casey felt as though a knife twisted in her heart. "Are you sure?"

"Yes. You see, Gabe never had anyone to look out for him after his ma died, except his sister Nora. His pa sure didn't."

Casey wasn't really listening to Betsy. She had heard the story before from Gabe himself.

She had thought he had betrayed her, and she was the one who had not believed in him. At the first test of their love, she had let him down. He had been innocent of everything she accused him of. He had tried to explain, but she hadn't let him.

She pushed the sandwich aside and stood. "I find I'm not hungry after all." She gave Betsy money and left as quickly as possible.

Casey felt ashamed. Gabe would probably never forgive her, and she didn't blame him.

Still, doubt nagged at her mind, and it followed her all the way home. Everything had pointed to Gabe's guilt.

Casey didn't know that Gabe rode behind her, keeping out of sight, just as he had on her ride into Mariposa Springs.

Chapter Twenty-six

Gabe emerged from the shadows and opened the door to the bunkhouse. He was careful not to make a sound as he stepped across the floor. The lone lantern cast a ring of light around the Ranger as he sat with his head bent over a book.

"Come on in, Gabe. I've been expecting you."

Gabe stepped into the light. "No one hears me if I don't want them to unless it's another Indian."

"Like you, I'm half Indian. My pa was a full-blood Cherokee." He motioned to a chair. "Sit down and ask your questions. I could see you were full of them today in town."

"I spoke to Murdock. He told me some of what I wanted to know. You must be really worried about Cyrus if you are actually working undercover here on the Spanish Spur."

"Murdock told me a few things about you as well. I imagine I know more about you than you'd be comfortable with."

"I don't care what you think about me. My only interest is keeping Casey and her family safe."

"She was shaken up about running into you in town. I don't care what happened between the two of you; I only want to do my job. You do know we have your pa's place staked out?"

"I'm comforted by that. It should have been done a long time ago."

"I met the two Hamilton kids today. Dammit, how can your pa have done what he did to them? That stampede could have killed them all."

"You need to understand about Cyrus—he cares nothing for anyone except himself. And when he wants something, he gets it one way or another."

"That's why I'm here . . . to make sure he doesn't get what he wants. People around here are fed up with him. That day when you came to see me, I figured it was time to act. If a man's own son don't trust him, who will?"

"It's about time someone did something," Gabe said, irritated. He stood and walked to the door. "I'll just be going now. But I'm not far away. I'll be keeping an eye on the Hamiltons, too."

"I know where you're camped. I know where Will Fletcher and your uncle are camped, too."

"Then if you need me for any reason, you know where to find me."

"You must love her a great deal."

Gabe glanced up at the ceiling with his hands on his hips. "More than you can imagine." He walked out onto the porch and stepped quickly back into the shadows. Jenny was running across the yard, and Sam was laughingly trying to catch her. Casey stood on the porch, lovingly watching over them.

Gabe felt the now familiar ache inside him. He moved silently away and melted into the shadows, but he could still hear their voices.

"You can't catch me," Jenny called breathlessly.

"Yes, I can," Sam said, grabbing her up and settling her in his arms.

Casey had been worrying for two days over what Betsy had told her about Gabe. She had to know everything, and there was only one person she could go to for the truth.

Kate was watering her plants on the porch when Casey approached her cabin.

"Looks like cold weather is coming," Kate said. "I'll be needing to move these plants indoors before long."

"It is much cooler. I have put quilts on our beds."

Kate broke a yellowed leaf from one of the plants. "You didn't come here to talk 'bout the weather or my plants, did ya?"

"No." Casey moved up the steps. "I could use a cup of tea, and a good dose of the truth."

Kate smiled. "I got hot water on the stove. I was just waiting for you to start questioning. I knowed you'd start putting the pieces together and see they didn't fit."

Casey followed Kate into the house and to the kitchen. "Betsy, the most unlikely person, made me question my conclusions. She told me Gabe despised his father."

"With his yardstick of honor, Gabe could not take to his pa's way of doing things. He could never forgive Cyrus for Nora's death."

Casey took the little woman's hand. "Can you ever forgive me for the unkind things I said to you?"

Kate patted Casey's hand. "Shucks, hon, you was just mixed up in your feelings. And it did look bad, Gabe not telling you that Cyrus was his pa. I'd have probably thought the same thing, if I'd been you."

Casey sat down at the table. "Tell me everything."

Kate grinned. "I can do better than that. I can tell you where Gabe is. He never left you at all. He's been watching over you like a guardian angel." Her grin widened. "Well, Gabe ain't exactly an angel. But he's watching over you all the same."

Flint had heard the rider approaching before the horse even came into view. With catlike quickness, he flattened himself behind a tree. Gabe had chosen this location because they had a clear view of the surrounding countryside.

He recognized that it was Miss Hamilton right away. Flint glanced at Gabe, who was asleep on his bedroll. Usually his cousin heard every sound, but right now he slept in total exhaustion.

He knelt down and shook Gabe. "Wake up. You're about to have company."

Gabe blinked groggily, trying to throw off his sleep-drugged state. Then he immediately became alert and rolled to his feet. Moving quickly, he hurriedly put on his boots.

"Your woman has come to you."

Flint moved away, blending in quickly with the countryside. Only someone with Gabe's hearing could have heard him lead his horse away and mount up in the distance.

Gabe pushed his hand through his hair and buttoned the top button of his shirt. When Casey drew up to him, he nodded.

She watched him tuck his shirt into his waistband. "Forgive my appearance. I was sleeping," he admitted.

It was midafternoon, and Gabe would never have been sleeping at this time of day if he had not been awake all night. Knowing him like she did, she suspected he had been watching her house to make sure her family was safe.

She dismounted in a flurry of petticoats. "I have come to talk to you."

"I know already what you want to say, so you can save your breath." He looked past her to Flint, who was just riding over the hill. "I'm not here to spy on you for my father's sake, if that's what you think."

He looked so tired and worried, she ached to take him in her arms and comfort him. "You're wrong. I don't think that way anymore."

His eyes widened slightly. "What made you arrive at that conclusion?"

"The most unlikely source—Betsy Turner."

"I seem to remember that name, but it was a very long time ago." He nodded as recognition hit him. "I do remember her."

Casey thought it was ironic that Betsy adored Gabe while he hardly remembered her at all. It was sad in a way.

"So," he said, breaking into her thoughts, "you don't object to my camping on your land?"

There were so many things she wanted to say to him. After talking to Kate, she knew Gabe's reason for guarding her family—it was out of love for his sister, Nora. The way Kate had put it, "Gabe didn't want to watch any more innocent people die."

She felt ashamed that she had misunderstood his motives that night by the river. She had thought he had been attracted to her as she had been to him. She had blatantly enticed him into making love to her. He never would have touched her if she hadn't been so forward.

She met his gaze squarely and said in a straightforward manner, "You are free to camp here as long as you want. I have no objections."

"And," he remarked dully, "you rode all the way out here to tell me this?"

"No, that was not my reason. When you left, you forgot to draw your wages. I have brought them to you."

"I . . . No. Don't do this."

She was puzzled by his response when she held several bills out to him, and he stepped away from her. "You earned this money. Please take it."

He ignored her offering. "I earned nothing! I wasn't there when you needed me the most."

"Kate told me where you were. It must have been frustrating for you to find out that the law wouldn't help you."

"Is there anything else?"

There was a long, uncomfortable silence between them. "No," she said at last. "Nothing else."

"Then there is no point to this, is there?" He angrily took the money out of her hand and stuffed it in her saddlebag. "You brought me the money, and I refused it. End of conversation."

She felt a heavy sadness. "If that's the way you want it. The money will be waiting for you should you change your mind."

"I won't."

She could almost see the young boy finding his sister dead from a self-inflicted gunshot wound. She remembered him telling her about the incident, and how her heart had gone out to that young boy. She'd never imagined that he had been speaking about himself.

There was nothing else to say, so she mounted her horse. "Stay here as long as you like."

His hand went instinctively toward her and tension corded his muscles. He quickly turned away, unwilling to watch her ride out of his life.

Chapter Twenty-seven

Gabe was not expecting his next visitor. He had just taken a drink from his canteen when he heard the rider approaching. The horse was coming from the direction of the river, so he knew it wasn't Flint returning.

Instinct drove him to the ground, and he rolled over until he could reach his rifle. Then he stood up, aiming it just as the rider came into view.

He lowered the rifle and waited for Cyrus to approach. His father halted and thumbed his hat back.

"I was told I'd find you here." His gaze dropped to the rifle. "You don't need that."

"I can't think of any reason you would feel it necessary to pay me a social visit."

Cyrus dismounted. "I've been doing some thinking since your visit, and something you said struck a chord with me."

"I didn't think you were listening to me."

"Well, I was. You said I had no friends or family, and for most of my life, that never mattered, but I find it matters now."

"It's too late. Anyone who would have been willing to love you is dead."

"You're not dead."

"I am as far as you're concerned, Cyrus. You've told me that plenty of times. I don't even think of you as my father." Gabe couldn't swallow his anger; it stuck in his throat. "If you don't think I won't shoot you dead, just try going near the Hamiltons again."

"Suppose I agreed to back off—would you come home then?"

Gabe heard a rifle cock just behind him, and he cursed himself for a fool to have trusted his father. He had Teague at his back and his father on the other side. He flipped his rifle up and spun around, but he was too late; there was no time to cock it. Ira Teague was not twenty paces away, and Gabe hadn't even heard him approach.

"I guess you got me this time. I should've known you'd have someone sneak up behind my back. Tell him to shoot, because if he doesn't, I will."

"Gabe, son—this is none of my doing."

The bullet rang out; Gabe dove for the ground and fired, but from his vantage point he didn't know if he'd hit Teague. He turned toward his father, thinking he might have drawn his gun, but he saw Cyrus slumping to his knees, the red spot on the front of his shirt growing wider.

Teague had shot his father! At the moment he didn't know whether the man had missed him and hit his father by mistake or shot him on purpose. He crawled forward, ripped off his shirt, and fell to his knees, pressing the wadded-up cloth against his father's wound.

Cyrus was coughing up blood as he put his hand on his son's. "I . . . didn't . . . do this."

Gabe pressed tighter against the wound, but there was too much blood. "Hold on. Flint will have heard the shot, and he'll be here in no time."

But he could tell by the position of the wound and how much it was bleeding that it was fatal, and the look his father gave him was evidence that he knew it too. For all he knew, Teague could be sneaking up on him right now, but it didn't seem to matter; he had to be with his father when he drew his last breath.

Gabe didn't love him, though he'd wanted to when he was younger, and he certainly didn't respect him, but no man should have to die alone, not even Cyrus.

Cyrus's hand clamped harder on Gabe's. "Sorry . . . sorr . . ." He went limp. Gabe felt like a fist had slammed into him, and then there was emptiness inside. He reached up and closed his father's eyes and turned to retrieve his rifle.

"I wouldn't do that if I was you," Teague said

from just behind him. "The last of the Slaughters will die here today."

"You've already spilled enough blood today. My father didn't even have a chance to defend himself."

Teague cocked the gun, releasing another bullet into the chamber. "Don't pretend you care when I know you don't."

"What you did is murder," Gabe said, straightening to his full height. "Cold-blooded murder."

"Why don't you pick your rifle up? You might stand a chance."

"I won't play your game. If you're going to shoot, do it." Gabe folded his arms over his chest. "You're a dirty coward, but have you ever shot a man who was looking at you?"

Gabe was playing for time, hoping Flint would arrive before it was too late. He didn't fear death; he just wanted to live long enough to see Casey again.

"You had everything I ever wanted. If Cyrus had been my pa, I'd've made him proud of me. You were just a little half-breed, and you didn't deserve to be his son."

"Apparently my father agreed with you."

Teague leveled the gun barrel at Gabe's heart. "So now you die beside him."

Gabe knew he had just run out of time. He knew Teague's marksmanship; he rarely missed. He waited for the impact.

A shot rang out, but it didn't come from the

foreman's rifle. It came from the small hill just to Gabe's right. He jumped to the side as Teague fell. He let out a relieved breath, expecting to see Flint.

Harwood laid his rifle aside and walked closer to see if Teague was dead. He nodded in satisfaction and stood. "It looks like I came along just in time."

Gabe nodded. "Thanks. You were almost too late."

"I followed Miss Hamilton when she rode out to meet you—just keeping an eye on her like we agreed. I was about to leave when I saw your pa riding up. So I hung around to see what was happening." Harwood smiled slowly. "Teague caught you by surprise, didn't he?"

"Yeah. I'm not as sharp as I should be."

"It's the woman." Harwood laughed. "Those females got a way of messing with a man's mind, making him careless, 'cause he's always thinking about her."

"I can't disagree with you there." Gabe stuck out his hand. "You saved my life, Ranger."

Harwood stepped over Teague's body and bent down beside Cyrus, making sure he was dead.

"He didn't know Teague was there. Otherwise he'd be alive."

"Too bad. All that money and all that power snuffed out with one pull of the trigger." He glanced up at Gabe. "I guess this makes you a wealthy man."

"I don't think so. My father would never have left Casa Mesa to me. And I wouldn't want it if he had."

Harwood nodded. "I can see how you'd feel that way. Your cousin is just over the rise."

"I know," Gabe said. "I *heard* him."

Chapter Twenty-eight

Ron Harwood stood on the porch with his hat in hand. "Can I talk to you, Miss Hamilton?"

Casey came out of the door, wiping her hands on her apron. "Of course you can, Ron."

"Well, ma'am, it's like this." He looked sheepish for a moment, dreading that he had to tell her the truth. "I kind of misrepresented myself to you. And I want to set everything right, because I'll be leaving in the morning."

She felt her hopes dashed, but she'd half expected him to leave—Cyrus cast a long shadow over the Spanish Spur. "I had hoped you would like it here, Ron. My brother tells me you are a good worker." She met his gaze with a probing one of her own. "You don't seem to me to be a man who could be scared off by Mr. Slaughter."

He thought she was such a sweet lady, and she had enough troubles without him adding to them. "It's not like that." He let out his breath and looked at her squarely. "This is going to take some telling."

"I have time," she said, crestfallen because they would be without help again. Where was she going to get someone else to work for them, with Mr. Slaughter threatening everyone to stay away from the Spanish Spur?

"You see, my name really is Ron Harwood, but I am a Texas Ranger, not a cowhand."

She was puzzled. "I don't understand. What is a Texas Ranger?"

"The Rangers are a branch of the law. Sometimes when someone is operating outside the law, they call us in to investigate or make an arrest."

Her eyes clouded. "Why would you ask to work for us if you are the law?"

"Because Gabriel Slaughter came to my office in San Bastion and asked me to have the Rangers look into Cyrus's dealings and to protect your family."

She nodded, beginning to understand more about what Gabe had done. "He went against his father to help us. I didn't know it at the time."

Harwood looked at the toe of his boot. "Cyrus Slaughter won't be a problem for you anymore, ma'am." He didn't know any other way to say it but to blurt out the truth. "He's dead."

Her head snapped up, and her hand went to her throat. "Gabe! Is he all right?"

"Gabe had a close call with a man named Teague. You may have heard of him; he was the old man's foreman. Anyway, Teague shot Cyrus, and he was getting ready to draw down on Gabe. I had to shoot the man."

She frowned, trying to sort out everything he was telling her. At last she nodded. "Gabe wasn't hurt at all?"

He felt the tension in Miss Hamilton, and he wanted to put her mind at ease. "There wasn't a single scratch on Gabe as far as I could tell."

"It's so difficult to believe that both those men are dead," she said as if she'd just realized how Mr. Slaughter's death might affect Gabe. "Mr. Slaughter was a wretched man, but I didn't wish him any harm."

"A man like Cyrus Slaughter has lots of enemies. He met the kind of death that comes to most men who think they can live above the law."

"Mr. Harwood, I appreciate what you have done for us, and we thank you for it. I'm sorry you have to leave—but I understand. What you did took a lot of courage."

"Miss Hamilton, I've done nothing compared to what Gabe Slaughter did. He hung in there doggedly, determined to help your family. So save your thanks for him."

"I will thank him. He is a very fine man."

He watched her eyes fill with sadness. Gabriel was one fortunate man. Harwood didn't think much time would pass before there would be a wedding in these parts.

* * *

Gabe was in a dark mood when he attended his father's funeral. He was one of the few who had come out in the cold rain to stand at the grave site. The only other mourners were people who worked on the Casa Mesa ranch.

Gabe tried to feel pity for the man who had ruined so many lives, but it was difficult not to think of Nora. He had not heard one word the preacher had said about his father. He stood stiffly as people filed past him to offer their condolences.

The one person he did smile at was Juanita, the cook and housekeeper.

Long after the others had gone he stood there in the rain, aching inside. He wasn't grieving for the life that had just ended, but for the lives that had been changed by Cyrus's greed.

Gabe knew of two small ranches and three farms his father had taken over in the last year, and who knew how many there had been before that?

How did one mourn a man who had destroyed lives for his own pleasure?

Omous and Flint had not attended the service. They did not believe in showing respect to a person who did not deserve it. He had considered going away with his uncle and cousin when they left, but he didn't belong with them any more than he belonged at Casa Mesa.

"Gabe."

He turned around to face Casey. She hadn't

attended the service, so she must have just arrived. She was dressed in the appropriate black for the occasion. He couldn't tell whether tears or raindrops clung to her lashes.

"Do you weep for me?" he asked.

Even now she blinked back fresh tears that threatened to fall down her cheeks. "Yes, I do. I stood back from the other mourners because I could tell you wanted to be alone. I waited until everyone left to speak to you."

He breathed in and out. "I don't think this has hit me yet. It probably will in a day or two. I don't want you to think I am heartless, but you are aware that my father and I were not the best of friends. I'm not mourning his passing."

She touched his hand and then clasped it in hers. "I do know. But it's all right if you grieve for what might have been between the two of you."

"There could have been nothing between us."

"I'll be leaving now. I just wanted you to know that my family is thinking about you in this terrible time."

"Casey," he said, clamping her hand tighter. "Your family is safe now. You don't need me to protect you."

She would need him for the rest of her life. When she was an old woman, she would still remember the way he looked today, with torture in his silver eyes. She would never forget that he had ridden into her life and made everything all right.

She would never love another man, because her

heart would go with Gabe wherever he went.

Her hand slid away from his and Gabe felt the first sense of loss—not the loss of his father, but the loss of something meaningful and beautiful. "I want you to know . . . I need you to know that I'll be heading out tomorrow."

His words came as no surprise to Casey, but they hit her hard all the same. "You are leaving Texas?"

"Yes. For good."

Her heart cried out to him not to leave her. How could she go on without him? "Wherever you go, remember there is someone wishing you happiness."

She did not say another word as she stepped away from him and headed down the hill.

Gabe watched Sam jump down from the buckboard and help Casey aboard. As they disappeared into the rain, he walked the few paces to Nora's grave just on the other side of his father's.

He clutched his hat in his hand as the rain fell on him. "Are you with Frank now, Nora? Have you found the happiness that was denied you in life?" He closed his eyes. "I pray that it is so."

Gabe realized someone was behind him, waiting a few paces away. He turned to see Fletcher standing near the road.

With his shoulders straight, he walked down the hill, where Fletcher fell into step beside him.

"Gabe, the men, well . . . they asked me to be

spokesman. They want to know what they should do."

"Do? I hope none of them are under the mistaken impression that Casa Mesa belongs to me. I can't tell any of them what to do, and I don't know who the new owner is, but I am sure Cyrus picked someone to be his heir. I always thought it would be Teague.

"I'll be leaving now." He shook hands with Fletcher and nodded at the others who had gathered in a group near the wagons.

With those words, Gabe mounted his horse and rode away.

Chapter Twenty-nine

Casey watched the rain make wide runnels against the window, her heart troubled, her sadness deep.

When she had gone to Mr. Slaughter's graveside service, she had not intended to approach Gabe at all. But when she had seen him standing there, looking dejected and so alone, she knew she couldn't leave without speaking to him. She had wanted only to reach out to him, to let him know that at least her family was thinking of him in his pain.

But her sorrow had bitten deep when she had looked into his tormented eyes. He was still alone, maybe even more so now.

She stepped outside onto the porch and listened to the rain peppering the roof. She had always loved it when it rained because she thought of the water's nurturing power, but tonight she felt as if the sky were weeping with her.

She glanced toward the barn as the figure of a

man detached itself from the evening shadows. Her hand went to her mouth. It was Gabe; she was sure of it!

What could he be doing there?

Ignoring the downpour, she ran across the yard toward him and caught up with him just as he was about to mount his horse.

She was soaked to the skin, and so was he. "You were going to leave without seeing me?"

Gabe took her hand. "Let's get you out of this weather."

He led her into the dark interior of the barn, his hand lingering on her arm. "I only came to leave something for Jenny."

She already knew what it was; she could hear the yelp of a puppy coming from the tack room. "You are the kindest man I have ever known, Gabe."

"You didn't always feel that way."

"I know, and I'm sorry."

He felt her shiver with cold. He didn't know how it happened, but the next moment he slid his arm around her and brought her body against his heat.

In the darkness their hungry mouths crushed together, fingers intertwined, and desire burned inside them.

"Sweetheart, I didn't mean for this to happen."

She pressed her hands to his face. "I know. It just happens when we are near each other."

Wet clothing was stripped away and thrown

aside. They couldn't get close enough. In a fury of passion, Gabe tore the canvas covering off the buckboard and threw it onto the ground. He then picked Casey up in his arms and laid her on top of it.

When he came down to her, Casey's arms opened for him. For a long moment she just held him, brushing her fingers through his damp hair, rubbing the other hand up and down his back. This was the only way she could think of to comfort him.

Gabe lay against Casey's naked body, his passion forgotten for the moment. He needed something deeper than desire from her. He needed her closeness, the touch of her hand, his head lying against her breast in comfort.

"Rest, Gabe. Close your eyes and don't think about today." She felt him settle against her, and she bore the full weight of his body. Time passed as she nestled him in her arms, touching her lips to his face, whispering comforting words much as she would to Jenny when the child was troubled about something.

"Even in your day of sorrow," she said, her hand settling on his back, "you thought of Jenny."

In Casey's arms, Gabe seemed to throw off all the troubling shadows that had darkened his life for so long. Her gentleness had healing power; it was like a warmth spreading throughout his body. And he wanted all she had to give him.

After a moment the soft body beneath him became more than a comfort; it became a temptation. Gabe nestled his face against hers. "I want to make love to you," he said almost pleadingly. "Give yourself to me and hold nothing back."

"Yes," she moaned.

There was not a place on Casey's body that Gabe didn't touch while he kissed her into burning submission. He spoke seductive words, and she ached for him to do the things to her that he was whispering in her ear.

Casey ground her lower body against his, and she felt rather than heard him hiss through his teeth.

A cry of longing escaped her throat when he dipped his head, his tongue sliding around her nipple, then drew it into his mouth.

Gabe could stand no more. He opened her legs and eased inside her, gritting his teeth at the intense pleasure that stabbed through him.

Casey felt her emptiness fill with his warmth. She wanted to hold on to this moment for the rest of her life. When he probed deeper, she sighed with even greater pleasure.

It was hard for Gabe to harness his desire. For so many nights he had lain awake thinking about doing this to Casey. Now it was almost impossible to hold back, but he did manage to slow his movements.

Casey was overcome with emotions. One had hardly registered before another took its place, making her tremble beneath Gabe.

When the tremor hit them both, they clung to each other as they reached for the moon.

After they caught their breath, Gabe rolled to his side and adjusted Casey to his body. Long moments passed as his fingers interlocked with hers, and he raised her hand to his lips. She slid her hand from his and pushed his hair back, kissing his full mouth.

"Will you marry me, Casey?"

She still had the same questions as before. "Why?"

His hand swept across her back. "Because we are good together."

"That's not much of a reason."

"Casey, I could have gotten you with child."

"That's a reason, but not enough of one. The last time I talked to you, Gabe, you wanted to leave town."

"I still do."

She closed her eyes, her heart aching. He was running away, just as he had when he had left to join the Confederacy. He had to stop running from the past, from Nora's death. But that was something he would have to decide for himself.

"You want to leave me?"

"No, Casey. I don't. You, Sam, and Jenny can come with me."

She pushed his arm away and sat up. There was such strength in him when it came to helping others, but he didn't know how to help himself. And she couldn't help him either. "We can't go with you, Gabe."

He had known what her answer would be. He grasped her arm and pulled her to her feet. "It sounds like it's stopped raining."

Casey fumbled around in the dark and found her clothing. If it were just her, she would go anywhere with Gabe, but she had Sam and Jenny to consider.

When she was dressed, he took her hand and raised it to his lips. "I do want to marry you, Casey."

She tiptoed and kissed his mouth. "I'm going to go in now because I don't want to watch you ride away."

"Casey!"

"Yes?"

"I will spend the rest of my life remembering tonight."

She waited. She needed to hear him say he would spend his life loving her. "Is there anything else you want to say to me?"

"Casey, you have to understand—I can't stay here. There are too many memories."

"Good-bye, Gabe."

She hurried across the yard and didn't stop until she was inside the house. She closed the door and leaned against it, clamping her hands over her ears so she could not hear the sound of departing hoofbeats.

Chapter Thirty

Gabe lay on a lumpy bed in the Randolph Hotel, his hands clasped behind his head, an empty feeling in his gut.

He wasn't sorry he'd come back to Texas. And he wasn't sorry to be leaving. He would be sorry that he'd be leaving behind the woman who'd enabled him to feel emotion again.

With Casey he had found hope and, for a few short hours, joy. He might have been better off if he had never met her. Then he wouldn't know what he would be missing for the rest of his life.

There was a rap on the door, and he called out in irritation, "It's open."

Harwood poked his head around the door. "I was told you were here. And I heard you were heading out in the morning. So I've come to try to recruit you into the Rangers."

Gabe sat up and waved the Ranger to a chair. "What makes you think I'd be interested?"

"You're just the kind of man we're looking for: dedicated, honest, not afraid of a damned thing."

"I'm not your man, Harwood. I'll be leaving Texas."

"Is that right? I thought you'd be sticking around."

"I'm getting out of here as fast as I can." Gabe smiled slightly. "Thank you for what you did for me out there. I'd be dead if it weren't for you. I find myself in your debt."

"Think nothing of it. All in the line of duty." Harwood rose from the chair and walked to the door. "I kind of thought you'd be staying around here for a certain young lady."

"I can't see why you'd think that."

"Well, I tried to get you to join us. If you change your mind, the Rangers could always use you." He turned with his hand on the doorknob. "By the way, Mr. Murdock has been tearing the town up looking for you. Unless I miss my guess, he'll be coming up those stairs anytime. He's a very persistent man."

"Good-bye, Harwood."

When the door closed, Gabe lay back and stared at the ceiling. What was Casey doing at that very moment?

He had not meant to see her when he'd delivered the pup for Jenny. But when he touched her, his resolve went right out the window, just as it always did. He couldn't be anywhere near her and not want to touch her.

Gabe closed his eyes, remembering the feel of her soft skin. His body tightened, and he swore under his breath.

He had to let her go.

Since he'd been camping out on the Spanish Spur, he hadn't slept in a bed for a long time. He shifted his weight, trying to find a comfortable position. He was weary, and he just wanted to sleep and forget about the last two weeks.

Tomorrow he would sell his horse and saddle at the livery stable and take the noon stage for Arizona.

At first Gabe thought he was dreaming the loud noise that pounded in his ears, sounding like gunshots. The old nightmare had returned. In his dream he was trying to get to Nora and prevent her from shooting herself. But the banging noise wouldn't go away.

He sat up, staring into the dark, his body covered with sweat. The banging persisted, and he realized someone was knocking on the door. He grabbed the towel that hung on the wrought-iron headboard and dabbed the sweat from his face.

Rolling off the bed, he wrenched the door open to find Bart Murdock standing in the hallway.

"I was afraid you'd already left town when you didn't answer my knock right away."

Gabe planted himself in the doorway, not issuing an invitation for the attorney to enter. "Do you have any idea what time it is?"

Murdock brushed past Gabe, clutching a brown leather satchel to his chest. "I don't care what time it is. It's critical that I speak with you."

"If you came here thinking you could convince me to go to court to try to gain title to my father's estate, you're talking to the wrong man. I don't give a damn about Casa Mesa or any of Cyrus's other holdings."

The attorney settled in a chair and dabbed his face with a snow-white handkerchief before opening his satchel and thumbing through it.

"What I have to tell you won't take very long. When I'm finished, then you can have your say."

Gabe pushed his tumbled hair out of his face, glad that Murdock had woken him from the nightmare. But he didn't want to talk about Cyrus. Not tonight, not ever.

"I see I'm not going to get any sleep until you've said all you came to say." He swept his hand toward the attorney. "Go ahead, tell me what's on your mind."

"The document I have here," he said, studying a single sheet of paper, "was drawn up at your father's request when he came to see me just the day before his death. Cyrus had me take down his words exactly as he said them. Then he insisted that the document be filed at once. Looking back to that day, I think he knew something was going to happen to him."

"I buried Cyrus today; I don't want to hear anything he had to say that concerns me."

"Gabriel," the attorney said in an imposing tone of voice. "Sit down and shut up until I've had my say; then you can have yours."

Gabriel grinned and sat back on the bed. "Go ahead."

"Now," Murdock began, studying the document. "It's not very lengthy as wills go." He cleared his throat. "These are Cyrus Slaughter's words: 'I, Cyrus Slaughter, being of sound mind and body, do hereby bequeath all my lands, holdings, titles, money, and all thereupon to my only son, Gabriel Slaughter, and his heirs. There will be no bequest to any other living person.' "

Gabe stared at Murdock as if he'd lost his mind. A dark hand seemed to settle on his shoulder, weighing him down. "Cyrus wouldn't leave me a damned thing."

"I can assure you he has left you everything. After I drew up this document, he insisted that we go directly to the courthouse where Judge Whitney notarized it, and Dave Hargrove and two other men witnessed it."

Gabe was stunned. He couldn't find his voice for a moment. When he did speak, his tone was grave. "Why would Cyrus do such a thing? I never expected him to leave the . . ." He stood up. "No. I can't do this. I won't."

"I'm not quite finished, Gabriel. There is a personal message from Cyrus. Do you want to hear it?"

"No," he said gravely. Then, "Yes."

"Cyrus wrote this down in his own hand, so bear with me as I try to read it. Or perhaps you'd like to read it yourself?"

Gabe looked at the sheet of paper clutched in Murdock's hand, still reluctant to hear anything his father had to say to him. "No. You read it."

"It says here, 'Gabriel, my son, I leave you everything I own, wondering if you will walk away from it or take what by birth belongs to you. Sometimes this much money and power corrupts a man's mind. But I'm betting it won't corrupt you. And I'm hoping you won't walk away from what rightfully belongs to you.' "

Gabe was not even tempted. "I don't want any part of it."

"He didn't even sign it. As your attorney—"

"I don't have an attorney."

"As your *attorney,* I feel it necessary to advise you that you have just been given responsibility for the welfare and well-being of over a hundred people who work at various positions on Casa Mesa and other holdings that belonged to your father. Many of the folks on the ranch were born there and have lived there all their lives, like Juanita, the cook, her husband, Carlos, and their seven children."

"Enough." Gabe groaned, remembering how

the Casa Mesa cowhands had convinced Fletcher to find out if they still had a job.

"You can't walk away from this, son. Your father was worth"—he glanced at another paper—"in the vicinity of seven million dollars. And that doesn't even include the land, cattle, horses, and houses."

"When the stage leaves for Arizona in a few hours, I will be on it."

"Stay and make Casa Mesa a place to be proud of. Make it into the kind of ranch you would one day want to leave to your son. The land isn't tainted. It was only your father's way of thinking and doing business that were corrupt."

Gabe stared at Murdock. His son? That thought rocked him like a heavy fist slamming into him. He wanted nothing more than to see Casey's stomach swollen with his child.

He wanted that more than he wanted his father's money and all his land.

"If I stay—and I'm not saying I will—there will be many changes made at Casa Mesa. I would want the land my father took by force to be returned to the rightful owners, or if they still want to sell, I'd want them to get a fair price for it. You would have to agree to manage that undertaking, or I will walk away."

Murdock grinned, knowing he had won. "I believe I can be of assistance to you in that matter, Gabriel."

Chapter Thirty-one

When Gabe rode up to Casa Mesa, he hardly noticed that the rainstorm of the night before had moved off, leaving the air crisp and clear. Reluctance twisted inside him as he looked toward the house. He dismounted and waited for Murdock to do the same.

Before he could reach the step leading to the porch, he was approached by some of the hands who worked for the ranch. He noticed that Teague's friends, Richard Bates and Charley Latter, were not among them. He assumed they must have left quickly when they heard he was the new owner of the ranch.

Fletcher stepped forward, once more becoming the spokesman for the others. "We're glad you're here, Mr. Slaughter. I guess we're all wondering what you want us to do."

"Fletcher, first of all, I have always been Gabe to you, and I don't expect that to change." He allowed his gaze to move over each face. "Starting tomorrow, I'll want to speak to each of you in private so I can tell you what I expect out of you and find out what your job is. I don't know most of you, so I'll expect you to tell me about yourselves. You will find that I do things differently than my father did. There will be changes. If any of you can't live with that, you need to ride for another brand."

There was nodding and muttering as the men spoke among themselves, but none of them left. And they soon moved away to begin their appointed tasks.

"Fletcher," Gabe called after the man. "I'll need to speak to you later on today. There are some things I need you to do for me concerning the Hamilton family."

Fletcher nodded his head and squared his hat across his forehead. "Sure, Gabe. You'll find me in the barn when you need me."

Gabe turned back to the attorney, dreading the moment he had to enter that house. "Let's get this over with."

The door swung open, and Juanita smiled in welcome. "Do you remember me, Señor Gabe?"

"Of course I do, Juanita. I never forget a friend."

Her smile widened. "I was so happy to see you return." She looked almost shy. "I would be honored to present my seven children to you, Señor Gabe."

"I would like that very much." He thought there could be nothing better to chase the bad memories of this house away than the sight of children.

Juanita walked to the door and called for them to come in. There was a shuffling of feet as seven young boys rushed in, stumbling over each other into the room. Juanita scolded them with a stern look. One of the boys received a particularly long stare. He blinked his eyes as if trying to think what he had done wrong, then quickly reached up and snatched his hat off his head, looking somewhat sheepish.

"I would like you to meet first our oldest son, Ignacio," she said proudly. "Then there is Rafael, Juan, Manuel, Eduardo, Roberto, and Javier." She nodded at her sons. "Say hello to the *patrón*," she told them, tapping her foot.

Seven voices spoke at once, and Gabe smiled back at them. "You have every right to be proud, Juanita." He looked into seven pairs of dark eyes. "But no daughter?"

Juanita patted her stomach. "I have hopes that this one will be a girl so she can help me with the housework." She shooed all the children toward the door and followed them out.

"That is one of the reasons I honored my father's bequest," Gabe told the attorney.

Murdock was already assessing the room. "You said you wanted all the furnishings removed." He shook his head. "There are some very well known paintings here, and the furniture will be difficult to replace. There are some very fine pieces."

"I want every stick of furniture, every painting, every book and table gone. I want those sofas out of here today and everything in the study as well. I want nothing left to remind me that Cyrus ever lived here."

Murdock nodded. Gabe had his own way of getting rid of the past, and if it meant getting everything out of this house, then that was the way it would be.

"I understand they are building a new orphanage in El Paso. The committee is asking around for donations. I'm sure they could use most of the things here."

Gabe stared down the hallway toward his father's study. "Then give it to them."

"What about your father's private papers?"

"You take charge of them. If there is something in them that I need to know, you can draw it to my attention."

Murdock was already moving through the room, making notations as he went.

The noon meal had been placed on the table, and Jenny was scooping her soup into her mouth with a slurping sound.

"Jenny, remember your manners," Casey reminded her. "Food should never be heard."

"When I crunch hard candy, you can hear it," Jenny reasoned.

"Yes, but that isn't a sound you make; it's the candy."

Sam had noticed that Casey rarely ever laughed anymore, and he knew she was missing Gabe. He missed him, too, and so did Jenny.

Jenny slid off her chair and placed her napkin beside her plate. "I'm going to see Miss Kate."

"Tell her we are expecting her for dinner," Casey reminded her.

Sam took a sip of milk as he watched his sister over the rim of the glass. "There is something I haven't told you, Casey, and I feel real bad about it."

"What have you done, Sam?"

"On that second night when you were suffering from your concussion, Gabe came to the house."

"Did he? I don't remember that." She did remember the next morning, when she had said all those horrid things to him.

"That's because you were asleep. Gabe wouldn't go away until he saw for himself that you were all right. I couldn't keep him out."

"I see."

"He stood over you, and I saw something soft when he looked at you. I asked him if he loved you, and he didn't answer, but I saw it in his eyes—I couldn't be wrong about that, Casey."

Casey glanced up. "I do believe he loves me, but not enough to stay so we can make a life together."

"Maybe he'll be back."

She studied her uneaten bowl of soup. "I don't think so, Sam. He told me he was leaving Texas for good."

"Omous and Flint came by this morning. They asked if they could have their jobs back."

Casey blinked her eyes. "What?"

"They said they want to work for us."

Casey stared at her brother long and hard. She had encouraged him to make some of the decisions, and apparently he had. "So you hired them?"

"I was going to ask you, but I was afraid you'd say no."

"I'm glad they are working for us again, Sam."

"Fletcher's back, too."

She shook her head, and her eyes widened. "He is? What I don't understand is why any of them would want to work for us after we dismissed them so unfairly."

"I feel real bad about that, but they don't seem to hold a grudge. I have the strange notion that Gabe asked them to help us out before he left."

She paused with her spoon halfway to her mouth. "Kind of looking out for us even though he's gone?"

"That's the way I see it."

"Finish your soup, Sam. We have to move those bales of hay into the loft this afternoon."

The dust cloud rising from the herd of cattle being driven onto the Spanish Spur struck no fear in Casey's heart. Fletcher had brought word that the new owner of Casa Mesa had discovered three hundred head of Spanish Spur cattle that had been mingled with his own. Today they were being herded home.

Sam had ridden out to meet them, and he came back smiling. "Casey, we now have enough cattle to drive to the railhead! Also, three of Slaughter's hands asked if they could work for us. With them, we have more than enough hands to get the job done."

She felt her heart lighten. They had lived under the dark cloud of fear and indecision for so long, it was difficult to grasp the fact that the bad times might be behind them now.

"Who is the new owner?"

"They didn't say, and I didn't ask. But Fletcher said he sent a message to you, and that I was to get it just right." Sam looked puzzled. "His boss said to tell you he was partial to apple pie, if you were interested."

Casey's hand went to her mouth, and her heart thudded inside her.

Could it be Gabe?

It had to be him! No one else would have sent her such a cryptic message. What did it mean?

"Sam," she said, tears clinging to her lashes. "I am going to make an apple pie, and I want you to take it to the boss of Casa Mesa today."

Later in the day, when Sam delivered the apple

pie, he was told that the owner was away. When he asked who now owned the ranch, the housekeeper smilingly told him it was Señor Gabriel Slaughter.

Chapter Thirty-two

The next day passed; then another day wore away, and still Gabe did not come. Fletcher and the rest of the hands had rounded up the cattle and were preparing to drive them to the railhead in a few days.

Life at the ranch went on just as before, but Casey was waiting . . . waiting. It took all her fortitude not to ride over to Casa Mesa and see Gabe for herself. But she must not do that. He must come to her this time.

Doubts plagued her mind. Had she been mistaken and read too much into the message Gabe had sent her?

The third day passed and still there was no word from him, and her doubts multiplied.

Sam had gone to bed early, and Jenny had been sleepy when she had tucked her in right after dinner.

Casey had just dried the last dish when she

heard a light tap on the door behind her.

With hope in her heart, she spun around, and he was there!

"Gabe."

He balanced her empty pie pan in his hand. "May I come in?"

She opened the door, and he handed her the pan. "I ate every bite myself."

"I've been waiting for you, Gabe."

"I wasn't sure." He reached for her hand, and she moved toward him. "I hoped you would want to see me."

"I wronged you, Gabe. And I wanted to say again how sorry I am that I didn't trust you."

He pulled her closer. "Is that the only reason you wanted to see me?"

She moved just the smallest bit, bringing her head to his chest. "No. I also wanted to thank you for sending our cattle back to us."

"Is that all?"

She raised her face to him. "I said it before, Gabe. Are you going to make me say it again?"

"I want to hear it again."

In his own way he was making her pay penance for not believing in him, although she doubted he even realized it himself. She was willing to pay his price. "I love you. I never stopped loving you for a moment, not even when I thought you had betrayed me, Gabe."

His hand rubbed up and down her arm as he absorbed the sweetest words he had ever heard.

"I have needed to hold you like this. You must know how much I want you."

She nodded. "Want and need, I do understand those feelings. But I still need something more from you."

He pressed his face against her hair. "What would you have me say?"

"I have confessed several times that I love you, Gabe. But you admit only to wanting me. You have never told me what your true feelings are."

"I can hardly make it through each day without wanting to see you. And the nights are the worst, because I want you beside me so I can make love to you."

She threw back her head, and their gazes locked, saying more than words ever could. "You are talking about desire; I'm talking about something else."

If Gabe couldn't confess that he loved her, they would not stand a chance.

His eyes drifted shut, and he touched his lips to her forehead. "I don't know what more you want from me. I've given you more of myself than I've ever given anyone else."

"Gabe, I know in my heart that I will only love one man in my lifetime, and you are that man."

He crushed her against him, scattering kisses over her face. "I need to be alone with you," he whispered against her ear, his voice filled with trembling need. "I need to do more than just hold you."

Gabe jerked away from Casey when he felt a tug on his shirt. Both he and Casey glanced down at Jenny, who had edged her way between them with a serious expression on her face.

"If you are going to kiss my sister, you'd better marry her. Are you going to marry us, Gabe?" the child demanded to know. " 'Cause if you aren't, let Casey go."

Casey could hardly keep from laughing, and Gabe bent down to Jenny, who was clasping the new pup he had given her tightly in her arms.

"If I asked your permission to marry your sister, would you give it?"

"She's getting pretty old," the child admitted. "And if you don't marry her, I don't think anyone else will."

Casey was frowning in mortification and had arched her brow at her sister. "Jenny, what a thing to say."

Gabe was shaking with laughter as he said, "If you put it that way, Jenny, I guess I'd better marry her real quick."

Jenny yawned as the pup licked her face. "If you marry her, you have to take me and Sam, and my dog, Molly, with you, too. Casey doesn't go anywhere without us!"

He felt a warmth spread through him. This was the family he had never had, the one he had wanted to be a part of almost from the first time he'd met them. The house in Casa Mesa needed

Jenny's laughter, Sam's steadiness, and Casey's loving devotion to make it a home.

"I'm glad I have your permission. Shall we ask Casey if she'll have me?"

Jenny yawned again. "You ask her. I'm sleepy." The child trudged back to bed.

Gabe stood up and took Casey's hand in his. "Will you marry me, Casey?"

"Why?" she persisted.

"Because, dammit—I love you!"

She smiled and propelled herself into his arms. "Yes! Yes, I will."

He clasped her to him, feeling the last remnants of his torture fall away. It felt as though sunshine, dazzling and bright, had burst through him. There were no shadows lingering in his mind because he had found something pure and beautiful in a woman's smile.

He had found love, and he was able to give love. "When will you marry me? I want it to be soon."

"It should be soon, Gabe," she admitted, pressing her face against his wide chest. "That night by the river you left me with something of yours."

She could hear his heart rate accelerate.

"You're pregnant?"

She had suspected she was going to have a baby for some time. She had been sure of it the day she had ridden out to see Gabe just before his father had been killed. "I believe so."

His arms tightened, and he touched his mouth

to hers ever so gently. His face lit up with a dazzling smile. "We will be married tomorrow."

"And how will you arrange that? We have so much to talk about. I have Sam and Jenny to think of."

"You heard Jenny. She said wherever you go, you have to take her and Sam. And that's the way I see it."

"I do come with a family."

"They'll be my family, too. I'll make sure you have enough good hands to work the Spanish Spur to help Sam. He'll live with us until he's old enough to take over here for himself. By that time he should know everything we can teach him."

She laughed as happiness spilled from her heart. "You have it all figured out, don't you, Gabe?"

His hand went to her stomach. "I like the thought of you carrying my child." He raised her face so he could look into her eyes. "You have changed my life, Casey. You have given me a family, and now you are going to give me a baby."

"I wanted to be what you needed. I've always wanted to help you."

He was frowning. "So you knew about the baby that night in the barn when I asked you to marry me? And yet you refused my marriage proposal. I don't understand. You let me go away not knowing I had fathered a child?"

"I wanted you to stay for the right reasons, not because you thought you had to."

"You would have borne the stigma of having a child out of wedlock rather than accept me at that time?"

"No. For the child's sake I had decided that we would sell the ranch and go back to Virginia. I couldn't let my baby grow up without a last name. I love this child because it is the part of you that I can keep with me."

He lifted her in his arms and sat down in a chair. He had to swallow several tries before he could speak. "I don't deserve you, Casey, but I love you so damned much it hurts. You have my oath, with God as my witness, I will make you a good husband."

"I know you will. We've gone through some hard times, but it was worth it."

He tilted her chin and made her look at him again. "I am a Slaughter." His hand moved across her stomach. "This child is a Slaughter; you will be taking the name as well."

She touched her cheek to his. "You have made the name a proud and noble one. I will be honored to be Mrs. Gabriel Slaughter."

"I'll be taking you to Casa Mesa, and I have to warn you, there is not a stick of furniture in the house."

"That's nothing. When we arrived here, there was no furniture either. But I have to know," she asked with humor in her smile, "do you have chickens in your house?"

Epilogue

Gabe hurried through the house, up the stairs, and into the bedroom. He stopped still when he saw how pale Casey was, lying against the stark-white pillowcase.

She smiled at him. "You got here quickly."

"I damned near broke my neck getting here."

Casey had known when she awoke that morning that her baby was about to be born. Kate had been staying with them for the last three weeks so she would be with Casey when her time came. That morning Casey had encouraged Gabe to ride over to the Spanish Spur with Sam to supervise the spring roundup.

"Come and meet your baby, Gabe."

He came to her, going down on his knees and kissing her lips. "I wouldn't have gone this morning if I had known you were going to have the baby."

She pressed a fingertip against the worried

frown on his brow. "Kate informed me that husbands just get in the way at a time like this. I thought you would be better off elsewhere."

He kissed her fingers. "Are you sure you are all right?"

"I have never been better."

He heard a soft noise and glanced down for the first time upon the face of his child. His breath caught as the baby shoved a small fist in its mouth.

"Casey," he said, gently touching the soft head that was covered with dark hair, just like his. "It's so small. I never knew babies could be this little."

"He's your son, Gabe. He's so lucky to have a father like you."

Emotions hit him hard and fast. As the small hand curled around his finger, he leaned forward and touched his lips to the soft cheek, loving the tiny creature who had made him a father.

"He's wonderful."

"Yes, he is. See how dark his skin is—he will carry on your mother's heritage."

"Yes," he said as his finger drifted into her hair. "I see that."

She tugged on his hand, urging him to sit beside them.

"I'm dusty from the cattle drive."

"Your son won't mind, and neither will I."

Gabe carefully moved onto the bed and looked questioningly at his wife. "Can I pick him up?"

"Of course you can. He belongs to you. You will

guide him and shape him into the kind of man you can be proud of as a son."

Gently he lifted the child, but he panicked when the little head bobbled, and he quickly caught it and braced it in his hand. "I never knew that there could be such a strong feeling."

"It's the love a father has for his child, I would imagine."

Gabe's eyes were bright as he held his son to him. "You have made me very happy, Casey."

She smiled. "And this is just our beginning, Gabe. We have such adventures awaiting us. Each day I discover more wonderful things about you."

He grinned. "Do you now?" His eyes flamed with sudden passion. "Hurry and recover from the birth. I have more wonderful things to do to you."

Her laughter rang out just as Jenny burst through the door. "Where's my baby? Kate told me he was in here."

Gabe laid the baby down and lifted Jenny onto the bed. "You will have to be careful with your sister until she is stronger, so don't shake the bed."

Jenny bent over and looked at the tiny face peeping out of the blanket. "He's all wrinkly."

Casey laughed. "Yes, he is, but he'll grow out of it."

Jenny was satisfied to sit beside the baby and hold his small hand in hers. "He's much better than a puppy."

Sam came running into the room and went directly to Casey's side of the bed. "Are you all right?"

"I am just fine. And you, Samuel, are an uncle now."

He grinned down at the baby in wonderment. "Do you think I could hold him?"

"Sure. But you'll have to support his head," Gabe said, acting as if he were already an expert on the matter.

Casey watched the four people she loved most. They were a close family, a happy one. There were no longer nightmares to disturb Gabe's sleep, because she slept in his arms every night.

Jenny was still as precocious and delightful as ever. She seemed to look upon Gabe almost as a father. And he adored her.

Sam was growing up. She could swear he had grown two inches in the last few weeks. He took his guidance from Gabe, and he was learning responsibility so he could one day take over the running of the Spanish Spur.

Casey looked into her husband's eyes. He would be there, guiding them all with his strength. He was still watching over them, just as he had from the beginning.

Chapter One

The Bar T Ranch
Outside of Hard Luck, Texas
1874

It was a hot late August afternoon. Young Casey Turner had been out working with some hands from her family's ranch, checking on strays since early morning. She'd ridden away from the men to look for stock along the river that marked the property line between the Bar T and the Donovan ranch, the Circle D.

Casey stopped for a minute on the shady bank. She was hot and tired, and the water looked mighty inviting. The notion of taking a break was all too tempting, but she couldn't allow herself the luxury.

Times were hard on the Bar T.

Money was tight.

She had work to do.

There was no time to relax, no time for play.

Urging her mount on, Casey followed the river's edge. When she heard splashing from around the bend just up ahead, she expected to find cattle. She quietly rode closer, not wanting to spook the cows, ready to drive them back onto Bar T land.

Then she rounded the bend.

Casey's eyes widened in shock and amazement at the scene before her, and she quickly reined in.

There, standing in the waist-deep water with his back to her, was none other than the Donovans' sixteen-year-old son Michael, and he was—as best she could tell—skinny-dipping.

Michael hadn't heard her approach, and she was glad. She'd never seen a naked man before. As embarrassed as she was curious, she took her time looking him over. His shoulders were broad and strongly muscled, and his waist was lean. Casey was really glad he was staying put, though, for she'd seen all of Michael Donovan she wanted to see.

The Donovans and the Turners had been feuding for years. Frank Donovan, Michael's father, had done everything he could to cause trouble for her and her father. He'd refused to let them join the trail drive to market, which cost them a lot of money, and he'd even accused them of rustling, which wasn't true. Casey knew she and her father had only managed to keep the Bar T in business because they had the best water in the area. She worked hard side by side with her father every day to try to make things better, but there were times when she wondered if they would ever start showing a good profit.

Suddenly Casey realized this was the perfect time to take a little revenge on Michael. He was pretty much helpless.

The thought of getting even with him made her smile.

Just a few weeks before she'd been in town picking up supplies, and Michael had walked into the general store at the same time. When he'd seen her, he'd made fun of the way she was dressed. She always wore boys' clothes because it was easier to get her ranch work done that way. She had one dress for church, but that was all. There was no money for extras like pretty dresses.

Casey hadn't wanted to admit it at the time, but Michael's comments had hurt her. Arrogant, rich Donovan that he was, he deserved what he was about to get as a payback for being so mean.

She smiled. Michael was still unaware of her presence. She looked around to make sure he was alone. Her grin broadened when she saw his horse tied up nearby and his clothes hanging over a low tree limb. True, the clothes were on the Donovan side of the river, but that wasn't going to stop her—not today.

A wild plan began to form in her mind as she stared at his clothing. He had made fun of her clothes in town; now she had the opportunity to take the perfect revenge. She knew exactly what she had to do.

Casey drew her rifle, then urged her mount closer to the water's edge. She stayed just far enough back to be out of Michael's reach in case he tried to come after her.

"Hey, Donovan!" she called out, enjoying herself tremendously.

Startled, Michael turned to find himself staring up at Casey Turner.

"What are you doing here?" he demanded as he moved into deeper water to keep himself shielded from her view.

"I'm checking for strays—but all I found was you." She was enjoying his discomfort.

"Well, just keep on riding," Michael ordered. "There isn't any Bar T stock around here."

"You sure?"

"Yes, I'm sure," he ground out as he glared up at her, not appreciating her amusement over his situation. "Go on—get out of here."

Michael wanted her gone, the sooner, the better. Everyone knew Casey was trouble. Though she was only twelve, she already had a reputation as a hellion. Her mother had died when she was five, and the lack of any female influence in her life showed. She was as wild and untamed as the land. She dressed like a boy, and acted like one most of the time, too. She kept her dark hair cut short, and the only time he'd ever seen her wear a dress was at church, and even then she'd had her boots on.

"I don't have to do anything you tell me to do, Michael Donovan," she shouted back. "I'm on Bar T land. I can stay right here all day if I want to. I don't have to go anywhere." She sat there staring down at him, looking quite relaxed in the saddle.

Michael's scowl deepened. He wasn't sure what she was up to, but he didn't trust her. She was Jack Turner's daughter. That alone gave him reason to worry. He was just about ready to challenge her, to walk right out of the water in front of her. He was almost certain that that would send her off at a dead run; he hesitated only because his mother had taught him to be a gentleman around ladies. Not that Casey was a lady, but . . .

A sense of power filled Casey as she watched Michael. She had him right where she wanted him. His pa acted like he owned the whole county, and it felt good to have the upper hand for a change.

"So, how's the water?"

"The water's fine."

"I was thinking as I rode up here that cooling off in the river probably would feel real good today, so there's no reason why you shouldn't just enjoy yourself a while longer. I'll be going now—"

"Good. Good-bye." Michael wished she'd stop talking and start riding.

"Yeah, I've got to get on back." Casey urged her mount across the low-running river.

"Why are you heading for Donovan land? I told you there weren't any strays around here."

Casey didn't answer. She just rode to the tree where his clothes were hanging, yanked them down and held them up for him to see. "I didn't find any strays, but I found these. I think I'll take them with me—"

"You can't take my clothes!"

"Oh, yes, I can. You said I needed new ones when you were making fun of me in town, so I'll just take yours!"

"You do and you'll regret it!" he threatened.

"I don't think so. What can you do about it?" Casey laughed out loud at him.

"You can laugh now, but you'll get yours! I'll see to it!" Michael started to charge through the water toward her, intent on getting his clothes.

It was then that she lifted her rifle for him to see. "Stay right there, Donovan."

He stood still, glowering up at her in silence.

"Enjoy your swim!"

Casey was still laughing as she rode to where his horse was tied up. She stopped just long enough to free his mount, then slapped it on the rump to chase it off. She crossed back to the Turner side and galloped away. She did not look back.

Michael climbed out of the water and up the riverbank just as Casey disappeared from sight. He swore loudly in humiliation and frustration. He wanted to chase her down. He wanted to teach her a lesson for doing this to him, but it wasn't going to happen—at least not right now.

Silently he vowed that one day Casey Turner would pay for what she'd done.

But first, he had to figure out how he was going to get home.

He looked around for something to cover himself with as he tried to figure out what to do. He spotted his boots and was grateful for that much. What he was going to do next, he wasn't sure. He only hoped that his horse would return to him on its own. If not . . .

After riding for about half a mile, Casey reined in and glanced over her shoulder toward the river. There was no sign of Michael chasing after her, and she was relieved. His threat of revenge had scared her a little, but she decided the risk had been worth it.

She dropped Michael's clothes on the ground. If he came that far, he was welcome to them. All that mattered was that she'd gotten them away from him in the first place. She was quite proud of herself.

Casey was smiling again as she rode off to join up with the ranch hands. She might not have rounded up any strays, but she'd certainly had an adventure. She almost regretted not keeping a piece of Michael's clothing, just to prove to everybody what she'd done.

Chapter Two

Five Years Later
On the Circle D Ranch

The gunman smiled to himself when Frank Donovan rode into view. He had been waiting, hidden among the brush and rocks on the hillside with his rifle in hand. The hired gun took careful aim at the lean, powerful, silver-haired rancher, and when he came within range, the killer got off his shot. He watched as Donovan was hit and fell from his horse. The boss had said to make it look like a robbery, so he mounted up and rode down to where the rancher lay unmoving on the ground. He took what money Donovan had on him, then rode away without a backward glance.

"Mrs. Donovan!" called out Tom Richards, the foreman on the Circle D, as he led the boss's horse up to the main house.

Fifty-year-old Elizabeth Donovan was busy in the kitchen when she heard Tom's call. She knew it had to be important if Tom had come looking for her, so she hurried outside. Elizabeth was surprised to find the foreman waiting for her at the foot of the porch steps with her husband's horse. "What is it, Tom? Where's Frank?" She looked around for her husband.

"His horse just came back in without him!"

She went down to check the mount. It was obvious it had been running hard and fast. "You'd better get some men together and ride out to look for him. He said he was going to check stock in the south pasture when he left this morning."

"We'll head out right away."

Elizabeth wasn't too worried about her husband as she went back inside. Frank was an excellent horseman. It wasn't often his horse got away from him. She found herself smiling at the thought of Frank being forced to walk home. The hands would find him, but she knew he wasn't going to be a very happy man when he did get back to the ranch.

A good two hours passed before Elizabeth heard the riders returning. She went outside, expecting to see Frank riding in along with them. Instead, she was shocked to see the men bringing him home on a makeshift travois.

"Frank!" She ran frantically to her husband's side. He was unconscious, and his shirt was blood-soaked. She looked up at Tom in horrified disbelief. "What happened?"

"He must have been ambushed. He was shot in the back and robbed," Tom quickly explained as he dismounted and went to her. "I already sent Harry to town for the doctor—and the sheriff."

"Who did it? Did Frank say anything?" Elizabeth asked tearfully, kneeling down and taking her husband's hand. His grip was usually strong and firm, but now his hand was limp in hers.

"No. He was unconscious when we found him."

"Let's get him inside," she directed quickly, desperate to do all she could to save him.

With great care, the men lifted Frank off the travois and carried him inside and upstairs. It wasn't easy, for he was a big man. They laid him carefully on his bed. Tom stayed on to help Elizabeth, while the other hands went back outside.

Elizabeth stripped off Frank's shirt and removed the makeshift bandage Tom had put on the wound when they'd found him. She cleansed the wound as best she could, but there was little more she could do. The bullet was still in him.

They waited anxiously for Dr. Murray to arrive.

"Why would anyone do this?" she whispered to Tom.

"I don't know, but whoever did do it was a coward—back-shooting him this way," Tom answered solemnly.

Tom left Elizabeth with Frank then and went downstairs to wait. He had been the foreman on the Circle D for five years, and he admired and respected Frank. If he'd had any idea who'd ambushed his boss, he would have been riding after the culprit to seek revenge, but he had no clue. There had been no talk of trouble in the area or of any outlaw gangs around.

Tom knew the Donovans had had some run-ins with neighboring rancher Jack Turner over the years. Old man Turner had no use for Frank, and Frank felt the same way about him, but their hatred for each other had never resulted in bloodshed—before.

Elizabeth stayed by her husband's side, anxiously awaiting the doctor's arrival. Each minute seemed an eternity as he lay so deathly still before her, his breathing shallow and labored. She desperately offered prayers that the doctor would be able to save him.

The moment Elizabeth heard the sound of a carriage pulling up, she hurried to the window to look out. When she saw it was the doctor, she rushed from the bedroom to meet him downstairs.

"Thank God, you're here!" she exclaimed.

"I came as soon as I got word from Harry." Dr. Murray quickly grabbed his bag and climbed down from the carriage. He could see how distraught the normally dignified, elegant Elizabeth was, and knew Frank's condition had to be as serious as the ranch hand had said. "Harry will be along soon. He was on his way to see Sheriff Montgomery when I left."

Elizabeth led him inside to the bedroom.

Her usually vibrant, handsome husband looked so pale when she reentered the room that for an instant Elizabeth feared he'd died in the moments she'd been gone from his side.

"Is he—?" she asked, terrified.

Dr. Murray went to examine Frank and quickly reassured her, "No, He's still alive."

"Thank God."

"Why don't you wait in the parlor? I'll call you as soon as I'm done."

Elizabeth left the room and went downstairs to find Harry had returned and was talking quietly with Tom in the front hall.

"Sheriff Montgomery wasn't in his office, so I left word with his deputy about what happened," Harry explained as she joined them. "He said he'd send him right out when he got back."

"Thank you, Harry."

"If you need anything, let us know," Tom and Harry said, looking as if they wished there was something more they could do.

"I will."

After they left her, time passed slowly for Elizabeth. Not for the first time in all the years she'd lived on the Circle D, she cursed the place. None of this would have happened if Frank had listened to her and moved back to Philadelphia as she'd wanted to do. Her family was there, and she and

Frank would have been safe and happy in that civilized world. Now here she was, waiting in agony to hear if her husband was going to live or die—and all because someone had shot him down in cold blood.

Tears filled her eyes. Frank was a strong man, a powerful man. She loved him dearly, but she had never understood his passion for this ranch and this way of life. That was why she'd wanted Michael to go back East to college four years before. She'd wanted her son to know there was a bigger, more refined world out there beyond the Circle D and Hard Luck, Texas. Frank had been reluctant to let Michael go, but she had insisted.

Elizabeth realized she would have to send one of the men into town to wire Michael as soon as she talked with Dr. Murray. Michael had just completed his studies, along with his cousin Nick, and they were scheduled to embark on a trip to Europe to celebrate very shortly. She wanted to get word to him of the shooting before they sailed. She needed Michael here with her.

Nearly half an hour passed before Dr. Murray sought her out in the parlor. She got tiredly to her feet when the physician appeared in the doorway.

"Is Frank going to be all right?" Elizabeth asked nervously, seeing his serious expression.

Dr. Murray went to her. "I think you'd better sit down."

Horror filled Elizabeth. She sank down on the sofa, and he joined her there.

"Frank's not—?" she began, terrified.

"No," he quickly reassured her. "He's regained consciousness. He's going to live."

"Thank God." Tears of relief and joy welled up in her eyes.

"But there is something you need to know," the doctor went on solemnly.

"Yes?" Elizabeth was cautious, wondering why he was so grim after telling her such good news.

"The gunshot wound was serious, very serious. It's left him paralyzed from the waist down."

Elizabeth stared at the doctor in disbelief as she tried to grasp what he'd just revealed. "Frank is paralyzed?"

"Yes."

"But it's only temporary. He'll get better, won't he?"

"I'm sorry, Mrs. Donovan, but no. He's not going to get better. Your husband will never walk again." Dr. Murray hated being the bearer of such tragic news, but he didn't want to give her any false hope. He waited a moment in silence, seeing her shock and giving her a moment to come to grips with what she'd learned. "Frank has been asking for you. Are you up to seeing him?"

Elizabeth nodded and slowly walked with the doctor to the bedroom. She paused in the doorway to stare at her husband as he lay as pale as death on the bed.

"Frank," she softly said.

At the sound of her voice, Frank opened his eyes and turned his head slightly toward her. "Elizabeth—" It took all his strength just to say her name.

"Thank God you're alive!" She ran to the bedside crying and pressed a tender kiss to his cheek.

"Send for Michael," he whispered hoarsely. "You must send for Michael."

Philadelphia

"So tomorrow is the big day," James Paden said with great pleasure as he went to the bar in his walnut-paneled study. "I think this deserves a drink in celebration."

He poured healthy servings of whiskey into three crystal tumblers, then handed one to his son Nick and one to his nephew Michael Donovan. He took the third glass for himself and lifted it in a toast.

"To you, Nick, and to you, Michael. Congratulations."

"Thank you, sir," they replied.

They all took a drink.

James smiled at the two young men who stood before him. He was proud of them and what they'd accomplished. They had graduated from the university and were ready to embark on their trip to the Continent.

James's gaze settled approvingly on Michael.

He'd been worried when his nephew had first arrived in Philadelphia four years earlier. Michael had been a rough-and-tumble cowboy then, but no visible trace of his Western background remained now. Tall, darkly handsome, and perfectly well-groomed, Michael had matured into a polished gentleman and fit easily into sophisticated society. James knew that that had been his sister Elizabeth's hope when she'd sent him there to attend the university, and he was glad Michael had made the transformation so successfully.

"I'm sure your mother and father are very proud of you, Michael. It's just a shame that they couldn't join us here for the ceremony."

"It's a busy time on the ranch right now," Michael told him, fully understanding why his parents hadn't made the trip.

"You plan to go see them when you get back from Europe, don't you?"

"Yes. I'll go home for a visit then."

"Good. Now, Nick has been to Europe before, so he'll be more than happy to show you the sights," James said, glancing over at his son and smiling.

"I'm looking forward to it."

"We're going to enjoy every minute," Nick said confidently.

"I'm sure you will," his father agreed. "Michael, have you thought about what you want to do now that you are done with school? Do you want to return to ranching, or stay here with us?"

Before Michael could answer, Nick put in, "He does have certain interests here, you know."

"You do?" James looked at his nephew.

"Karen Whittington, for one, Father," Nick finished.

"Well, should you decide you want to stay on and work here in Philadelphia, there will always be a position open for you with Paden Shipping."

"Thank you." Michael was honored by his uncle's offer.

"As for Miss Whittington—you could do far worse," James went on thoughtfully. "Her family is quite affluent and very influential. Have you proposed to her yet?"

"No," Michael answered quickly. He found Karen an attractive woman, but their relationship hadn't progressed that far. He wasn't sure it ever would.

"Are you planning to see Karen again before we set sail?" Nick asked.

"Yes, I'm meeting her later tonight."

"I don't think she's happy that you're leaving."

"She hasn't said anything—"

"From what I know about Karen, I'm sure she would prefer you to stay right here in Philadelphia with her." Nick knew how spoiled the rich, beautiful blond debutante was, and he had cautioned his cousin about getting too involved with her. Karen had a reputation for being a very controlling young woman.

"What about all your women?" Michael countered. "Do they know you're leaving?"

Nick was one of the most sought-after bachelors in town. Many a mother had set her sights on him as potential husband material for her marriageable-age daughter. He had money and the Paden dark good looks, but he didn't see the logic in settling for just one woman, when he could have them all.

Nick chuckled at his cousin's question. "They know. In fact, I was wondering who was going to show up to see us off."

"Why don't you hire several carriages to transport all your admirers down to the station?"

All three men laughed good-naturedly.

A knock came at the study door, and the Padens' butler, Jonathan, came in.

"This telegram just arrived for Michael, sir," Jonathan announced.

Michael smiled as he took the telegram. He was certain it was from his parents, wishing him well on his trip. He tore open the envelope and quickly read the message.

Nick watched him as he read, and he noticed how serious Michael's expression became. "What's wrong?"

Michael looked up at him, his eyes dark with worry. Any thought of going to Europe had been instantly banished from his mind.

"I have to go home." There was no uncertainty in his voice.

"Why?"

"My father's been injured."

"What happened?" James asked worriedly.

"I don't know the details. Mother didn't say. She only said he's been paralyzed." Michael frowned, trying to imagine his strong, vibrant father crippled.

"What? Paralyzed?" James was shocked. "You've got to get back home at once."

"And I'll go with you," Nick offered, ready to help Michael in any way he could.

"But the trip to Europe—I can't ask you to give it up. I know how much you've been looking forward to going."

"You didn't ask me to give up the trip. I just offered. Besides, that's what family is for. I'm going to Texas with you. You might need me."

Michael smiled in appreciation of his cousin's support. "I'll check at the train depot right away and see how soon we can depart."

"How long will it take us to get there?"

"Depending on connections, it could take a week, maybe longer, to reach Hard Luck."

"Then we'd better get going."

"Do you need any money?" James offered.

"No, Uncle James, but thanks."

"Is there anything your aunt Sarah and I can do to help?"

Michael looked up at him. "Just pray."